Merciless

Villains

ALSO BY MARION BLACKWOOD

Marion Blackwood has written lots of books across multiple series, and new books are constantly added to her catalogue. To see the most recently updated list of books, please visit: www.marionblackwood.com

CONTENT WARNINGS

The *Ruthless Villains* series is intended for mature readers. It contains graphic violence and sexual content. Not to mention that the two main characters are villains who do immoral things both to others and to each other. If you have specific triggers, you can find the full list of content warnings at: www.marionblackwood.com/content-warnings

Merciless Villains

Ruthless Villains
Book Five

Marion Blackwood

Copyright © 2023 by Marion Blackwood

All rights reserved. No part of this book may be reproduced in any form or by any electronic or mechanical means, including information storage and retrieval systems, without permission in writing from the publisher, except by reviewers, who may quote brief passages in a review. For more information, contact info@marionblackwood.com

First edition

ISBN 978-91-988024-4-3 (hardcover)
ISBN 978-91-988024-3-6 (paperback)
ISBN 978-91-988024-2-9 (ebook)

Editing by Julia Gibbs
Cover design by Claire Holt with
Luminescence Covers (www.luminescencecovers.com)

This is a work of fiction. Names, characters, places, and incidents either are the product of the author's imagination or are used fictitiously. Any resemblance to actual persons, living or dead, events, or locales is entirely coincidental.

www.marionblackwood.com

I'm dedicating this one to myself.

This time last year, I was still writing books while I also worked a normal job. A job that drained me and that ruined both my physical and mental health.

Now I'm a full-time author, sitting here in my armchair, drinking a glass of wine, and writing about stabby villains fucking each other.

It's funny how life turns out :)

Chapter 1

Callan

The people of Eldar believed that dark mages were selfish and power-hungry. That we craved control over everything and everyone around us, and that we enjoyed seeing the fear and awe in our victims' eyes as they bowed in submission and begged us for mercy. That we lied and cheated and killed without conscience or remorse. And that we would burn the whole fucking world down to get what we wanted. Unfortunately for them, they were absolutely right.

A vibrating force scythe shot through the air, severing a constable's arm from his shoulder. I followed it up with another spinning arc that cut his head off. It plummeted to the grass along with the rest of his body while blood misted the warm afternoon air.

"Go left," Audrey snapped from behind my back.

Not hesitating a second, I immediately took a step to the left while raising a force wall to block the combined wind and fire attack that the constables threw at me from straight ahead. Lightning shot past me on the right a fraction of a second later, coming from behind.

Audrey let out a low snarl of annoyance.

I couldn't spare her side of the battle any attention, but the rapid flashing of glittering green light on the grass around us suggested that she had increased her attack speed even more. We were fighting back to back so I couldn't see what was happening on her side, and since she didn't have any defensive magic with which to block, she had to warn me if an attack went through. So far, I had managed to dodge them all, but I could tell that it irritated her when a strike slipped past her.

A boom echoed across the hills as a blast of wind magic slammed into my force shield. I released it the moment it had stopped the attack and instead hurled a wide arc towards the five constables who still drew breath on my side. Three of them blocked it with a wall of water while the others shot more attacks at me. A fireball and a lightning bolt zapped through the air, but I managed to shove them off course with a well-timed shield, and then threw another spinning arc. It cleaved the constable on the left halfway down her chest.

I had almost forgotten how to fight against people who were connected to the Great Current. After battling our way up the dark mage mountain in Castlebourne and then dealing with Johnson and Kane's gang of vengeful idiots in Malgrave, I had gotten used to fighting people who possessed raw power. *One* power. These constables weren't nearly as powerful as Johnson's gang had been, but each one of them could switch between several different magic types. And that was annoying. There were also quite a lot of them.

Heat washed over me as two simultaneous fire attacks crashed into my defending force wall. I shoved it sideways before calling up a massive scythe and hurling it at the constables across the now bloodstained grass.

Only two of them managed to block it in time.

Fear flashed across their faces as they tried desperately to hold off the sudden barrage I started up. Wind and water smacked into my attacks, but their power levels were so much lower than mine. Stumbling backwards, they whipped their heads around in search of back-up. But there was none.

There had been twenty of them when they had ambushed us. Fortunately, Audrey's quick reflexes had managed to take out five of them before they could even get the first shot off. The remaining fifteen had pushed in on us from two sides, trying to split our focus and take us down separately. But Audrey and I had done this dance quite a lot at this point. I trusted her to watch my back, just as I watched hers, which gave us seven to one odds. And against normal magic users, that wasn't too much of a problem for dark mages like us.

Green poison magic suddenly shot past me and slammed into the two constables who had been busy blocking my force arcs. They collapsed to the ground immediately. With shock still lingering on their faces, their lifeless eyes stared unseeing up into the bright blue sky.

Turning slowly, I arched an eyebrow at the poison mage who now stood next to me.

She lifted her shoulders in a nonchalant shrug. "You were taking too long."

"I was just about to finish them off." I shot her a pointed look. "If you had just waited ten more seconds, they would've been dead."

"Uh-huh. Ten more seconds was still too long."

Reaching out, I took her jaw in a firm grip and leaned down closer to her face. "Don't steal my kills."

"I won't." A smirk played over her lips as she lifted a hand and gave my cheek a couple of brisk pats. "When you stop being so inefficient."

I slid my hand from her jaw and instead wrapped it around her throat while slanting my lips over hers. "Oh the things I could do to you."

"I know." Her dark laugh danced over my mouth. "So let's go kill Chancellor Quill and Lance Carmichael and everyone else so that we can finally get to that part."

With my hand still locked around her throat, I pulled her the final bit to me and claimed those wicked lips for myself. She grabbed the back of my neck, holding me firmly against her as she answered the possessive kiss.

My heart still beat twice as hard every time she did that. Every time she touched me and kissed me as if she was declaring to the whole damn world that I was hers. And I was. Every blackened piece of my soul belonged to this vicious little poisoner.

All I wanted to do was lift her up and feel her wrap her legs around my waist. But we had people to slaughter and a war to win, so I grudgingly released my grip on her throat and stepped back.

She ran her tongue over those luscious lips and flashed me a smirk, informing me that she knew exactly what I'd been thinking, before she swept her gaze across the rolling grasslands.

"The horses are gone," she observed.

"Yeah." They had run off quickly when we were ambushed by the squad of constables. "But it shouldn't be that far to Grant's mansion now."

"That's what worries me. If Quill sent this patrol," she motioned towards the dead men and women around us, "out here, it must mean that his main force isn't far off either. We need to get to the mansion before they do."

"Agreed."

I jerked my chin and started forward. Audrey scanned the corpses littering the grass before falling in beside me as we continued on foot towards Harvey Grant's mansion.

While Audrey and I were in Malgrave trying to persuade Levi to help us, Henry had sent a message saying that he and

Paige and Sam had reached Grant's mansion safely. Since Grant's mansion was protected by that massive magic-infused garden, we had decided that it was the best place for them to lie low until we could come back with Levi's people. We hadn't heard anything from them since, but hopefully that just meant that there was nothing to tell.

"I wonder where Malcolm and Sienna are," Audrey said after a while. "Back in Castlebourne, Sam just said that Malcolm was on the run and Sienna was unaccounted for. But that was weeks ago. We'll need them if we're going to win this war."

"I'm sure they're out here somewhere. Malcolm is too smart to get caught. And Sienna is too unpredictable, so they won't be able to capture her either."

"I agree. But the problem is, how the hell do *we* find them then?"

"Let's just meet up with Henry and Paige and the others first. Then we can make a plan while we wait for Levi to show up with his people."

"Yeah."

After telling Levi how to get to Grant's mansion, we had left the King of Metal in Malgrave to clean up the rest of Trevor Gale's gang on his own. With one exception. Audrey and I had tracked down the water mage and the lightning mage who had worked for Trevor and who had tortured us in that warehouse when they tested our loyalty. And when we found them, *we* had tortured *them* to death instead. Brutal revenge at its finest.

It hadn't surprise me that Levi had given us permission to do that. He understood the concept of getting even, more than most. What *had* surprised me was that he'd had his healer fix all of our injuries before we left. It hadn't been part of our original deal, and the King of Metal wasn't exactly known for his selfless generosity. Especially not where I was concerned. But maybe he really had been satisfied with how we had dealt with the threat to his wife.

"Do you hear that?" Audrey asked, pulling me out of my thoughts, after a long stretch of silence.

Cocking my head, I listened. My heart sank. "Yeah."

Audrey blew out an annoyed breath. Her dark hair rippled in the golden sunlight as she pushed it back over her shoulder and adjusted the straps on her pack. "Let's approach carefully."

"I thought you liked to make an entrance."

A brief smile blew across her lips, but it didn't stick. She was worried. And so was I, to be honest. If the noise coming from below the hill was what we thought it was, Henry and Paige were in more trouble than we had feared.

Tension crackled in the air around us as we snuck across the sloping grass and approached the edge. When we were almost there, we dropped to the ground and crawled the final stretch so that we wouldn't be spotted against the clear sky behind us.

The air around me smelled like warm grass and soil, but it did little to dispel the dread that pulsed through me with every beat of my heart. Henry had to be okay. He was strong and capable. And I wasn't sure if I could handle it if Quill had somehow managed to take him. So he had to be okay.

Sunlight beat down on me, warming my back through my leather armor as Audrey and I closed the final distance to the edge. Bracing myself on my elbows, I peered down into the valley below the slope.

Another wave of dread washed over me. *Fuck*.

Harvey Grant's mansion sat nestled like a white jewel in the thick greenery that served as both his gardens and his defense against enemies. But that was not what made my heart thump in my chest.

The gardens were surrounded.

A massive ring of people had laid siege to the mansion. As

far as I could tell, all of them were still stuck outside the gardens, but they had circled them so that no one would be able to get in or out.

I stared at the sheer number of people. These couldn't only be constables. It had to be other volunteers who were decently skilled in combat too. They really hadn't been exaggerating when they said that they had mustered the whole city for war.

Lying on her stomach beside me, Audrey heaved a frustrated sigh.

"Well, this war is off to a great start."

Chapter 2

The sun was slipping closer to the horizon with every passing minute. Walking from the ambush site to Grant's mansion had taken a lot longer than riding would have, and the fact that there was an army camped right below the hill wasn't exactly helping our efforts either. Finding what we needed would become next to impossible once darkness fell, so we were going to have to pick up the pace.

"Tell me again what the message said," I prompted as I pushed aside bush number five hundred and twenty-three and peered down at the ground below.

From a few steps away, Callan straightened from his own search and dragged a hand through his messy black hair. "That there was an escape tunnel hidden in a copse of trees on the ridge and that it would take us halfway into Grant's gardens."

The message that Henry had sent to Callan weeks ago when they had arrived at Grant's mansion had been written in code, so I hadn't been able to read it myself. And now as I trudged through the underbrush and shoved aside yet another cluster of leaves, I was starting to wonder if that damn force mage hadn't actually been able to read the letter either.

"*Which* copse of trees?" Straightening, I threw my arms out in a frustrated gesture. "And *which* ridge?"

"He didn't say. Grant probably wouldn't let him, in case it fell into the wrong hands."

"It was written in code!"

"Yeah, but it's Grant. He's so damn secretive that his left hand is probably keeping secrets from his right."

Tilting my head back, I raked my fingers through my hair and stared up at the orange and purple streaks that now painted the sky. I let out a groan.

"And besides," Callan continued, "I doubt he thought we'd have to search for it while also dodging Quill's entire army."

I tipped my head back down and scowled at him. "When the hell did you become so calm and rational? I distinctly remember you almost strangling me to death just because I happened to send you to wait right next to where some constables were taking a break."

A laugh tore from his chest. Raising his eyebrows, he shot me a pointed look. "What do you mean? That was a perfectly rational response."

I snorted.

But before I could retort, the sound of thundering hooves rolled across the landscape.

Panic shot up my spine.

Callan and I darted behind the closest tree trunks right as a large group of horses became visible on the slope. They weren't coming from the camp around Grant's mansion, but rather from the direction that we had come from. From the ambush site where we had left twenty dead bodies behind. *Shit.*

While staying behind the cover of the tree, I discreetly scanned the approaching riders. By my best estimate, there were twenty-five of them. If we could ambush them before they realized that we were here, it would probably be another relatively easy win.

My gaze drifted towards the army camped below the ridge on the other side.

Taking out twenty-five normal magic users in an ambush might not be a problem, but if they managed to alert the rest of their army before we could kill them all, then we would be in serious trouble.

I opened my mouth to tell Callan as much when the five people riding at the front of the squad at last came close enough for me to make out their faces.

Another wave of panic, mixed with indecision, pulsed through me.

Chancellor Godric Quill was riding at the head of the squad, and four twenty-year-olds flanked him. Lance Carmichael, his girlfriend Jessica, and their friends Leoni and Darren. Behind them were what looked like twenty constables.

I slid my gaze to Callan. His expression mirrored my own.

We might be able to take out twenty-five constables before they could alert the army down below, if we were lucky. But add four people with the undiluted power levels of dark mages, plus the Chancellor, into the mix, and we were looking at a recipe for disaster.

"Spread out!" Quill called. "They can't have gotten far."

The rough bark scraped against my skin as I pressed myself harder against the tree trunk. We couldn't stay there. It was only a matter of time before they found us, so hiding was out of the question. And so was open battle.

"We need a hostage," I whispered as I met Callan's gaze.

He nodded before casting another glance towards the approaching search party. "Lance?"

"Yes."

"Alright."

"Get ready to create a distraction when I tell you to."

He nodded again.

Leaves rustled around us as a warm summer breeze swirled through the copse of trees. After motioning for Callan to follow, I snuck towards the other side of the grove. The company of riders had split up into pairs as they searched the ridge for any sign of us. A few of the constables had already reached the other small thicket that we had checked out before we moved on to this one. But if Lance and Jessica stayed the course they were currently on, they would be passing by the far side of this grove soon.

"Are you sure it's them, Chancellor?" Darren called from a short distance to our right.

Godric Quill looked up from the patch of grass he had been staring at before replying, "Yes. You saw the state of the bodies back there. Some were missing limbs or heads while others had no injuries at all. It's the work of Callan Blackwell and Audrey Sable. I would stake my career on it."

"I knew it," Leoni growled. She shook her head while she kept riding next to Darren. "As soon as that patrol didn't return, I knew that it was those two villains who had attacked them. They finally come back to Eldar from wherever they've been hiding these past weeks, and the first thing they do is to start slaughtering people again. By the Current, I hate them so much that I can barely breathe."

I rolled my eyes. First of all, *they* were the ones who had attacked us. Secondly, we hadn't been hiding. And thirdly... Well, she *was* right about the rest, I supposed.

Drawing myself up against the tree at the edge of the grove, I glanced over at Callan and then judged the distance to Jessica and Lance. They were almost upon us now. I met Callan's gaze and then nodded towards a spot behind the two approaching students. Callan nodded back and then brushed his palms together.

"We'll get them this time, Leoni," Jessica called across the grass. "And then this will all be over and we can go home."

From this close, even I could see the doubt that swirled in Lance's blue eyes at her words. But he said nothing.

They kept riding closer.

My pulse thrummed in my ears.

We had to time this perfectly.

"Now," I hissed while touching my palms together and calling up a glittering green tendril.

Callan shot a small force blast towards a tree farther down. It slammed into the trunk, sending chips of bark flying through the air. The noise made both Lance and Jessica whip around in their saddles.

Using their second of inattention, I expanded my poison cloud and threw it at them. The glittering green color caught their attention before it could strike and they flung themselves sideways, practically toppling off their horses. Lance managed to avoid getting hit by a mere second and crashed down on the thick grass while his horse reared and then bolted. Jessica wasn't so lucky.

Since she had been riding on the side closest to the trees, the poison slammed into her before she could duck. She crashed down on the ground a few steps from Lance while her horse galloped after his. The Binder shot to his feet, whipping his head from side to side. Jessica didn't.

I kept part of the poison cloud hovering around her head, to make it clear to everyone around us what was happening, while she lay on the grass, fighting for breath as the rest of the lethal mist swirled through her throat and lungs.

"They're here!" Lance bellowed towards Quill before snapping his gaze back to his girlfriend. "Jessica, get up and…"

He trailed off, and fear pulsed in his eyes as he took in the poison cloud around her.

Callan and I had stepped out of the trees the moment that the two of them toppled from their horses. And with Jessica riding so close to the grove, we had reached her before Lance could even get back up on his feet.

Technically, Callan could have used that time to throw an attack at him. But Callan couldn't keep people hostage with his magic the way that I could, and killing the Binder right now would only lead to a battle we couldn't win. And since I couldn't poison Lance without first releasing my grip on the magic currently inside Jessica's body, we would have to make do with just one hostage.

So far it was enough, because Lance was only staring at the two of us where we stood a single stride from his girlfriend. Jessica lay writhing on the ground, choking and dry heaving from my poison.

Shouts rang out across the grasslands as Quill called back the other constables while Leoni and Darren raced towards us. Lance stood frozen a few steps away from us on the other side of Jessica. He had managed to get the black dye out of his hair, so it was now back to its usual golden color, and it gleamed like molten metal in the light from the setting sun as he looked up to meet our gazes.

"I'm sure you can guess what I will do if you so much as twitch your fingers in a way I don't like," I said to the Binder.

His blue eyes darted down to Jessica again. Then he dragged them back up to me and swallowed. True dread and fear shone across his whole face as he met my gaze and pleaded, "Don't."

"That depends entirely on how the rest of this conversation plays out."

Before he could reply, Darren and Leoni's horses skidded to a halt behind him. Their horses' hooves created ruts in the soft ground as they stopped abruptly. Neither of them dismounted.

"You!" Leoni spat. Lightning flashed in her brown eyes and her curly brown hair rippled around her face as she shook her head violently at me. "Drop your magic right now or I swear I will—"

"Does it look like you are in any position to make demands right now?" I interrupted, and raised my eyebrows expectantly.

While holding her gaze with mercilessly cold eyes, I increased the strength of my poison. Jessica thrashed on the ground as the green mist forced its way deeper into her body. Fury crackled across Leoni's face as she stared down at me from atop her horse.

"Stop," Lance pleaded. "Please."

I eased up a bit, and Jessica went back to simply dry heaving.

"You should—" Darren began.

But he was cut off by a commanding voice before he could finish.

"Audrey Sable," Chancellor Quill said as he reined in his horse on Lance's other side. His blue eyes slid to the force mage standing next to me with his arms crossed. "And Callan Blackwell. I knew I'd find you eventually."

The rest of Quill's company slowly formed up behind him until all twenty constables were positioned in two neat lines. Several horses snorted and stomped their hooves as they came to a halt.

I let a smile full of sweet poison slide home on my lips as I met Quill's gaze and said in a mocking voice, "Aww, have you missed us that much?"

A summer wind blew through the hills, ruffling his gray hair as he glared down at us. "You slaughtered an entire patrol. They were good people. Men and women with families. Loved ones. Friends."

"They shouldn't have ambushed us. And you shouldn't have sent them out here in the first place." I lifted my shoulders in a nonchalant shrug. "So really, I think the villain in this situation is actually you."

"I am not the one currently torturing a student with poison."

"Which I wouldn't have had to do if you had just left us alone. But you didn't. So here we are."

Righteous fury blazed on Quill's features as he raised his chin. "I will see you brought to justice if it's the last thing I do."

Callan snorted. "Good luck with that."

"Please let her breathe normally," Lance interjected before the Chancellor could retort. His worried gaze flicked between my face and Jessica's.

I rolled my eyes and blew out an annoyed sigh, but pulled back my magic enough that Jessica could now suck in a few deeper breaths. The poison cloud stayed around her head, though.

"Thank you," Lance whispered, his gaze fixed on her as she struggled into a kneeling position.

"Don't thank them," Quill snapped. Then he composed himself again before returning his attention to me and Callan. His horse paced a step back and forth as he shifted his weight in the saddle. "They don't deserve gratitude."

"You'd do well to *show* some gratitude, Chancellor," Callan said, a mocking smile on his lips. "Unless you want us to kill this poor girl."

"No!" Lance blurted out.

But Quill just held up his hand, silencing him. The orange and deep red light from the slowly setting sun cast ominous shadows across his unforgiving face. Then a smug smile drifted across his mouth.

"You know, we searched the hills," he began, a sharp glint in his eyes. "Very thoroughly. And there are no dark mages there."

A hint of worry swirled through my chest, but I kept a taunting smirk on my lips as I said, "Is that what you think?"

"I know it. All the other hills and valleys and mansions are deserted. We were led to believe that there were hundreds of you out here, but it can't have been more than ten. And now, all that's left is the two of you." He nodded towards the sloping ridge on the other side of the grove. "And that troublesome emotion mage in that mansion."

Callan and I exchanged a look.

And then I burst out laughing.

Thankfully, Callan did too.

"You really have no idea who you're up against, do you?" I said while making a show of wiping away tears of amusement and shaking my head.

Callan, who fortunately understood what we needed to do, chuckled as well. I really hadn't given him enough credit when it came to his skills regarding lies and deceit.

"Do you have any idea how many dark mages are inside that massive mansion right now?" Callan challenged, and jerked his chin in the direction of Grant's home.

"It can't be more than a handful," Quill answered. "No one has gone in or out since we laid siege to it weeks ago."

"That you know of."

"What does that mean?"

"Did you forget the part about us being dark mages?" I picked up, sensing where Callan was going with this.

Quill narrowed his eyes. "What does that have to do with anything? You still can't have moved a massive army in through those accursed gardens without us seeing it."

"Except..." A wicked smile spread across my lips. "A worldwalker doesn't have to go through the garden."

Everything went silent. I swore even the wind stopped for a few seconds. Confusion danced across Darren and Leoni's faces as they turned towards the Chancellor. Lance kept his eyes locked on Jessica. Red light from the setting sun fell across his face, turning his eyes a strange purple color.

"You're bluffing," Godric Quill said at last. His horse paced again as he shook his head. "There hasn't been a worldwalker in centuries."

Callan smirked. "That you know of."

"I would have known about it."

"Would you? How much do you really know about dark mages, Chancellor?"

Quill opened his mouth to retort, but then closed it again.

It was a bluff, of course. And a rather outrageous one at that. Worldwalkers were mages who could travel from one place to the next in the blink of an eye, but nowadays, they were so incredibly rare that no one was really sure how their magic even worked. No one could say for certain whether worldwalkers could only move through space themselves, or if they could bring people with them. Which was why the bluff worked so perfectly when combined with the fact that the Chancellor knew absolutely nothing about our dark mage society. He *was* right, of course. While there were rumors about one existing somewhere up north, the city of Eldar hadn't seen a worldwalker in centuries. But there was no way for him to know that for certain.

"Trust me, Chancellor, this is a war you really can't win," Callan said, and flashed him a wolfish smile. "Better back off while you still can."

At last, Quill seemed to recover from his shock. Giving his

head a few quick shakes, he sat up straighter and then raised his hand as if to give a signal.

I immediately strengthened the poison again until Jessica was doubled over on the grass, choking violently.

"Ah, ah, ah," I warned, and shook my head. "Make one move, and she dies."

Godric tightened his grip on the reins until his knuckles turned white. Hell, he really was furious now. But was it because we were threatening Jessica or because of the news about the worldwalker?

"I'm sure Jessica would be honored to sacrifice her life in order to bring the two of you to justice," he said, his voice tight with anger.

Lance whipped around to face him. Shock danced across the Binder's features as he stared up at his leader in utter disbelief.

Worry swept through my chest. If Quill was truly prepared to sacrifice Jessica, we would be in deep shit. A battle against twenty constables on horseback, the leader of the parliament of Eldar, and three students with the power levels of dark mages who would also be fueled by rage and grief from Jessica's death, would not end well for us.

"Did you hear that, Lance?" I said in an effort to shift the situation back in our favor. "That's how much your beloved Chancellor truly cares about you. He doesn't give a shit what happens to you as long as he gets what he wants." My lips curled in a cruel smile. "Doesn't that sound familiar? What was it you said about dark mages again?"

Quill blinked, as if realizing what his words had sounded like. His blue eyes darted between the four students, and his face softened slightly as he said, "Don't listen to her. She's just trying to drive a wedge between us."

Leoni and Darren gave him a determined nod and turned

back towards us, hatred once again seeping into their brown eyes. But Lance's gaze lingered on the side of Godric's face for a few more seconds before he returned his attention to us.

"Here's what's gonna happen," Callan began. Raising a hand, he spun it in the air. "You take all of your constables and ride back to your little camp. And then, once you're long gone, we'll let poor Jessica go."

"Why should we trust you?" Leoni spat. Her horse walked a few steps to the side as she leaned forward in the saddle. "You might kill her anyway as soon as we're gone."

I shrugged, and the glittering green mist around Jessica swirled slightly. "Yes, we might. But if you don't leave now, we *will* kill her. And then she will definitely be dead."

"If we leave, they will let her go," Lance said before Leoni or any of the others could respond.

They all turned to look at him. I did too. Based on the tone of his voice, it was impossible to tell if that had been a statement or a plea. The Binder, however, didn't seem to notice their stares. His eyes were fixed on Jessica's.

"You will be alright," he said. "Just do as they say. I'll see you soon."

I decreased the strength of the poison enough for her to draw in a deep breath and nod.

Lance dragged his blue eyes back up to us. For a few seconds, no one said anything. The Binder only held my gaze before shifting it to Callan and doing the same. Then, without another word, he turned and walked away.

Darren and Leoni exchanged a glance before flicking their gazes towards the Chancellor. Still seated atop his horse, Quill glared down at us in tension-filled silence for another couple of seconds. Then he flashed some kind of hand signal.

Horses snorted and neighed as the constables turned them

around and started after the retreating Binder. Leoni and Darren did the same.

The low-hanging sun painted Quill's face in a deep red color, making it look like it was covered in blood. That righteous fury on his face had hardened into something cold and unyielding as he held our gazes.

"I will *personally*," he said, biting out each word like a curse, "drain every drop of magic from your bodies before this is over."

Matching smiles that were pure evil spread across my and Callan's lips.

He jerked his chin. "Run along now, Chancellor."

"While we still let you."

Chapter 3

Callan

As soon as Chancellor Quill and Lance and the rest of their people had disappeared beyond the ridge, Audrey released the grip on her magic and let the glittering green mist around Jessica's head fade out. The water mage sucked in a deep breath.

Her long blond hair fell down to cover her face as she bent forward and coughed before drawing in another rattling breath. Still on her knees, she curled her fingers in the thick green grass as if bracing herself while she tried to recover from Audrey's magic. I glanced over at my poison mage. She just shrugged.

The move made the red and purple light ripple in her shining black hair. I shifted my gaze to the sun dipping lower towards the horizon. We would lose the light soon. Finding Grant's hidden exit would be impossible in the dark, and camping out here in the open was out of the question, so we had to finish this up quickly.

"How big is Quill's army?" I demanded.

For a couple of seconds, Jessica only continued focusing on her breathing. Then she at last raised her head and looked up at us. Based on the tight set of her mouth, she was angry. Or at least trying to look angry. But then she cast a quick glance over her shoulder towards where Lance had disappeared, and dread flooded her eyes instead.

"How many?" I pushed.

"You..." she began as she met my gaze once more, but she had to pause and clear her throat before trying again. "You promised to let me go."

"Yes, we did. But we said nothing of the state you'd be in."

Her eyes widened, and she cast another panicked look over her shoulder.

By all hell, she wouldn't have survived a single day as a dark mage. When she was with her friends, she seemed confident enough, but now she just looked terrified. Didn't she know that even if you were hopelessly outclassed, you were supposed to fake power and confidence? It was the first thing any dark mage learned. And those who didn't, died. But then again, I supposed that she had never had to face any real dangers before now.

"Don't make me ask again," I said.

"I don't know," she blurted out. Shaking her head, she stared up at me, her blue eyes still wide with fear. "I don't know how many."

Blowing out a long exhale, I touched my palms together and called up a force blade.

Jessica flinched and tried to scoot backwards on her knees, but before she could, I leveled the half-translucent gray sword at her throat. It wasn't close enough to actually cut her, but I knew that she would at least be feeling the vibrations pulsing against her skin.

"I don't!" she protested, raising her hands in a pleading gesture. "I don't know how many. I swear, it's the truth."

She sounded sincere, so I was pretty sure that she *was* telling the truth. I glanced over at Audrey. Her head was tilted slightly to the side, and she had crossed her arms while she studied the water mage before us. Then she slid her gaze to me and nodded, confirming that she also believed her.

"Alright," I said, shifting my attention back to Jessica. "Then where's the rest of the army?"

Confusion flickered across her features. "What do you mean?"

Since I didn't want to give away any of our potential plans, I had to phrase my questions carefully. Quill would no doubt interrogate her afterwards, so even if Jessica didn't pick up on anything I said right now, the Chancellor might.

"There has to be others," I said. "Apart from the ones surrounding the mansion."

"Oh." She sounded almost relieved. Raising a hand, she hooked a lock of straight blond hair behind her ear. "Yes, there are some patrols moving around the grasslands too."

Which meant that everyone else was here. That was good at least. Having to fight a battle on several fronts would have been difficult for us considering how few people we had on our side.

"And Quill's plan is to... what?" I asked. "Starve us out?"

"I... I don't know. I think so." When we only continued watching her, she went on. "I mean, the first plan was to attack the mansion. But those woodlands around it are... strange."

Thank hell for Harvey Grant and his clever use of emotion magic and desire for privacy. Otherwise, this war would have already been over by the time we got back from Malgrave.

I slid my gaze to Audrey. Interrogating Jessica was a two-way street. Anything we asked about would be reported back to Quill, which meant that the information we received might become useless by the end of the day anyway. And it might allow him to start plotting countermeasures.

Audrey heaved a soft sigh, as if she had come to the same conclusion. Then she met my gaze and lifted her shoulders in a casual shrug.

I supposed that was as much as we would be able to get out of Jessica without risking our own plans.

We could have interrogated her more thoroughly and then just killed her afterwards, of course. But she didn't seem to know all that much about Quill's schemes anyway, and the violent response we would get from Lance if we did that wasn't worth it. Until Levi showed up with his people, we had to play this carefully.

"Why are you here?" Audrey asked while I let my force blade fade out.

Annoyance rippled across Jessica's features as she glared up at her. "Because you took me hostage."

A cold and dangerous smile that made Jessica flinch curled Audrey's lips. "I'd be careful with that tongue, if I were you."

Jessica opened her mouth as if to say something while casting another panicked look at the empty grasslands around her, but then she just closed it again.

"Why are you here?" Audrey repeated. "In this war?"

"Because..." Her pale brows furrowed slightly, and she trailed off. "Well... Because it's... the right thing to do, I guess."

"Are you asking me or telling me?"

"I..." Uncertainty danced in her eyes. "Well, Chancellor Quill said that it was the best way to once and for all deal with the threat you pose."

"I know what Quill thinks. What do *you* think?"

The uncertainty suddenly disappeared from her eyes, and she raised her chin in a defiant move. "I think what you're doing is despicable. Killing people is *wrong*."

Audrey let out a short humorless laugh. "We weren't killing anyone in Eldar. But guess what? Now that you've started a war against us, people will definitely die."

"I..." She opened and closed her mouth a few times as if

trying to figure out what to say. "It was the only way to stop you."

"To stop us from doing what? Choosing how we want to live our lives?"

"From hoarding magic."

"So instead, you forcibly rip it from our souls against our will?"

"I..." Scrunching up her brows, she opened and closed her mouth once more.

Audrey pinched the bridge of her nose for a few seconds before casting a glance at the red and purple streaks that lined the heavens. "We're losing the light. Callan?"

I shook my head in silent reply that I didn't have any other questions for Jessica either.

"Alright." Audrey twitched her fingers at the water mage. "Stand up."

A hint of wariness blew across Jessica's face, but she slowly climbed to her feet. She was quite tall. About half a head taller than Audrey. But because of the power and authority pulsing from Audrey's whole being, Jessica looked like a frightened child in front of her.

Audrey jerked her chin. "Go."

Jessica hesitated. Remaining where she was, she glanced around as if checking to see if this was some kind of test.

"You're free to leave," Audrey said.

She shifted wary blue eyes back to the poison mage. "Just like that?"

"Just like that."

For another few seconds, the blond water mage only stared at us in silence. Then she slowly took a step backwards.

She paused.

When nothing happened, she took a few more steps. We remained where we were, only studying her as she edged away.

Did she think that we were toying with her? That we were letting her walk a short distance before we hunted her down again or something? Though, to be fair, that did sound like something I would have done to Audrey back when we were still trying to kill each other.

Once Jessica had reached a spot that most people would assume was out of our range, she whirled around and sprinted across the thick green grass. Neither one of us made any move to follow. Instead, we turned towards the grove behind us.

The tree trunks looked like they were coated in liquid fire. It wouldn't be long before that colorful light disappeared completely.

And before it did, we had a secret tunnel to find.

Chapter 4

By the time we had found the tunnel and made it through to the other side, the sun had slipped almost entirely beyond the horizon. Only a splash of yellow remained to the west while the rest of the sky was drenched in ever darkening shades of blue. I squinted at the gloomy gardens before us.

"So... we bypassed the army." I looked over my shoulder even though the foliage was far too dense to provide any views of Quill's army on the other side. Then I turned back to the equally thick woodlands still ahead. "But how the hell are we supposed to make it through the rest of the gardens?"

As far as I could tell, the escape tunnel had only taken us halfway to the mansion. I supposed it made sense. Grant being the paranoid sort that he was probably didn't want people to be able to just walk right up to his home, in case the tunnel was ever compromised. And while I understood his reasoning, it posed a serious obstacle for us right now.

Callan shrugged. "I guess we'll just have to hope that Grant finds us before we can slaughter each other while lost in some kind of magic-induced psychosis."

For a while, we just stood there. Side by side. Watching the dusky woods.

Deep purple flowers that glittered as if they had been dusted with starlight dotted the trees up ahead, and along the branches to our left were some sort of round fruits that pulsed with orange light. The thick grass that covered the ground looked untouched. As if no one had passed through here in years.

Once again, I looked behind me in an effort to try to estimate how far from the border we were. But in the dark, it was impossible. I turned back around and met Callan's gaze while lifting my shoulders in a shrug.

"Well..." I smacked my lips. "If we haven't managed to kill each other for five years, despite our best efforts, I'm sure we'll survive this too."

Callan huffed out a laugh. "True."

After drawing in a bracing breath, we started towards the mansion. I flicked a suspicious glance up at the sparkling flowers above, wondering what sort of emotion they had been created to summon. I wasn't sure I wanted to find out. But at least they provided some much-needed light to the otherwise dark path.

"No dreamfoil," Callan said after a couple of minutes of silence.

I swept my gaze around the area again while we walked. "No. But it's a pretty weak plant compared to what Grant can create with his magic, so I guess it's only used at the very edge of the gardens."

"Weak? It made me think I was stranded on a pillar above a chasm."

"I said *compared to* what he can create with his magic." Bitterness crawled up my throat as I shot him an irritated look. "Did you even listen to what I said?"

He glared back at me. "You're the one trying to downplay the dangers."

"No, I'm not."

"Yes, you are."

"Just keep your damn eyes on the path."

"Fine."

"Fine."

We stalked forward in sullen silence. It was such a waste. We were walking through a beautiful garden, full of glittering flowers and magical plants, but Callan was ruining the whole experience with his damn attitude. Maybe it would have been better if we had split up.

However, before I could voice those thoughts, something moved at the corner of my eye.

Jerking to a halt, I whipped towards it.

Shock pulsed through me.

For a few seconds, I just stood there, staring at the scene before me. It was a kitchen. Or rather, half of a kitchen. The one from my childhood home. Three people were inside. By one of the polished wooden counters, my father poured coffee into a red ceramic mug, while my mother looked over the papers that were fanned out around her on the table. Next to her was my sister, Jenny. She was drinking from a tall glass of water. Sweat trickled down her neck, and her shirt was damp with it too.

And then, I showed up.

Appearing out of thin air, a younger version of me walked through the doorway and into the kitchen. Younger me dragged a hand through her hair and then stretched her arms above her head, as if she had been sitting in the same position for a long time.

"Audrey," my father said, looking up from his now full cup. "We just got back." He moved over to stand behind my sister's chair and clapped her on the shoulder. "Did you know that your sister ran ten miles today?"

My fifteen-year-old self looked between the two of them. "No, I didn't."

He patted her on the shoulder again before taking a large gulp of coffee. "Well, she did. What did you do today?"

Bitterness swelled in my throat, but I couldn't tear my eyes from the scene. Or rather the memory.

"Studied," my younger self replied while an iron mask descended over her features.

"Well, that's good. But remember what your athletics teacher said? You need to improve both your speed and your agility if you're going to catch up to Jenny someday."

Fifteen-year-old me stared back at them in silence for two seconds before turning around and walking back out of the kitchen while saying, "I'll keep that in mind."

The bitterness inside me was so potent that I could almost taste it as it burned its way down my throat and into my stomach.

"What are you doing?" Callan growled from my other side. "Why do you always act as if you know best when all you do right now is to slow us down?"

I whirled towards him, ready to spit a retort back at him, but something tapped at the corner of my mind. Bitterness. Why was I feeling so bitter all of a sudden? Both bitter at Callan and at...

Bitterness.

Fuck. Not again.

"It's the flowers," I said, trying to force my mind back into the present. "Callan, the flowers. They're like that fruit we ate back in your dining room. The one we stole from this garden."

Callan looked like he was about to argue. Then he blinked and shook his head violently. "Shit."

"Yeah."

Leaving the kitchen scene behind, I hurried over to Callan

and took his hand in a firm grip. "Walk. And no matter how much bitterness you feel towards me right now, don't say anything. This is meant to make us fight and drive us apart. Just hold my hand and walk."

His strong hand was warm against mine as he held it tightly. The kitchen scene faded behind me as we continued towards the mansion, but another one soon took its place. I gritted my teeth and squeezed Callan's hand harder as another half-formed room appeared between the dark trees.

My parents were sitting on the couch in our living room, going through papers and talking softly. I was younger in this memory, somewhere between ten and eleven, and I was standing right outside the doorway, hidden in the shadows.

"Audrey learned to throw her magic today," my mother said. Looking up from the document she had been reading, she met my father's eyes. "I mean, not as well as Jenny, of course. But still."

My younger self, who had been about to knock on the doorframe and go inside, turned and disappeared back into the shadows.

I ground my teeth so hard that I thought they were going to shatter. Why was Callan walking so fucking slowly? I just wanted to get out of here. We should split up so that I could go on ahead instead of having to linger here because he didn't have it in him to move faster. Hell damn it, why...

Shaking my head violently, I tried to dispel the effects of Grant's magic. It didn't work. Bitterness welled up inside me like a flood, and it took everything I had to stop myself from yanking my hand out of Callan's and taking out all of my misery on him.

A blurry classroom materialized on my right. I didn't want to look at it, but my eyes were somehow still drawn to the thirteen-year-old Audrey who sat there. The teacher, an older woman with grey hair pulled into a bun, read the names of her new students from the paper in her hands.

"Audrey Sable," she said eventually. Her gaze landed on me, and recognition sparked in her brown eyes as she repeated, "Sable. You're Jenny Sable's little sister, aren't you?"

"Yes," my younger self replied with a perfectly blank face.

The teacher waved her hand in the air while a smile spread across her face. "Oh, your sister was such a pleasure to teach. Bright, kind, polite, and top of the class on every test." She gave the younger me another smile. "I'm sure you'll live up to her standards too."

I was one second away from yanking my hand from Callan's grip and throwing an attack at the figures from my memory, or at the damn force mage himself, but right then he tightened his grip on my hand. It was so intense that a pulse of pain shot through my bones, and it snapped me out of the bitterness for a few seconds.

Glancing up, I found Callan glaring at the darkened trees on his left. I had no idea what he was seeing, but if his memories were as delightfully *pleasant* as mine, he wasn't having a great time either. Forcing out a long breath through my nose, I tried to keep my mind in the present. But once again, another room from another bitter memory shimmered to life on my right.

This was going to be a long damn walk.

Chapter 5

Callan

We should have reached the mansion long ago. If we had walked in a straight line from the tunnel mouth and towards Grant's house, we should have already been there. But we weren't. Only trees and glittering flowers and glowing fruits stared back at us as Audrey and I stalked across the grass.

"Are we walking in circles?" I ground out.

Those intensely bitter emotions from earlier were gone, along with the purple flowers, but my already tense mood hadn't exactly improved by having to relive all those damn memories.

"I don't know," Audrey replied. "It feels like we're walking straight towards the mansion at least."

"Except we can't trust our feelings," I snapped. "Because that is exactly what Grant is manipulating."

"I know that," Audrey sniped back, her voice sharp. "But you asked a question, and I answered as best as I could. I have no fucking idea if we're walking around in circles or not, so don't blame me."

Her eyes flashed like hardened gemstones as she glared up at me. The anger inside me fizzled out. Tilting my head back, I raked my fingers through my hair and blew out a long breath.

"You're right. I'm sorry." I rubbed my forehead before meeting her gaze again. "Fuck, I hate this. I can't tell which of my feelings are actually mine and which are just there because some bloody plant is messing with me."

Her features softened and she heaved a deep sigh, as if she too had been caught up in feelings that weren't necessarily her own. "I know. Same."

The crackling tension around us eased up a bit as we continued walking. I looked over my shoulder again, trying to estimate how far away we now were from the tunnel. But with the trees and bushes blocking the view, not to mention the darkness, it was hard to tell. I turned back to the path ahead.

Panic flashed through me.

Throwing out my hand, I grabbed Audrey by the arm and yanked her backwards.

"What the hell," she snapped as she stumbled back and almost crashed into me. "What are you—"

"We can't go through here," I interrupted.

Before she could respond, I forcibly hauled her backwards and away from the flowers that had begun appearing on the trees. Audrey tried to yank out of my grip, but I was much stronger than her so it didn't work. She let out a low snarl but could do nothing except follow me.

Only once we were a safe distance away did I release her.

She yanked her arm away and rolled her shoulder while glaring up at me. "What the hell is going on? Are you affected by some kind of magic right now or what?"

"Those flowers." Raising an arm, I pointed towards the area we had just left. "They were the same ones I saw in that cavern in the mountain in Castlebourne."

"The..." She trailed off as realization slammed home on her

features. With her mouth still open, she turned and looked towards the now no longer visible flowers. "Oh."

"Yeah."

My heart pounded in my chest. The last time I had breathed in the pollen from those red and gold glittering flowers, I had hunted Audrey through twisting tunnels and almost strangled her to death. Those flowers were infused with a magic that stripped a person of every emotion except one. The overwhelming need to slaughter everything and everyone around them. That loss of control had been one of the most terrifying things I had ever experienced.

"Alright," Audrey said as she turned back to me. "We'll go around that section then."

Lingering dread was still bouncing around inside me, so I only managed a nod. Audrey brushed the back of her hand against mine and then started towards the left. Her touch helped pull me out of those dreadful memories, and I rolled my shoulders back before following her.

Nocturnal insects hummed in the foliage around us. It mingled with the soft rustling of leaves to create an almost soothing effect. I knew that it was just a lie. A ruse to distract people right before the next danger materialized. My pulse thrummed in my ears as I scanned the bushes and trees around us, looking for threats.

Clusters of what looked like giant raspberries hung from the thick branches above, and between them were long yellow fruits that shone like lanterns. I glared at them, but nothing dangerous jumped out to attack us.

A snarl cut through the soft singing of the insects.

I snapped my gaze back down to the ground right as Audrey leaped back and called up a cloud of poison.

"Callan," she hissed while I summoned a force blade and whipped my head from side to side. "There are wolves here."

Indeed, dark shapes prowled in a circle around us. Just out of sight.

Fucking hell.

I released the blade and instead called up a force wall. "Can you poison them from here?"

Glittering green mist swirled in front of Audrey as she turned slightly. "I think so. Cover my back."

"Always."

Her poison magic shot through the air and towards the closest shape. I squinted against the darkness.

"Did it hit?" I asked.

For a few seconds, she said nothing. "I don't know."

Calling up another cloud, she hurled it at the next prowling shadow. Leaves rustled and a branch snapped behind us. I whirled towards it, my force wall ready to block an attack at a moment's notice. But nothing leaped out.

One of the wolves let out a rumbling growl.

Audrey shot several whips of poison into the darkness. More snarls followed, but if anything, the prowling shapes seemed to be growing in number. Fear surged through me.

"Audrey," I said.

"I know," she snapped back. "I'm trying."

Green light flashed between the tree trunks. The wolves snarled and growled with increasing ferocity.

My gaze flicked back and forth, tracking their shapes as they circled us again and again. The fear inside my chest intensified until I could feel it seeping through my veins like cold poison. We wouldn't be able to fight them all off if they attacked at the same time.

Fear.

It felt like jogging in mud to try to get my brain to follow that thought down to where it had come from.

Fear. Why was I so afraid of wolves? I shouldn't be. Which meant that this...

"Why won't they die?" Audrey pressed out. The terror in her voice was clearly audible.

Poison tendrils shot out around her as she threw more and more magic at the growling wolves. Their dark shapes lunged a step towards us before continuing to circle us. And their numbers kept growing.

"They're..." I began, trying desperately to grasp that slippery thread in my mind that I had just discovered.

"Do something, Callan! They'll attack any second now and I can't hold them off on my own!"

Blinking hard, I shook my head to clear it. "They're not..." It was an incredible struggle to keep that precious thought strung together in the right order. "Real."

The moment I said it, it was as if the thought finally lodged itself firmly in my mind.

"They're not real," I repeated, with more conviction this time.

"They're coming! Callan, on your left."

Turning in the direction she was pointing, I stalked straight for the dark shadows that prowled there. My heart slammed against my ribs. But I was sure that I was right.

"What are you doing?" Audrey yelled from behind me, trying to snatch at my clothes to keep me from going.

I yanked out of her grip and met her gaze for a few seconds. "They're not real, Audrey. The wolves, they're not real. Here, I'll show you."

And then I turned around and ran right into the mass of prowling shapes.

Chapter 6

Pink flowers and pale purple fruit sparkled in the foliage around us. I glared at them before bending down to pull out a waterskin from inside my pack. Opposite me, Callan set his pack down as well and did the same.

It was impossible to tell how much time had passed since we left the tunnel. It might have been half an hour. Or five hours. With all of these damn plants constantly messing with my emotions, I was starting to lose touch with reality.

At least the wolves hadn't actually been real, and the irrational terror that had gripped me had disappeared as soon as we left that part of the gardens behind. But it was only a matter of time before the next piece of emotion magic hit.

I shook my head at the glowing woodlands around us before taking a swig from my waterskin. *Hell fucking damn Harvey Grant.*

"Hell fucking damn Harvey Grant," Callan muttered after wiping the back of his hand across his mouth.

A surprised laugh escaped my lips.

Callan scowled at me. "What?"

"I was just thinking the exact same thing."

His lips twitched in a small smile. Then he heaved a deep sigh and shoved his waterskin back into his pack. "We should be out there, slaughtering Quill and the rest of his damn parliament. Not here..." Straightening, he flung out an arm to indicate the gardens. "Fighting Grant's unruly vegetation."

A pulse of desire flickered through me at the way Callan's muscles rippled when he moved. I shook my head. *Focus.*

"Yeah," I said instead. "But at least it explains how he came to be one of the six surviving dark mages. And why Quill and his massive army haven't been able to take the mansion. I doubt anyone has ever gotten through these gardens without Grant's permission."

Callan raked his gaze up and down my body, and his eyes darkened. It made heat pool at my core.

Clearing his throat, he gave his head a couple of quick shakes and said, "Agreed."

"We should get going."

"Yes."

For a few seconds, we only watched each other in silence. The sparkling pink and violet light cast colorful highlights in his dark hair. Fuck, I wanted to run my hands through it so badly. Actually, I wanted to rip his clothes off and run my hands *all over him.*

With great effort, I tore my gaze from his body and bent down to put my waterskin back into my pack. This really wasn't the time for distractions. But the sudden need to feel his naked body against mine was so intense that I could barely think straight.

Drawing in a deep breath, I straightened again.

I blinked in surprise when I found Callan standing right in front of me. So close that I could almost feel his breath on my skin. His gaze seared into my very soul as he raked hungry eyes up and down my body.

My pussy throbbed with the need for him. To touch him. To reach out and just—

His lips crashed against mine. With his fist buried in my collar, he yanked my body the final distance towards him and kissed me as if the world might end any second. I raked my fingers through his hair before taking it in a firm grip while I answered the kiss with the same desperate need.

A moan tore from my chest as he slid his hands down my sides and grabbed the hem of my shirt. I could barely convince myself to draw back from his mouth enough for him to yank my shirt over my head. It fluttered through the warm evening air as Callan threw it down on the thick grass.

The rest of the glowing forest seemed to disappear as Callan and I ripped off the rest of our clothes. He was the only thing that mattered. *We* were the only thing that mattered.

A small part of my mind was trying to say something. Scream something. That there was something else that we should be doing right now. Something important. But the voice was quickly drowned out by the tidal wave of lust that crashed over me when I took in Callan's naked body.

Glittering light illuminated the sharp ridges of his abs and painted his muscled chest with shifting contours. Blazing desire shot through me as my eyes dipped down to his hard cock.

Before the final piece of clothing had even finished hitting the ground, I lurched forward and grabbed the back of his neck, pulling his firm body flush against mine. He slid his strong arms around my ass and lifted me up. Wrapping my legs around his waist and locking my fingers behind his neck, I claimed his mouth with furious passion while he walked us towards the nearest tree trunk.

The bark scraped against my naked back as Callan pushed me against it while continuing to ravage my lips.

In a synchronized move, I shifted my hips while Callan

lifted me up and then slid me down onto his cock. A deep groan rumbled from his chest and into my mouth. With my legs still wrapped around his waist, I braced myself on his shoulders as I started moving.

Pleasure rippled through me at the feeling of his cock inside me. Angling my hips, I ground my clit against his shaft as I slid up and down the thick length. A whimper spilled from my lips.

Fuck, had he always felt this good? I just wanted to get lost in this feeling forever.

Callan's hands roamed across my heated skin while I rode his cock, making sparkles skitter over my body in their wake. Intense pleasure pulsed through me, soaring to terrifying heights. I dug my fingers into his shoulders. A dark moan rolled from Callan's tongue, and he bit my bottom lip while continuing to claim my mouth.

The friction against my pussy was driving me insane. I shifted my position slightly before rolling my hips at a faster pace.

Release exploded through my body. I gasped against Callan's lips as my pussy trembled around his cock. Tightening my grip on his shoulders, I tried desperately to keep myself from falling while pleasure ricocheted through my limbs. He braced his hands on my sides, helping my movements along until release shot through him as well.

I should have felt satisfied when the orgasm wore off, but I didn't. It wasn't enough. I wanted more.

Callan must have felt the same way because after he lifted me off his cock and set my bare feet down on the grass again, he grabbed my hips and spun me around so that my back was pressed against his hard chest.

Gray force magic wrapped around his right hand as he brushed his palms together. My legs were still wobbly, so I almost collapsed against his chest when he took his hands from my hips.

Reaching up, Callan wrapped his left hand around my throat, keeping me steady and holding me firmly against him while he drew his right hand down my stomach and over my pussy.

A small whimper escaped my lips as his vibrating force magic pulsed against my clit. It was still sensitive from the previous orgasm, and I squirmed slightly against him as he rubbed a finger over it.

With his hand still around my throat, Callan leaned down and kissed his way along my jaw while his fingers traced gentle circles around my clit. Pleasure crackled through my veins. Fuck, I wanted his lips on me, his hands on me, his cock in me, all the time. Nothing else in the world mattered. Only this. Right here.

I sucked in a breath as Callan plunged two fingers inside me. A tremor coursed through my body as he positioned his thumb against my clit, sending his magic pulsing against it, while he began pumping his fingers in and out. Lights flickered through my brain. I wiggled my hips, trying to increase the friction. Callan tightened his grip on my throat in response and began a circling motion with his thumb.

Pleasure pulsed through me. I sucked in desperate breaths underneath his strong hand while his lips brushed over my jaw, inching closer to that spot below my ear. His fingers pumped in and out of my pussy.

A pleading moan slipped from my mouth.

Callan increased the pace and the strength of his magic.

My chest heaved.

Keeping my eyes squeezed shut, I squirmed against his muscular body as the pleasure trapped inside me grew. It was so close. So close now.

He kissed that perfect spot below my ear right as his vibrations shoved me straight over the edge.

I cried out as the orgasm crashed through me. My whole body shook. Only Callan's hand around my throat kept me upright as I came hard all over his hand. He kept pumping his fingers into my trembling pussy throughout the entire climax.

When he at last pulled his fingers out and relaxed his grip on my throat, we both just collapsed to the ground. My chest rose and fell with deep breaths as I lay there on the soft grass, staring up at the dark blue heavens visible between the glowing pink flowers.

But once I had recovered my breath, that feeling came creeping back in again. It wasn't enough. I wanted more. I *needed* more.

Sitting up, I slung my leg over Callan's naked body so that I was straddling him. His brown eyes were dark with desire and need too as he met my gaze. Grabbing the back of my neck, he pulled my mouth down to his in a violent kiss. I dragged my fingers over his chest, tracing the lines of his muscles. He slid his hands down to rest on my sides.

In one fluid motion, he flipped us around and rolled over so that I was lying on my back and he was straddling me instead. Lightning crackled across my skin as he drew his hands up my chest and then along my arms before taking my wrists in a firm grip. My pussy throbbed with need as he forced my hands down onto the grass, keeping them trapped there while he repositioned his hips.

A satisfied groan tore from deep within my chest as he shoved his cock inside me.

I angled my hips and spread my legs wider to give him better access as he started up a rough pace.

The world could be ending for all I cared. I didn't need food. Or water. Didn't need sleep or air. I only needed this. This pleasure that pulsed through my body and filled my whole being. Nothing else in the world mattered. I was going to stay right here in this garden for the rest of my life.

Soft grass tickled my skin as Callan slammed into me, sending my body jerking back and forth on the ground. Still keeping my wrists trapped beside me, he leaned down and stole a desperate kiss from my lips. I deepened it.

My heart slammed against my ribs in tune with his pounding.

Curling my fingers into fists, I sucked in rapid breaths as incredible pleasure pulsed through me. This was it. This was all I would ever need in life.

Callan changed up the pace, and a moan tore from my throat.

The tension inside me was so intense that I thought I was going to shatter. Just one more push. One more and—

That all-consuming haze of lust vanished in a flash, as if someone had ripped off a veil that had been blocking my vision.

I blinked up at Callan, who had abruptly stopped with his cock still inside me. He looked about as confused as I felt. What the hell were we doing?

However, before I could open my mouth to ask that question out loud, an amused voice drifted through the warm evening air.

"Well, this was certainly an interesting way to end an otherwise dreadfully boring day."

Chapter 7

Callan

For a few seconds, all I could do was stare. Stare down at Audrey who was lying naked beneath me. At my hands keeping her wrists trapped beside her head on the grass. At my own naked body. I knew exactly what we had been doing these past minutes, and while it was something that I always very much enjoyed, I didn't understand why we had decided to do it here. And now. In Grant's garden.

Then the words that I had just heard spoken registered, and everything clicked into place.

Releasing Audrey's wrists, I gently pulled my cock out of her pussy and climbed off her. She sat up and flicked a glance between me and the person behind me before she slowly pushed to her feet. Her face was flushed, and blades of grass clung to her tangled hair.

Embarrassment seared through me. But I refused to let it show, so I drew in a bracing breath before standing up and turning to face the source of the voice.

A very average-looking man with brown hair was standing a few steps away. Harvey Grant. Amusement danced across his features as he swept his gaze over our utterly naked bodies. That burning embarrassment tried to resurface again, and I glanced towards where our clothes lay scattered on the ground a short distance behind Grant.

Clearing my throat, I managed a somewhat strained, "Grant."

"Callan," he replied, mirth still sparkling in his blue eyes. His gaze slid to Audrey and, fortunately for him, stayed on her face. "Audrey. Impressive show. I almost wish I could have seen the whole thing."

Audrey flashed him a sly smile. "Need inspiration for your own sex life?"

He chuckled but didn't respond. Instead, he shifted his attention back to me. For a second, his gaze dipped down to my still hard cock, and he gave me a half nod in what looked like approval. I wasn't sure whether to grin or throw a force wall at him.

"Mind throwing our clothes over here?" I said instead.

Grant returned his gaze to our faces. "In a minute."

"Excuse me?" Audrey challenged, a sharp note to her voice.

She didn't look embarrassed in the slightest even though we were currently standing stark naked in front of another dark mage.

"First, you need to do something," Grant replied in a calm voice. His expression was suddenly dead serious as he looked from face to face. "You need to swear a blood oath that you will never reveal any of my mansion's secrets or use them against me."

"I'm getting dressed," I announced, and took a step forward to go and get the clothes myself.

However, before I could take another one, that intense feeling of lust crashed over me again. Trailing to a halt, I looked over at Audrey. Fuck, I wanted to yank her back to me and wrap my arms around her and feel her hands all over my body. I wanted to—

I shook my head and blinked hard. *Hell damn it.*

"Grant," I ground out as I turned back to the emotion mage. "Do I need to remind you that you swore a blood oath to never do anything to hurt me or Audrey?"

"I did indeed." He looked back at me with a no-nonsense expression on his face. "And I will uphold that oath. I will never do anything to hurt you. And if you don't swear this blood oath to me, to keep my secrets, I won't do anything to you. I will just leave."

My gaze was involuntarily drawn back to Audrey as another wave of overwhelming need for her slammed into me. It took all of my self-control to drag my gaze back to Grant.

"And when I leave, the protection that I was previously extending to you, the protection from the effects of those flowers up there, will disappear with me." Grant shrugged. "At which point you will succumb to the effects fully once more. And based on what I just walked in on, it will most likely end with the two of you fucking each other nonstop until you die of dehydration."

"We're in the middle of a bloody war, Grant."

"A war that, as you have already noticed, I will be able to weather perfectly fine in here. So, if you want my help in this war, you will swear a blood oath to never reveal any of my mansion's secrets and to never use them against me."

It was getting increasingly difficult to concentrate on his words when Audrey's whole being seemed to be calling out to mine, just two steps away. Based on the expression on her face, she was having similar difficulties. And no matter how much I tried to pretend otherwise, I was pretty sure that Grant was right.

Bitterness and fear were emotions I didn't often feel, so

those had been a bit easier to manage. But the burning passion that existed between me and Audrey was already so strong that Grant's magic would be able to push it to intensities that were impossible to break. If he left, we *would* probably fuck each other in a lust-filled haze until we died.

Steel sang into the darkened woodlands as Grant pulled out a short knife and tossed it towards us. It landed in the grass before our feet.

"The choice is yours," he said simply.

"Fucking hell," I growled as I snatched up the knife.

Due to his casual manner and his non-combative personality, I often forgot that Harvey Grant was a dark mage. A *true* dark mage who knew exactly how to leverage his power and bend others to his will. As I stood there completely naked in front of him and ready to cut my own palm to give him the blood oath he wanted, I couldn't help but wonder how dangerous Grant could have been if he'd had any sort of interest in expanding his power and influence instead of just staying here, secluded in his mansion, with his extravagant parties. In all honesty, I was pretty sure that I didn't want to find out.

A thin line of red appeared on my skin as I drew the blade across my palm and spoke the words of the blood oath.

To be fair, it was a reasonable ask. I wouldn't have wanted to share the security protocols for my mansion with anyone else either, and Grant was even more secretive than most. And besides, I had no plans to actually attack his mansion either, now or in the future, so the oath didn't change anything.

Grant gave me a nod as I finished and passed the knife to Audrey, who did the same. As soon as her blood oath was complete as well, Grant brushed his palms together, making his shimmering purple magic float into the air around us once more. All the lingering feelings of lust disappeared in a heartbeat. I dragged a hand through my hair and blew out a short breath.

Across the grass, Grant took a step to the side and motioned towards our clothes. Audrey and I exchanged a glance before we stalked past the emotion mage and grabbed our discarded garments.

Once we were finally dressed again, we turned back around to face him.

"Damn." Audrey cocked her head and flicked her gaze up and down his body. "I had forgotten how ruthless you can be, Grant."

A small smile ghosted across his lips. "Yes, it seems people often do."

"Can we just get on with it?" I muttered as I hoisted my pack.

"Certainly." Grant raised his arm in the direction of the mansion. "Follow me."

The walk through the dense gardens was a lot easier with Grant's magic protecting us from the effects of the plants. Audrey and I must have been walking in circles at some point, because now we reached the white stone mansion in no time. Glass domes in different colors hung all throughout the gardens closest to the building. However, the candles inside them were unlit. These areas had once been filled with happy partygoers, but now they lay empty and dark.

I raised my eyebrows as Grant led us away from the back door and towards the other side of the building. Only crawling vines covered the smooth wall. There were no windows on this side. Or doors.

Leaves rustled as Grant stuck his hand into a cluster of thick vines. A moment later, there was a click. And then part of the wall swung open to reveal a doorway.

Audrey let out a low whistle. "So that's how you get into the actual mansion."

The corridor that led from the front entrance to the back door and the gardens beyond didn't contain any other doors or staircases, so no one had been sure how Grant got into the rest of his home. But I supposed now we knew.

Grant looked over his shoulder at Audrey. She held up a hand as if to say that she remembered the blood oath. After watching us with serious eyes for another two seconds, he strode across the threshold. We followed.

Behind us, the door swung shut again with a soft click.

After the darkness in the gardens, the sudden bright light that filled the room we stepped into almost blinded me. I blinked repeatedly in order to get my eyes to adjust.

"Audrey!" a cheerful voice called.

Still squinting against the light, I barely managed to avoid getting mowed down by Paige as she raced past me and threw her arms around Audrey.

"I knew it," Paige said as she stepped back. With her hands still on Audrey's shoulders, she gave Audrey's body a little shake. "If anyone would be able to go to Malgrave and convince Levi Arden to help us and then survive the trip back and then through the gardens and all that, it was you because you've always been resourceful like that and—"

"Paige," Audrey interrupted. Her green eyes glittered as she gave her friend a smile. "Breathe."

The blond forger sucked in a deep breath and then let out a rippling laugh. I turned towards the rest of the room right as a mountain of a man stopped in front of me and clapped me on the shoulder. Relief pulsed through me at the sight of him, and I reached up to give his muscular arm a couple of friendly pats.

"Glad to see your head's still attach to the rest of your body, boss," Henry said while a grin tugged at his lips.

I snorted. "You and me both."

"So you pulled it off then?"

"Yeah." I slid my gaze to Grant, who had stopped halfway into the room. "Where's Sam? We should probably get him too before we tell that story."

Grant waved a hand towards the doorway set into the spotless marble wall. "This way."

Henry clapped me on the shoulder again before following the emotion mage through the door. I glanced back to see Paige speaking rapidly to Audrey. Both of them wore expressions of relief. They started forward too as I strode after Henry and Grant.

Grant's mansion looked pretty much how I had expected it to look. Smooth white marble inlaid with veins of gold, beautiful paintings depicting different nature scenes in gilded frames, and expensive furniture made of pale wood. I let my eyes sweep over the corridors and rooms as we made our way upstairs and then followed Grant through a doorway and into another room.

Bookshelves lined most of the walls inside while a rich carpet in dark green and gold covered the floor. A cluster of leather couches and armchairs were arranged around a low table in the middle of the space. I stopped short as my gaze fell on the people inside.

"Callan," Malcolm Griffith said in greeting as he looked up from the book he had been reading.

"Malcolm," I said while Audrey and Paige trailed inside as well. "Last I heard, you were on the run." My gaze slid to the attractive redhead pacing back and forth in front of the windows. "And you were unaccounted for."

"I detest running," Malcolm announced, and flicked imaginary dirt off his impeccable black suit.

"I don't even know what it means to be unaccounted for,"

Sienna stated while tossing her long red hair behind her shoulder.

"I'm so glad you're back!" Sam interrupted. His gray eyes lit up as he took in both me and Audrey. "Does that mean you did it? Did you actually manage to get Levi Arden to come?"

"Oh, calm down, children," Grant said before I could respond. While rolling his eyes, he strolled over to the oversized armchair next to the one Malcolm was currently occupying. The cushions let out a soft huff as he plopped down. "I found Malcolm and Sienna lurking outside my gardens shortly after the attacks on their mansions, so I invited them in." He waved a hand at us. "Now, have a seat so that we can bring each other up to speed."

Henry glanced back at me before moving over to one of the couches. I joined him.

"I don't lurk," Sienna proclaimed while Audrey and Paige set course for the sofa opposite ours.

"No," Grant agreed. "You tried to burn your way into my garden instead."

"Exactly. That's not lurking."

The leather couch creaked slightly as Henry and I sat down on it and adjusted our weight.

"But *you* most definitely lurk," Grant said, and shot a pointed look at Malcolm.

A hint of a smile drifted across the shadow mage's lips as he put his book down on the low table. "Yes. I do."

Sam, who had been sitting cross-legged in the armchair opposite Malcolm, leaped to his feet and started towards Audrey. She looked over at him in surprise as she and Paige sat down on the couch.

"Didn't I just ask you all to sit down?" Grant shook his head at him. "Why are you getting up?"

"You swore the blood oath about the secrets, right?" Sam

said, his eyes on Audrey. "I'll just fix the cut in your palm. And any other injuries from your trip to Malgrave."

"No need," I said.

They all turned to look at me.

I shrugged. "Levi's healer already did."

Next to me, Henry stared at me with wide eyes and eyebrows that almost reached his hairline. I waved a hand in front of my face to tell him that we'd get to that. Shimmering turquoise light joined the warm glow from the oil lamps and candles as Sam called up his magic and healed the cut on Audrey's palm.

"And you," Grant said while shooting a half exasperated, half amused look at Sienna. "Are you going to sit down?"

Sienna scrunched up her brows as if that was the most ridiculous thing she'd ever heard. "No."

From his position in the other armchair, Malcolm blew out a sigh and pinched the bridge of his nose.

It took great effort not to chuckle. If Malcolm and Sienna had shown up shortly after they were attacked, that meant that they had been staying here in Grant's mansion for weeks at this point. Those three trapped together for that long... It was a bloody miracle that all of them were still alive.

Once Sam had healed both my and Audrey's cuts, he returned to his armchair, which meant that everyone who was planning to sit down was now at last seated.

For a few seconds, the eight of us just watched each other in silence.

Then, Malcolm steepled his fingers.

"So, what happened in Malgrave?"

Chapter 8

"So... Mr. Arden will actually come?" Sam said, his eyebrows raised, once Callan had finished speaking. The expression on his face made him look both shocked and impressed. "And with a bunch of his people too?"

Callan nodded. "Yeah."

"Wow. I have to admit, I didn't really think you'd be able to pull that off."

Malcolm hummed in agreement. "Me neither."

"Thanks for the vote of confidence," I muttered.

Paige slapped my arm with the back of her hand. "I never doubted you for a second."

I chuckled and flashed her a small smile.

"So, we have a metal mage who can destroy the Blade of Equilibrium," Grant picked up. Waving a hand, he motioned towards the windows. "But we still have that army out there to deal with too."

"Yes!" Sienna interrupted. She stopped her pacing only long enough to stab a hand towards the dark garden outside. "So let's go out there and attack them now. Callan and Audrey are back, which means that our battle strength has almost doubled. So let's take the fight to them!"

Exasperation flickered in Malcolm's brown eyes as he slid his gaze to the fire mage. "Not before we make a plan."

"I am sick and tired of making plans! We've been sitting around in here for *weeks* now." Raising her arms, she raked both hands through her long red hair. "It's making me crazy!"

"As opposed to the usual mental stability that you're so famous for, you mean?"

Grant cleared his throat before Sienna could hurl a fireball at the shadow mage. Light from the candles throughout the room glinted in his blue eyes as he turned his head and looked from face to face as if to make sure that no one was about to start a fight in his library. When we all just looked back at him in silence, he nodded.

"Alright." He shifted his gaze between me and Callan. "So, when is Levi Arden coming?"

We exchanged a glance.

"Soon, hopefully," I said.

"He had to finish killing some people in Malgrave first," Callan supplied.

Henry snorted. "That does sound like Levi."

By the windows, Sienna threw out her arms in an exasperated gesture. "So we're just going to hide here until he comes?"

"We are not hiding," Malcolm retorted at the same time as Grant said, "Yes."

I massaged my brows. How in all hell had they managed weeks of this without slaughtering each other?

"Grant," Callan said before they could start fighting again. "Quill's army uses the Great Current. They can all access fire magic. What's to stop them from just burning your entire gardens down?"

A wicked grin slid home on Grant's mouth. "Oh, they've tried. But if it was that easy to get through, I wouldn't have survived this long, now would I?"

Sienna stabbed her hand at him. "If we don't do something soon, *I'm* going to burn them down myself!"

"You already tried that, remember? It didn't work."

"You thought that was a proper attempt? Oh, you haven't seen anything yet. Why don't we—"

"Enough," I snapped. "Fucking hell, this day has been infuriating enough as it is without your incessant bickering. Malcolm is right, we need to make a plan before we attack. But so is Sienna. We *should* attack." Drawing my eyebrows down, I scowled at the three arguing dark mages. "If only so that the three of you can take out all of your frustrations on the real enemy instead of each other."

Sienna's citrine eyes lit up like firebolts at the promise of battle. In his armchair, Malcolm just heaved a sigh and waved a hand in agreement. Grant gave me a nod.

The leather armchair to my left creaked faintly as Sam shifted his weight while holding up a hand. We all turned towards him.

"Uhm, not to bring down the mood or anything," he began while shifting his gaze from face to face. "But I'm not a battle mage." His blond hair fell down slightly across his forehead as he nodded towards our couch. "And neither is Paige. Which leaves the six of you. I mean, I know you're good. But six people... against an army?"

"We're not going to be fighting an army," I said. "How about this?"

Eyebrows rose and sly smiles spread across several faces as I explained what I had in mind. From the couch opposite me, Callan flashed me an approving grin.

"I like it!" Sienna said, and rubbed her hands together.

Grant drew a hand over his jaw. "I... approve too. And I have several more tunnels that we can use, so we won't need to go through the gardens."

"Perfect," I said.

"I approve too," Paige added. "On one condition."

Turning, I frowned at my friend. "You're not even a part of this attack plan."

"I still have a condition."

A surprised chuckle escaped my throat. "Alright. Let's hear it then."

"Get me one of the constables' uniforms."

This time, all seven of us frowned at her.

"Why?" I asked.

"Because we need eyes inside that camp. And I..." Touching her palms together, she called up a ball of fire before extinguishing it and then summoning water, followed by lightning. "Can pass as one of them. *You* cannot."

"Absolutely not."

She narrowed her eyes at me. "Get me a uniform, or I'll go out there and get one myself. Your choice."

Forcing out a breath, I gave her a flat look. "How had I forgotten just how stubborn you can be?"

While rolling her eyes, she snorted and slapped my arm with the back of her hand. "Like you're one to talk."

"It is actually an excellent idea," Malcolm said before I could retort.

I drew a hand through my hair while giving Paige a sideways look. Her blue eyes glittered in the light from the candles. Or with mischief. With her, it was sometimes hard to tell. I heaved a sigh.

"Fine."

"Then get one for me too," Henry said. His gray eyes were

serious as he met Paige's gaze from across the low table. "You're not going out there alone."

"Uhm, yes, I am." She gave her head a few quick shakes. "Because I won't draw attention. You will."

Still holding her gaze, Henry summoned wind and then water. "I'm not a dark mage either."

"No, but you're like eight feet tall!"

He crossed his muscular arms over his broad chest and muttered, "I'm actually only seven foot one."

"Fantastic, then that means you don't tower over people everywhere you go." She shot him a flat look. "Oh wait, you do."

"It's still risky—" I began, but Paige cut me off.

"Look, I get that you all feel like you should be protecting me or whatever because I'm not a super powerful dark mage or something, but let me remind you that while you..." There was a stubborn set to her mouth as she locked eyes with each and every one of us. "...have been living openly out here in the hills, I have been working as a forger. I have been breaking the law *inside* the city of Eldar *for six years* without getting caught." Crossing her arms, she threw herself back against the leather backrest and glared at us. "I know how to remain unnoticed."

Ringing silence followed her proclamation.

Guilt swirled up inside me. I saw it mirrored in Henry's eyes too.

She was right. She wasn't some normal civilian who needed to be protected while the rest of us schemed and fought. She was Paige. *The* Paige.

"You're right." Clearing my throat, I gave her an apologetic smile. "I'm sorry. We'll get you a uniform."

"Good." She tried to keep her face an imperious mask, but a grin tugged at her lips and her eyes sparkled with amusement. "Don't make me lecture you again."

I chuckled and then blew out a breath before turning towards the others.

"Alright, so who's up for some guerilla warfare?"

Leaves rustled faintly in the warm night wind as we left Grant's massive garden behind and snuck towards the wagons across the grass. Apparently, that paranoid emotion mage had several escape tunnels built into his mansion. The one we had just come through emptied out in a spot close to where Quill's army kept the wagons with some of their food supplies. Which was our target for the night.

Malcolm's shadows twisted around us as we moved in formation towards our targets. In the darkness, and with that added layer of magical protection, we were all but invisible. Grant was walking at the front, mostly just because we trusted him to keep his head on straight more than we trusted Sienna, who we had placed in the middle so that she couldn't suddenly decide to go rogue. And Malcolm brought up the rear so that he could cover us all with his shadows, while Callan and I occupied the flanks.

Since this was a stealth operation against a specific target, only the people who had skills that were necessary for its success had been allowed to come, which meant that we had left Paige, Henry, and Sam back at the mansion. Both to minimize the danger to them and also the risk of us being spotted.

A shape suddenly became visible on my side. I touched my palms together and shot a thin whip of poison straight towards it. Malcolm shifted his shadows aside to let it pass, and a second later, it slammed into the guard's face and shoved its way down her throat. She only managed to suck in one startled breath before she collapsed to the ground.

From somewhere on my right, another thud sounded, informing me that Callan had also assassinated an unwitting guard. While Malcolm kept us all covered, our job was to take out anyone who stood in our way.

My heart pattered in my chest as I swept my gaze back and forth across the grass on the left. My magic was lethal, but it was also green and glittering, which meant that it was much easier to see in the dark than Callan's force magic. But as long as I attacked while the person was looking in another direction, we would be fine.

Three more guards died on my side as we closed the distance to the target. One of them had been half a second away from getting a warning shout out of his mouth, but thankfully, my magic had hit him just in time.

Shadows continued swirling around us, covering us from view, as we stopped next to one of the wagons. Grant touched his hands together and moved up to the baskets and crates that were stacked on top of it. Shimmering magic of a pale violet color fluttered down like a blanket above it.

Still in the middle of the shadow bubble, Sienna jumped from foot to foot as if she couldn't contain her excitement. Which was probably the case. It looked like she wanted to yell at Grant to hurry up, but she fortunately kept her mouth shut while Grant did the same thing with the next wagon.

"Now?" she whispered once Grant was done.

"Wait," I answered while hurrying over to one of the constables that I had killed when we approached. While bending down, I flicked an impatient look at Grant. "A little help?"

With the two of us working simultaneously, we managed to quickly strip the dead constable of her uniform. I draped it over my shoulder while Callan grabbed the now half-naked corpse and dragged it over to the third wagon. After dusting off his hands, he returned to his position on the right flank.

"Now," I said to Sienna.

Before I had even finished getting the word out of my mouth, she leaped out of Malcolm's shadow shield and slapped her palms together. A second later, dark red flames tore across the grass like an inferno.

I jerked back slightly at the sheer force of it. Damn, I was glad that Sienna was on our side.

The roaring fire washed over the third wagon, and the fourth and fifth ones behind it too, setting everything aflame. I glanced down at the constable that I had murdered. Her corpse was now only a blackened husk, which hid the fact that her uniform had been stolen.

"Woohoo!" Sienna called as she torched the wagons.

Red flames licked the air and reached towards the dark blue heavens while heat washed over us. That, along with Sienna's mad cry, made shouts of alarm echo through the camp.

"Time to go," I said.

But Sienna only continued pouring flames over the three wagons as if they hadn't already been reduced to crackling firewood. Grant darted up to her and yanked her backwards while screams rose from the previously sleeping soldiers and boots pounded against the ground as they sprinted towards us.

At last, Sienna stopped resisting and whirled around to face us.

A wide grin split her face. And that, along with the fire that blazed behind her, made her look like some kind of lunatic demon from hell. I didn't know whether to laugh or shake my head. But we were out of time, so I did neither and instead followed the others as they took off at a run.

With Malcolm's shadows hiding us from view, we sprinted back to the hidden tunnel and left the roaring inferno behind.

Chapter 9

Callan

Running footsteps sounded in the corridor outside. I rammed the dagger I had been attending to back into its sheath and turned towards the doorway right as Paige skidded across the threshold. Her wavy blond hair bounced around her face as she grabbed the doorjamb to stop her momentum.

"It's time," she pressed out between gulps of air. "They're eating it right now."

"Excellent," Grant said while putting down the document he had been reading. After giving her a nod, he looked between the other six of us. "Then it should only be another twenty minutes before the effects start. Give or take a couple of minutes due to individual differences."

"How do you know?" Audrey asked, a cunning glint in her green eyes.

The same shrewdness gleamed in Grant's too as he shifted his gaze to her and gave her a slow smile. "The same way you know how long a person will be unconscious due to your poison, I suspect."

"Which is what?" Malcolm demanded from his place by the window.

Audrey and Grant exchanged a knowing smile and then turned towards the shadow mage and lifted their shoulders in a synchronized shrug. Malcolm looked about ready to strangle both of them, but thankfully, Sienna interrupted before he could.

"Who cares?" She jumped down from the table she had been sitting on and waved a hand in the air. "She said they're eating it, so let's go already!"

Paige hiked a thumb towards her. "I agree with the impatient fire lady. If we're gonna do this, we need to do it now."

The rest of the room murmured agreement and nodded. Chairs scraped against the floor and clothes rustled as almost everyone headed for the doorway. Paige rapped her knuckles against the doorjamb before taking the lead.

"Be careful," Sam called after us from where he remained by the pale wooden table. "Remember, I can heal you, but not if you're dead."

I huffed out a short chuckle and gave him a nod. "We'll try our best not to die."

"Good."

Our shoes thudded against the polished floor as we made our way towards one of the hidden doors that led to the outside.

"Everyone remembers where to find their tunnel, yes?" Grant said over his shoulder as we strode down the hall.

"Yeah," we all answered more or less in unison.

"Good. Then drink your antidotes now."

Faint pops sounded as we all took out the small glass vial that Grant had given each of us earlier, and pulled out the stopper. The pale violet liquid inside would give us temporary immunity to the effects of Grant's magical garden. I glanced down at the shimmering potion before downing it and then putting the empty vial back into my pocket. All around, the rest of them did the same.

"And *you*..." Grant began as we reached the door. Stopping with his hand on the handle, he turned to lock eyes with our resident pyromaniac. "Don't go overboard."

Sienna rolled her eyes. "First of all, I don't go overboard. I'm thorough. And secondly, you don't give me orders."

Several people opened their mouths to no doubt intervene, but Henry got there first. His steady gray eyes locked on hers, and he spoke with a calm and confident voice.

"If you accidentally burn down these gardens or this mansion, we will all be dead before the night is over."

Surprise flitted through me. Henry didn't usually get involved or speak his mind in these kinds of situations. Normally, he just lurked in the background, listening and watching. But then again, he had also ambushed Audrey and tried to interrogate her about her motives back when we traveled to Castlebourne, which I had only found out about later when he told me, so maybe he had been doing stuff like this for a while. And I had just never noticed. He had also been staying here with Sienna and the others for weeks, which I supposed had broken down some previous barriers too.

The fire mage blew out an annoyed sigh and rolled her eyes again. "Fine. I won't go overboard."

"And remember," Malcolm added before Grant could push the door open. "Don't be reckless. Kill as many as you can manage, but then pull back." His sharp brown eyes moved from face to face. "While I have no particular fondness for any of you, and would shed no tears if you died—"

Audrey put a hand on her chest and flashed him a sharp smile dripping with sarcasm. "I'm touched."

"I still need you for this war," Malcolm finished as if she hadn't interrupted. "We all need each other in order to win this war. So do whatever damage you can, but don't take any unnecessary risks. The real war hasn't even started yet."

As much as that suit-wearing bastard annoyed me, I had to admit that he was right. Levi and his people hadn't even gotten here yet, and if we died now, everything we had just gone through in Malgrave would have been for nothing. So I muttered an agreement and gave him a nod.

"And on that note, let's go slaughter people," Sienna said in a cheerful tone as she placed her hand over Grant's and shoved the handle down.

Evening air smelling of moss and summer flowers whirled into the white marble corridor as the door was pushed open. Sienna darted out as soon as the gap was big enough. Behind her, Grant shook his head but then stepped across the threshold as well once the door was fully open. The rest of us followed too.

Paige's blond hair fluttered behind her as she jogged towards the secret tunnel she had been given. The others began branching off as well.

A sudden flash of panic pulsed up my spine.

Before Audrey and Henry could move past me, my hands shot out and I grabbed their arms. Both of them turned to look at me with eyebrows raised.

I cleared my throat, suddenly feeling incredibly awkward. "Be careful."

Mirrored expressions spread across both of their faces as they looked back at me. Half... softness, or something, and half amusement. It just made me feel more awkward, and heat crept into my cheeks, so I abruptly released them and stalked away instead.

"We'll drink to our victory afterwards," Henry said while I

continued walking.

"And to our dead enemies," Audrey called.

I just gave them a halfhearted wave with the back of my hand and then jogged away towards my designated tunnel. *Fuck.* I loved Audrey, and Henry was like a brother to me. Both of them had somehow become my family, and I hated how much I now worried about them. About their safety. I didn't used to worry about anyone. Coldblooded Callan. I killed colleagues and casual friends alike without a second thought. But now I was suddenly worrying so much about two people that I could barely breathe.

We were about to head into a war with the whole damn city state of Eldar. People were bound to get hurt. Logically, I knew that both Audrey and Henry were lethal in their own right and could most certainly take care of themselves. But there was still no guarantee that they would survive all of this unharmed.

My heart pounded in my chest as I slipped into one of Grant's hidden tunnels and ran towards the other side.

What if they didn't make it?

Steel bands tightened around my chest at the mere thought of it.

They had to make it. We all had to make it. Because if something happened to them, then by all hell, I would tear this whole fucking world to pieces and drench the smoking ruins in blood.

Drawing in a deep breath, I tried to push aside that horrible fear and worry as I reached the end of the tunnel. I couldn't go into battle with my mind scattered. Then I would be the one who didn't make it back.

Moonlight fell across the grasslands outside the garden. I stopped at the very edge, hidden behind a thick tree trunk, and watched the scene ahead for a few minutes. Having something to study and analyze helped take my mind off

Audrey and Henry, and I soon found that steady calm returning.

The constables who were camped outside of Grant's gardens were currently in varying stages of wolfing down their evening meal. I scanned their faces. Light from the fire pits cast shifting colors over their features. As I studied them, it struck me that none of them looked frightened even though they were in the middle of a dark mage war, which was pretty different from what they were used to dealing with back in Eldar. But what was even stranger was that none of them looked particularly eager either. I couldn't help but wonder how many of them truly cared enough about dark mages not sharing their magic to warrant marching out here into a potentially very lethal battle.

That was why I hated democracy. It was too orderly. Too neat. Too many rules about what was right and wrong that you had to follow whether you liked it or not. The dark mage world might be brutal and bloody and completely merciless, but at least I got to make my own choices.

"Hey," one of the constables suddenly called to the guy who had just shot to his feet next to him. "What are you doing?"

The second guy just threw up his hands and started what looked like some kind of weird dance.

"Uhm... dude. What the hell?"

All around the fire pit, more people started twirling and moving around in strange patterns while blissful smiles spread across their faces. I suppressed a chuckle. Grant sure was good at what he did.

Sneaking a couple of steps out of the shadows, I touched my palms together and called up a wide force arc. In the darkness near the garden, the half-translucent gray color was nearly invisible. And even if it hadn't been, I doubted that any of the people by the fire would have seen it. All of them, even the first man who had spoken, were now thoroughly lost in whatever emotion Grant's magic had pulled from them and amplified.

With a snap of my wrist, I threw the arc at them. It spun around itself as it shot through the darkness and straight towards the blissfully ignorant constables.

A shout split the night.

But it hadn't come from these soldiers. In fact, they didn't even see my attack before it cleaved them in half. Blood sprayed into the air as their severed limbs and bodies fell to the ground.

Now, the screaming started near my location too.

A bit farther in, where people must not have eaten dinner yet, soldiers cried out in panic as they saw what happened from a distance. I called up another spinning arc and hurled it towards some of the other constables at the edge. They too were lost in their emotions and died quickly when my attack struck.

But now, others had begun racing towards their location, ready for battle.

I threw one more arc while edging a step back.

Right then, a terrible roaring sound echoed through the air and an entire section was lit up on my left as massive red flames exploded into the dusky evening. I blew out an exasperated sigh while cries of terror rose. What part of 'don't go overboard' did Sienna not understand?

My vibrating magic spun through the air as I shot my next attack. It killed another handful of constables and slashed through two rows of tents behind them.

Shouts of alarm were coming from every side now.

A grin spread across my mouth. What an excellent plan this had been. As they usually were, coming from my vicious little poison mage.

Since there were so few of us, we couldn't attack their forces outright. At least not without first stacking the deck in our favor. Which was what we had done last night.

When we snuck into their camp under the cover of Malcolm's shadows, Grant had infused the food in some of the wagons with his emotion magic. Then, we'd had Sienna torch the rest of the wagons so that the constables would unwittingly be forced to eat the tainted food today. Thanks to Paige's discreet surveillance, we'd been able to pinpoint exactly when they ate the food from those wagons, and therefore also time our attacks.

A simultaneous strike on all fronts, thanks to Grant's convenient tunnels, while the constables were lost in emotion magic and unable to defend themselves, had just given us a small win. And a rather impressive body count for such a short attack.

I let out a dark chuckle as I disappeared back into the trees before the still lucid constables could reach this spot.

Was this an honorable way to wage war? No.

Was it ethical? Also no.

Did we care? Hell no.

As long as we won, there was nothing we wouldn't do.

Chapter 10

Audrey

Colorful vegetables looked back at me from my plate. Using my fork, I poked at the fried pieces while studying them skeptically. The bright colors alone screamed of danger. Even though they had been chopped up and cooked in a frying pan along with herbs and some kind of thin dark sauce, they were still so alarmingly colorful that no normal animal would even dare to go near them. Let alone eat them. Add to that that they had come from *Grant's* garden, and every one of my survival instincts was screaming at me not to touch them.

I glanced up at Callan, who was sitting opposite me at the massive dining room table made of pale wood. The midday sun fell in through the windows and glittered in his dark eyes as he raised his head and met my gaze. Suspicion swirled in his eyes as well.

Next to me, Malcolm tracked Grant's kitchen staff as they set down the final plate in front of Sienna and then moved to stand silently by the wall. Malcolm's brown eyes drifted over the gigantic forest paintings that hung on the walls before his attention slid back to his plate, but he didn't touch the food either.

"There's no magic in it, if that's what you're worried about," Grant said from his seat at the head of the table. His blue eyes twinkled in the sunlight as he looked from face to face. "It's just food."

I glanced down at the white and gold plate again and used my fork to push a bright pink vegetable closer to the edge, but made no move to eat it. Next to Callan, Sienna unceremoniously speared two pale blue pieces and popped them in her mouth. Malcolm, Callan, and I all watched her as she chewed.

A soft chuckle drifted through the room. Leaning back in his ornate chair, Grant swirled the red wine in his glass while watching us with amusement on his face. "I thought we all trusted each other now."

For a few seconds, no one said anything. Sienna kept eating as if she hadn't been listening, but Callan, Grant, Malcolm, and I exchanged a look. Then Callan and Malcolm snorted while Grant and I let out a short chuckle.

Setting down my fork, I instead picked up my glass of wine and raised it in front of me. "To the absence of trust."

The others huffed out a laugh and did the same.

Once I had set my glass down, I looked over at Sienna again. She was almost halfway through her meal already, and since she wasn't acting strangely, or at least not any stranger than usual, I picked up my fork again and began eating as well.

Surprise flitted through me as I took a bite. It was actually really tasty. Spicy yet fresh, and full of flavors I had never experienced before.

"It's just as I suspected," a voice said from the doorway.

We all turned to find Sam strolling into the spacious dining room. Grant immediately lifted a hand and gave some sort of signal to one of the kitchen staff who was waiting by the wall. A young man in a crisp white shirt disappeared towards the kitchen.

"What is?" Malcolm asked.

Sam glanced towards me and Callan. "I've been trying to figure out how to bottle healing magic like you said that healer in Malgrave did, but it's not exactly a trick you learn overnight."

"Any estimated timeline?"

He shook his head, making his blond hair shift slightly around his face, as he dropped into the chair next to Callan. "Maybe a year. At least."

We all nodded. It was to be expected for something as advanced as that.

Right as Sam sat down, the young man reappeared and placed a plate full of those colorful fried vegetables in front of him. He picked up his fork and just dug right in.

A small smile blew across my lips. Sometimes I envied him. He was the only one of us who knew without a doubt that no other dark mage would ever do anything to hurt him.

"Oh, by the way," Sam said around a mouthful of food. "Paige and Henry are on their way back. I saw them through the window so they should be here any—"

"I have news," Paige announced as she and Henry came striding across the threshold.

"Second," Sam finished with a chuckle.

Paige, still wearing the stolen constables uniform, sauntered up to the table and threw herself down on an empty chair to my right. She had been running surveillance on Quill's camp all morning. Before she left, Henry had offered to go with her and watch from the edge of the garden in case something went wrong and she needed help getting out. To my surprise, Paige had let him.

While Grant once more signaled to his staff to bring out more plates, Henry sat down on Paige's other side. The ornate wooden chair creaked in alarm underneath his massive frame.

"Good news or bad news?" I asked.

Paige leaned over and snatched a bright green vegetable off my plate. After popping it in her mouth, she leaned back in her chair again and crossed her arms while chewing thoughtfully. "That depends on what we do with the information."

The young man returned with plates for her and Henry too. Once everything was in place, Grant flicked his wrist. Every member of his kitchen staff quickly disappeared out the door.

"There's a new shipment of food coming," Paige said once they were gone. "To replace what we torched and drugged."

Sienna's eyes finally snapped up from her plate. "So I get to burn all of that to ash too, right?"

"That's where the bad news comes in. It's a trap to lure us out and then ambush us. They're stealthily pulling people from other parts of the camp and sending them to protect that food as it comes in. So it'll be heavily guarded, specifically to make sure they overwhelm you and catch you when you try to go after those wagons."

"I still don't get where the good news part of this is," Sam said, his pale brows scrunched up.

Henry shrugged. "When they shift that many guards to the food delivery, it means that other parts of the camp will be less defended."

"Oh."

Silence fell across the dining room as we all looked at each other.

"So we could hit something else then?" Grant said eventually.

"The question is, should we risk it?" Malcolm slid his gaze to Callan. "When is Arden coming?"

Callan lifted his broad shoulders in a shrug. "I don't know."

"Oh, come on," Sienna interrupted. "Let's attack! Just sitting here won't help us win this war."

Grant heaved a sigh. "She has a point. We could take out their weapons tents. That would make them less likely to push for close combat once the fighting starts. As you already know, most of us here detest close combat."

Silence once more descended on the room while we all considered our options. Only the clinking of utensils broke it as Paige inhaled her food.

I drummed my fingers against the table. Sienna was right. Just hiding in here was pointless. For all I knew, Levi Arden could be a lying piece of shit who had no intention of holding up his end of the bargain. He still hadn't arrived, so who knew when or if he would even show up. And if he didn't, we would need to find a way to end this war on our own, which meant that we couldn't let chances like this one slip past.

"I agree," I said. "Let's hit their weapons tent while they're busy defending the food."

Malcolm straightened the cuffs of his suit jacket. "Just because it's less defended doesn't mean that it's undefended."

I shot him a taunting look. "Scared?"

Not bothering to even dignify such a statement with a reply, he just let a sharp smile full of threats slowly spread across his lips.

"We'll do a coordinated assault," Callan picked up before I could do something to wipe that smile off Malcolm's face. "If we all hit it simultaneously, we'll minimize the risk to us." His dark brown eyes slid to his friend. "Henry?"

Henry huffed out a short laugh and raised his eyebrows. "Do you even need to ask?"

"I'm coming too," Sam announced.

"No," we all blurted out in unison.

His gray eyes flashed as he looked from face to face. "You seem to be forgetting that I'm a dark mage too. I don't need your permission." Raising his chin, he stared us down. "And besides, it was different when you were all hitting different targets. Now, you'll be in the same place at the same time, so it's much easier if I'm there too. Like I keep telling you, I can heal you, but not if you're already dead."

"Yeah, then I'm coming too," Paige said.

Panic and fear crackled through me, and I snapped my gaze to her. "What? No. You're not a battle mage."

She heaved an exasperated sigh and raised her eyebrows at me. "Have you already forgotten that I warned you not to make me lecture you again?"

"No, but this is different. Paige, please. You—"

"Look, I know I'm not a battle mage. But I can block well enough." She pointed towards the blond healer across the table. "Which means that I can shield *him* while you do the fighting."

For a moment, we all just looked at each other.

"That's actually not a bad idea," Henry said at last.

Paige jabbed an elbow into his side and threw him a mock glare. "What do you mean *actually*?"

Red crept into his cheeks, but before he could say anything, Grant spoke up.

"I agree." He nodded to no one in particular. "We all go."

One by one, we nodded back. Malcolm was the last one, but eventually he jerked his chin down as well.

Anticipation crackled through my veins. As soon as Quill moved his people towards the food delivery, we would hit their weapons stash. I was at an incredible disadvantage in close-range fights, so destroying all of their swords and daggers and other weapons would help make sure that I survived the real battles to come.

Oh, I couldn't wait to see Quill's face when he realized that he had sent his people to protect the wrong target.

This was going to be fun.

Chapter 11

Callan

Blood sprayed through the air as the constable lost his head. It rolled off his shoulders and fell to the trampled grass while his body crumpled down next to it. The force scythe I had thrown faded out a couple of steps behind. I continued sneaking forward.

Behind the tent on my right, faint green light shone as Audrey no doubt shot her poison magic towards other unwitting soldiers. On my other side, black shadows whipped through the air as Malcolm did the same.

The golden afternoon sun glinted in a steel sword up ahead. I ducked behind a large brown tent. Leaning forward, I glanced around the edge.

Two constables were standing a short distance ahead. They were facing each other, and their mouths moved as if they were speaking, but I couldn't hear what they were saying. I drew back again. The one on the right was standing at an angle which would make it possible for her to see me. Drumming my fingers against the blade strapped to my thigh, I swept my gaze over the area behind me.

Sienna had almost reached this area now. I glanced from

side to side. The brief hints of Audrey and Malcolm's magic that I had spotted before were now nowhere to be seen, which meant that they had already continued on ahead. I couldn't linger here too long.

Since Sienna was the only one who possessed enough destructive power to actually destroy an entire tent full of steel weapons, she was the one who needed to get there. However, she wasn't exactly the stealthy kind. If she just started blasting her flames for everyone to see, we would have Quill's whole army descending on us in no time. And we couldn't afford that. Which was why Audrey, Malcolm, and I were in charge of clearing a path for Sienna so that she could just walk right up to the tent, while Henry, Paige, and Grant protected Sam and also guarded the rear.

I cast a quick glance around the tent again. What I needed was to divert their attention for a few seconds, so that my attack could take their heads off before they could see it and sound the alarm.

Shifting position, I brushed my palms together and called up a small force blast while calculating the trajectory. I blew out a soft breath. Then I shot the small blast right into a tent a short distance ahead and to the left.

It slammed into the fabric wall, making the whole structure shudder.

The two constables turned towards it in surprise.

That was all I needed.

The moment the force blast left my hand, I summoned a spinning arc and hurled it towards the constables. Since the woman on the right was staring towards the trembling tent, the attack was outside her field of vision. And the other one had never been in a position to see it, so it shot towards them unnoticed.

A wicked grin spread across my mouth as their severed

heads bounced down on the grass, leaving red stains on the otherwise green and brown surface. I darted forward again.

Casting a quick look over my shoulder, I found that Sienna had almost caught up with me now. I lengthened my stride to widen the gap between us again. That damn fire mage was one of the most impatient people I had ever met, and she might start throwing her fire everywhere if we didn't clear the path for her fast enough.

When the weapons tent that Paige had marked at last became visible, I had to suppress the urge to heave a deep sigh of relief. My heart was slamming against my ribs. Not from fear. No, my heart was racing from the stress of trying to complete this mission before Sienna flew off the handle and accidentally turned us all into ash.

While blowing out that sigh I had tried to stifle, I stopped behind the nearest tent and glanced from side to side. Audrey had come to a halt behind a tent directly to my right, while Malcolm was waiting behind one on the left. Both of them gave me a nod when I made eye contact.

Relief fluttered through my chest. So far so good.

There was an open patch of grass separating the large tent used for weapons storage and the smaller ones we were currently hiding behind. Based on Audrey and Malcolm's nods, all the people on their sides were dead. Just like the ones in my path. Moving out into the open would invite unnecessary risk, so we remained where we were until the others caught up.

"Any issues?" Henry asked as he and the other three at last reached my location.

"No," I replied. My gaze slid to Sienna. "Remember what we talked about? When you go into..."

I trailed off and raised my eyebrows because that damn fire mage just kept striding right past me and towards the tent without stopping. A low groan rumbled from my throat. Before she could move past entirely, my hand shot out and wrapped around her arm, yanking her back.

"Did you—" I began.

"What?" she interrupted, while trying to pull her arm out of my grip.

I didn't let her. "Remember what we said about keeping the fire small?"

"Callan Blackwell." Her voice was suddenly silky smooth. It made my skin prickle with a sudden alarming sense of danger. "If you don't take that hand off my arm in the next five seconds, I will melt it all the way to your elbow."

The problem was that I was pretty sure that she *would* do it, so I quickly released my grip on her arm and let my hand drop back down. It shocked me how fast her moods changed sometimes. Henry had once joked that maybe Sienna had more than one personality. I wasn't sure if that was true. But whatever it was, it made her unpredictable. And dangerous.

I opened my mouth to try to find another way to remind her that she couldn't just blast the whole tent to smithereens, but before I could, a deep and steady voice floated through the air.

"Sienna," Henry began. He locked eyes with her, and to my surprise, she kept her attention on him. "If you set a big fire, it will draw everyone here and we'll be outnumbered and captured. But your tiny fires have such incredible destructive power bundled into such small forms, which makes them incredibly beautiful, doesn't it?"

Her eyes took on a faraway look for a few seconds. Then she smiled. "Yes, it does."

Without another word, she turned around and sauntered towards the big weapons tent. A couple of steps behind us, Paige studied Henry while amusement danced across her features. Sam had a similar expression on his face, while Grant just massaged his brows in exasperation.

After scanning the area between us and the tent for enemies again, I flicked a glance towards Henry and raised my eyebrows. "Since when did you become the Sienna whisperer?"

He let out something between a snort and a chuckle. "Trust me, boss, it was a matter of necessity. A week into our stay at Grant's mansion, she was going so stir crazy that she almost set the whole building on fire. It was either figure out a way to talk her down or we'd all become ashes in the wind."

Grant shuddered, as if in horror from the memory.

I gave Henry an appraising look before shifting my attention to Sienna again. She had almost reached the tent flap now.

"You really—"

"Ambu—" Sienna's voice cut me off, but her shout of warning was drowned out.

The moment she had opened her mouth, I had slapped my palms together and hurled a force wall towards the tent flap that she had barely managed to push open. A *boom* reverberated through the air as part of my wall slammed into a massive water blast. But it hadn't made it fully in time.

Half of the water blast crashed straight into Sienna's chest, sending her flying through the air as if she weighed no more than a child's doll.

"Ambush!" I bellowed, finishing Sienna's warning, while all hell broke loose.

Constables poured out of the weapons tent in incredible numbers while a wave of them surged out of the other tents behind it as well. My heart lurched into my throat. Summoning another force wall, I shot it towards the opening in an effort to stem the tide.

Halfway between me and Audrey, Sienna's body crashed

into an empty tent, making the whole structure collapse around her.

"Sam," I called.

"On it," he replied while sprinting towards her.

"Paige."

She was already moving too. "Got it!"

Bringing her to shield Sam really had been a good call, because we would need everyone else in order to survive this.

Water and lightning and shadows and poison exploded around me as the soldiers threw everything they had at us while we desperately tried to block and form up an organized defense.

Henry and I quickly fell into our usual rhythm of him focusing on blocking the attacks while I shot my most lethal arcs and scythes at the enemies. Wood snapped and fabric tore as he used his wind magic to redirect a blast of water into the nearest tent. I hurled a wide arc towards the constables. Half of them managed to duck. Some blocked. The rest screamed as the vibrating force carved through flesh and bone.

Glittering green mist exploded across the grass, and people dropped like flies.

"Charge!" someone screamed from the back of the ranks.

A battle cry split the air as the soldiers surged forward. Feet pounded against the ground and magic crackled as they shot attacks while thundering towards us.

Panic pulsed through me. They were going to force us into a close-range battle. I whipped my head towards Audrey. She was backing up step after step while throwing clouds of poison towards her attackers. Walls of water and wind shoved her green mist aside.

"Henry," I snapped. "Get to Audrey."

"No way," he growled while pushing aside two lightning bolts with a blast of wind. "I'm not leaving—"

"Please."

His gray eyes flicked to me. I could only spare a quick glance back at him between shots and shields of force magic, but he must have seen the fear that flooded my soul and wrapped around my throat like a noose. I could handle close combat. Audrey couldn't.

"Alright," Henry said. Spinning around, he took off across the grass while calling over his shoulder, "But you'd better still be standing at the end of this battle, or I'll come drag you back from hell myself."

A *crack* sounded as I threw up a force wall to block another lightning strike right before it could hit me in the chest. I dropped it immediately and summoned a spinning arc that I hurled towards the charging soldiers. Two of them were split down the middle by it, but the rest managed to block. They kept coming.

From somewhere to my left, I was vaguely aware of Malcolm's black shadows and Grant's violet emotion magic, but I had no idea what they were doing. I only managed to steal one more glance towards Audrey. Henry was sprinting across the grass, his long legs eating up the distance as he tried to make it to her before the constables did.

Then the first wave of soldiers slammed into me.

Drawing my knife, I rammed it into the first man's throat while I kept my force shield up with my left hand. Blood sprayed through the air as I yanked the blade out after severing his artery. His pale eyes were wide with shock and pain as he tried to get a hand up to his throat to stop the bleeding. He collapsed to the ground before he could.

Steel flashed in the corner of my eye. I twisted away on instinct right before another enemy could bury a sword in the side of my ribs. Using my force shield, I shoved two constables aside while I slashed my knife through the air, cutting the throat of the guy who had tried to stab me.

Another one immediately took his place.

My pulse thrummed in my ears.

Expanding my shield, I tried to keep half of them at bay while I swiped towards the others. Metal clashed as they blocked my knife with their swords. I shoved my shield outwards. The left half of them stumbled backwards. It barely gave me enough space to leap out of the way as three more swords flashed through the air right in front of my chest.

My only saving grace was that none of these people could use their magic without the risk of hitting each other, which meant that they were forced to rely solely on blades for this part. But they had all obviously been trained in swordplay, and I could feel my control of the situation slipping through my fingers.

Air exploded from my lungs as a great weight slammed into me from behind and to the right.

Completely unprepared for the attack, I crashed down on the ground as a massive soldier tackled me. My mind screamed at me to move, and I barely managed to jerk my head sideways before a sword flashed down and buried itself in the ground where my neck had just been. Yanking up my arm, I slashed blindly at the man trying to pin me down.

A howl tore from his throat as my knife carved a deep rut across his collarbone. Warm blood ran down from the wound and dripped in my face as he struggled to get his weight into position over my chest.

Dread crackled through my veins as hands suddenly appeared on my ankles as well when some of the other soldiers tried to help him.

I had lost the grip on my force shield when he tackled me, so I had to drag my other hand towards my knife hand while also slashing wildly at the guy's face. It made him jerk back enough that I could touch my palms together.

Four people had already gotten a grip on my legs, keeping them trapped against the ground.

My heart hammered against my ribs.

Shoving my palm forward, I planted it on my attacker's chest.

And then I released the force wall.

Half-translucent gray magic shot out with enough force to send the bulky man flying off my body and crashing into the people behind him. I sucked in a desperate breath as his weight disappeared from my chest. A second later, the hands on my legs were gone too as the man slammed into his companions and knocked them down.

Rolling to the side, I tried to get back up to my feet before they could get close enough to grab me again.

"Down!" a female voice screamed loud enough to shatter the veil to hell.

Not hesitating a second, I dropped to my stomach and wrapped my arms over the back of my head.

A second later, dark red flames tore through the air above me.

Chapter 12

Terrible heat washed over me as I pressed myself into the trampled grass and covered my head with my hands. Next to me, Henry was doing the same. The air vibrated above my back as a seemingly unending torrent of dark red flames swept past over me. I barely dared breathe for fear of scorching my lungs.

By all hell, how much raw power did Sienna Hall actually possess?

"Run!" Paige called the second that the fire died down.

Henry buried his large hand in the back of my shirt and all but hauled me with him as he shot to his feet and took off towards Paige and the others. I stumbled before managing to get my feet underneath me properly. While we ran, I cast a glance over my shoulder.

A few constables had managed to throw themselves down on the grass too before the flames hit, and the ones farther away had been outside the blast radius, but the whole area where the weapons tent had previously been located, as well as the tents behind it, was now only a smoldering patch of black earth and melted metal. She must have directed the flames to slant downwards, so that they missed us but reached all the way to the ground behind us.

Incredulity bounced around inside me as I took in the completely obliterated crates of metal weapons as well as the sheer size of the scorched area. Fucking hell. If Sienna had possessed a more stable mind and an ability to actually make long-term plans that weren't solely based on whichever emotion she was feeling that very minute, every dark mage in Eldar would have been forced to bow at her feet. I had never met anyone who possessed this level of sheer destructive power.

The constables who had been fighting close to us jumped up from where they had taken cover on the ground as well. I checked to make sure that Callan, Malcolm, and Grant were out of the way and sprinting in the same direction as us before I slapped my palms together and shot a poison cloud over my shoulder. I had no idea if it hit because I had to return my attention to the scene ahead.

Fury crackled on Sienna's face, intense enough to burn the world down. Next to her, Sam was speaking rapidly while making calming gestures. It was at that moment that I realized how incredibly lucky we had been that Sienna had even had the presence of mind to scream that first warning for us to get down. Because based on the expression on her face, she was close to losing her mind with rage. Though to be fair, if I had been flung through the air in the way that she had been, I would have felt the same.

Paige was standing next to Sienna and Sam in front of the collapsed tent that the fire mage had crashed into. A hint of wariness flitted across her features when she looked at Sienna, but she appeared entirely unharmed, which made relief wash over me.

Callan positioned himself between us as we ran towards the

three of them. Malcolm and Grant were racing towards us from the next row of tents.

"You okay?" Callan demanded as soon as he reached us.

"Yes," Henry and I replied in unison. "You?"

He nodded.

"We need to get back to the gardens," Grant called as soon as we were within earshot.

Sienna still looked like she was planning to march right onto the smoking grass and rain hell down on the surviving soldiers. But even though her fire had taken out a large portion of them, there were still too many of them for us to fight without significant risk. Sam pulled desperately on her sleeve, trying to get her to run too.

When we reached them, she at last tore her furious gaze from the constables and let out a snarl. Then she whipped around and joined Paige and Sam as they took off towards the mansion too.

Behind us, orders rang out.

I sucked in a deep breath of air that smelled of ash and smoke as I tried to keep pace with Callan and Henry. Brown tents flashed past us as we hurried back through the same path we had already cleared.

We had only made it halfway when the sounds of a pursuing army echoed from behind our backs.

"How the hell did they know that we were coming?" Malcolm snapped as he and Grant joined the rest of us.

"I don't know," Paige pressed out between rapid breaths. "I swear, they were moving the bulk of their army towards the food delivery."

"And they did. If they hadn't, if we'd faced their whole army, we would be dead right now. So they must have just moved parts of it to the weapons tent. But how could they have known that we would hit that one?" His dark eyes flicked towards her. "Did they spot you?"

"No!"

"Are you sure?"

"Yes!"

"Then how—"

"Can we argue after we're safe inside the mansion?" Sam interrupted. "Please?"

"We still need—"

"Watch out!" Callan screamed.

I flew sideways as his arms shot up, shoving me and Henry to each side of him. White lightning crackled through the air a fraction of a second later. My heart squeezed tight as a pained grunt tore from Callan's lips.

Landing on my shoulder in the grass, I watched the lightning bolt sink into Callan's left shoulder with enough force to knock him back a step. His whole arm twitched and jerked uncontrollably as he collapsed to one knee.

Shadows shot up from the ground, high enough to block out the slanting sun, as Malcolm raised a black wall in front of us. A moment later, a combined attack of water, wind, and lightning crashed into the shadows with enough power to tear the darkness apart.

Through the rips in the shadows, five people became visible.

Chancellor Godric Quill, Lance Carmichael, and his three friends who possessed lightning, wind, and water magic at a dark mage's power level. Behind them, more constables were running in from the tents on both sides of their siege to block our way back to Grant's mansion.

My heart thrashed in my chest as I shoved myself to my feet and sprinted over to Callan. He was gritting his teeth so hard that a muscle in his jaw ticked, and he had wrapped his right hand around his left arm. That one still hung uselessly by his side while the fingers twitched.

"Sam," I called as I reached Callan.

Boots thudded against the ground on our other side as the pursuing soldiers closed in from behind our back.

"No," Callan growled. "We don't have time. We need to go before we're completely boxed in."

"Did you really think you could outsmart me?" Chancellor Quill called across the muddy grass. Smugness laced his voice. "You forget, I know exactly how you think. You attack the food. Then more food arrives. You assume I'll send people to protect the food, so you go for the second-best target instead. Did you learn nothing when we spoke below the mountain in Castlebourne? I can read you like an open book."

Water and lightning slammed into the remnants of Malcolm's shield, and the last of it faded away. Sienna answered it with a massive wave of fire that burned the tents between us and Quill to cinders.

"We can't get through that way," Malcolm snapped.

I whipped towards the emotion mage. "Grant, any other ways in?"

"Not from this location," he answered.

"Then we go into the hills and try to get around them." I spun towards our healer. "And Sam, fix Callan on the way. Let's go."

Before anyone could protest, I dragged Callan with me as I took off towards the only open space left. Paige and Henry flanked us. After another wave of fire, Sienna sprinted after Malcolm and Grant as well while Sam hurried over to us.

Orders to follow echoed across the burning grasslands as Quill's side and our original pursuers gave chase.

I tried to suppress the panic that crawled its way up my throat.

With great effort, I managed to relax my grip on Callan's arm and release him when Sam caught up with us. Shimmering turquoise magic appeared between his palms as he touched them together and then held them close to Callan's shoulder.

Lightning zapped through the air. We all ducked while continuing our mad dash towards the nearest hill. Slapping my palms together, I blindly threw a cloud of poison over my shoulder. Wind magic rushed somewhere behind me.

Sienna let out a scream. Fire tore across the grass, setting tents aflame and slowing our attackers. But not stopping them.

My heart pounded in my chest and it felt as though I was inhaling shards of glass. I sucked in desperate breaths as we at last cleared the final row of tents.

And came face to face with a wall of flat earth.

We all skidded to a halt.

Where the sloping ground should be was now only a flat wall, impossible to run up, as if someone had used wind and water and fire magic to carve a smooth surface into the hill. My heart sank, because that was exactly what Quill must have done.

I whipped my head from side to side, but the impassible barrier ran far to both the left and right.

"They're coming," Henry yelled.

A *boom* shook the warm afternoon air as a blast of wind magic collided with his own. Whirling around, I touched my hands together and shoved a massive poison cloud towards our hunters. Jessica and Darren yanked up two thick shields of water and wind that blocked the attack before it could strike.

Next to me, Sam was still trying to fix Callan's injured arm. Paige called up a water wall that blocked part of the lightning bolt that Leoni shot towards Callan, but because of Leoni's superior power levels, parts of it went through anyway. A low groan ripped from Callan's chest as the remnants of the lightning bolt cracked into the same arm that Sam was trying to heal.

Rage roared through my head.

Slamming my palms together, I sent a gigantic poison cloud towards that fucking insolent lightning mage. A grin danced on her features and her brown eyes glinted in the white light from her magic as she shot another bolt towards Callan. That time, a combined shield of wind from Henry and water from Paige managed to block it entirely.

Fire tore through the air as Sienna unleashed her wrath on the constables, and darkness whipped in its wake as Malcolm's shadows joined her. Soldiers screamed and turned to run when Grant's pale violet mist hit them. But more kept taking their places.

Both sides that had been pursuing us had now caught up. And with the unscalable wall behind us, we had nowhere left to run.

I shot attack after attack at the growing semicircle of soldiers. Their sheer numbers, combined with the fact that they had Leoni, Darren, and Jessica on their side as well, put us at a severe disadvantage. And if they decided to rush us again, we were doomed. Lance was here now. All he would need was one touch while someone else pinned us to the ground, and it would all be over.

Fucking hell. We should never have gone out here. *I* should never have convinced them that we should carry out this attack. And now Callan was hurt and we were trapped out here and fucking Levi Arden had forsaken his promise to us.

Anger and dread and panic all mixed into a terrible storm inside me. I cast desperate glances between Paige and Callan. I couldn't let them get hurt. Not because of me. I had to find some way to make sure that they got out.

But as I met Callan's gaze, I realized that he was thinking

the same thing. His eyes were swimming with soul-shattering terror as he looked between me and Henry. Sam was still trying to heal his unresponsive left arm, but the second lightning bolt must have reopened some of the damage.

For a few seconds, it felt as if the whole world went silent. As if nothing and no one else existed apart from the two of us. I saw the moment that he made his decision. A steely sense of determination fell across his features.

Then the rest of the world crashed back in around us.

Callan pushed Sam aside.

Flicking his gaze between me and Henry, he said, "Climb."

Panic squeezed my heart like an iron fist as he lurched forward as if to sprint right into enemy lines in order to buy us enough time to somehow get over the wall behind us.

"No!" The word tore from my throat as I threw myself towards him to stop him while Henry did the same.

Fireworks exploded into the rows of constables.

We all threw up an arm to shield our eyes as purple and orange and yellow and red light lit up the grasslands before us. It stunned Callan enough that Henry and I managed to yank him back before he could start running again.

I blinked desperately against the lingering blindness as I tried to figure out what had just happened.

Screams echoed across the landscape.

Followed by deafening booms. And more light.

Then shadows streaked across the blue sky above our heads.

They were followed by a gigantic sheet of metal that temporarily blocked out the entire sun.

Shock crackled through me as I whipped around and stared up at the hill above us.

Levi Arden slashed his arm through the air, sending another sheet of metal flashing above our heads and slamming right into the constables, as he strode down the hill. Two explosion mages on his left shot a barrage of firework into their ranks as well, while a shadow mage poured darkness towards the other side.

My mouth dropped open as I watched what had to be a hundred dark mages stride down the hill in a massive line while throwing battle magic at our enemies.

The King of Metal had come.

Chapter 13

Callan

Relief crashed over me like a tidal wave. And gratitude. Normally, all I wanted to do was to punch Levi in the face, but at this moment, I could've kissed the bastard. Magic crackled through the air and slammed into Quill's defending forces as Levi and his army rained hell down on them from their position at the edge of the ridge. A sigh escaped my lips. Audrey and Henry would be safe now.

"Fall back!" Chancellor Quill bellowed across the trampled grass. "Everybody, fall back!"

Booms echoed through the air as Levi and his people kept assaulting them while they beat a hasty retreat.

"What was that you said about reading us like an open book?" Audrey suddenly called to Quill while he backed away. "Didn't see this ambush coming, did you?"

He was too far away for me to see the expression on his face, but I could imagine pretty clearly the annoyance that must be present there. A soft chuckle rolled off my tongue. We most certainly hadn't set up this ambush knowingly. But Quill didn't need to know that.

"Henry," a commanding voice cut through the noise.

Next to me, Henry flinched slightly. It was only a barely perceptible stiffening of his posture, but I could feel it ripple through the air because I knew exactly what had caused it.

While keeping his face blank, Henry turned around to face the King of Metal. I did the same.

A dangerous smile curled Levi's lips, but all he did was to shoot a pointed look towards the ground.

Henry slowly touched his palms together and called up wind magic. Without a hint of hesitation, Levi stepped right off the tall ledge above and plummeted towards the ground. However, before he could break his legs, Henry used his wind magic to soften the fall and help him land comfortably.

Immediately afterwards, six other wind mages stepped off the ledge as well. They turned around and began helping the rest of their companions down while Levi sauntered up to us.

A smirk played over his lips as he swept his gaze over us. "Damn, what a bloody mess you've managed to get yourselves in."

"Levi," I said in greeting since I couldn't very well call him *sir* in front of other dark mages.

His gray eyes glinted as he held my gaze for a few seconds, as if he knew exactly what I was thinking. But thankfully, he didn't push the matter.

"So, you're Levi Arden," Malcolm said while flicking scrutinizing eyes up and down the metal mage's body.

Levi spread his arms in a cocky gesture. "One and the same."

"You're a lot hotter than I thought you'd be," Sienna announced.

He slid his gaze to her and gave her an assessing once-over before replying, "I'm married."

"So?" She scrunched up her brows. "I wasn't trying to flirt

with you. I was just acknowledging that you're objectively very hot. And I should know. I'm a fire mage."

Confusion flitted across Levi's face. For a few seconds, he just looked back at her as if he couldn't figure out if she was being rude or not. I didn't know whether to chuckle or shake my head at the crazy fire mage. At least she kept things interesting.

"Perhaps we should save the rest of this meet and greet for when we're back inside the mansion?" Malcolm interjected before Levi could reach a conclusion.

I glanced back towards the hill. Only about ten of Levi's people remained on the ledge now, waiting for a wind mage to assist them with their descent.

"Yeah," I agreed, and then turned towards the man next to him. "Grant?"

Harvey Grant looked as if he wanted to say something else, but then his gaze shifted from Levi and towards the direction that Quill and his people had disappeared to. He blew out a sigh.

"Follow me," he said before turning around and taking off at a run.

Irritation rippled across Malcolm's features, but he jogged after him regardless. The rest of us did the same.

Quill's troops had retreated far to the sides, leaving the path back to the mansion clear for now. But we didn't know how long it would remain like that, so we had to hurry.

I glanced down at Audrey as we ran. Relief washed over me to find her more or less unharmed. My left arm still wasn't working properly, and it felt as though lightning bolts were ricocheting through it constantly. But Sam could fix that as soon as we stopped moving around so much. I opened my mouth to say something about that to Audrey, but right then she looked up and met my gaze.

Fury burned in her eyes as she glared up at me.

It took me by surprise, so I just blinked at her instead, my mouth slightly open. She snapped her gaze back to the path ahead. I had no idea why she was so angry, and this wasn't the time or the place to ask, so I just closed my mouth again and kept running.

A thin mist of pale violet magic rose up from Grant and floated back to cover the rest of us as we at last reached the edge of the gardens and disappeared into the vegetation. Levi shot me a sharp look. I shook my head in silent answer to let him know that it was protection rather than an attack.

When we had gotten halfway through the gardens, Grant stopped. We all trailed to a halt as well. I cast a quick glance back at Levi's people, who had stopped a respectful distance behind us, while Grant slowly turned around to face us. Or rather, to face Levi.

Glowing dark red flowers and fruits hung from the thick branches around us, and the green leaves rustled in the wind as it whirled through the treetops.

Suspicion rose inside me as I looked between Grant and the King of Metal. *Fuck*. This couldn't be good.

"Before we go any farther, you are going to swear a blood oath," Grant said in a tone that left no room for discussion. "A blood oath swearing that you will never reveal any of this mansion's secrets or use them against me."

Dread sluiced through my veins like ice.

Across the grass, Levi stared at the emotion mage with a look of utter disbelief on his face. The tension was so palpable that the very air seemed to crackle with it.

Then Levi cocked his head in a move that was pure predator. "What did you just say?"

"You heard me perfectly well."

"Look, Grant..." I began, and took a step forward, positioning myself between the two of them.

There was no way in hell that Levi would ever swear a blood oath to someone else. That Grant had even dared suggest such a thing would in Levi's mind be a grave insult. And a challenge to his power.

"I am not interested in what you have to say, Callan," Grant said. His eyes remained locked on the King of Metal as he repeated, "You and all of your people will swear the blood oath. Or this is as far as you go."

Levi let out a cold laugh full of disbelief. Then his gray eyes slid to me, and he lifted his broad shoulders in a shrug. "Well then, good luck with your war, Callan."

He began turning around as if he was going to leave. Panic surged up inside me.

"Wait," I said before snapping my gaze to the infuriating emotion mage. "Grant, what the hell? We need him."

"No." Grant's eyes were hard as he stared back at me. "*You* need him. As I have already told you, I am perfectly capable of weathering this war here inside my gardens. So if you want to use my mansion as a base, you will do as I say. My house. My rules."

At that point, Levi had already turned around and taken a step back towards his people. With a few quick strides, I positioned myself in front of him.

"Get out of the way, Callan." His whole being was pulsing with the threat of violence. "You know how it ends."

"We have a deal," I said instead. Holding his gaze, I remained firmly in his way. "We held up our end of the bargain. This is yours."

"My end of the bargain did not entail swearing a blood oath to someone," he growled between his teeth.

"If that's what it takes for you to help us with this war, then yes, it did."

"I am one second away from slaughtering you all. Step aside, Callan."

"What does it matter? The blood oath doesn't change anything. It won't limit you in any way. It's not as if you're planning to go to Eldar later to attack one random mansion."

"Now there's a thought." A lethal smile spread across Levi's mouth as he turned back around to face Grant. He swept his gaze over all of us. "This is all there is, isn't it? All the dark mages left in Eldar. Maybe I should just kill you all right here and conquer Eldar on my own."

Shadows sprang to life around Malcolm's shoulders, whipping like black snakes, while dark red flames whooshed down Sienna's arms. The red light glinted in Levi's metal shoulder plates as he took a threatening step forward and touched his palms together.

Alarm shot up my spine.

Moving my right hand, I managed to press it against my unresponsive left and summon a force wall. But before I could do anything else, Levi and his whole army flinched.

I snapped my gaze towards them.

It was so faint that it could barely be seen in here, but if I concentrated, I noticed that Grant's pale violet mist had shifted so that it no longer covered Levi and his people.

Gasps ripped from several dark mages, and fear flooded their faces. Even the King of Metal stumbled a step back and blinked hard as if trying to clear his head. Slapping his palms together, he hurled a sheet of metal straight towards Grant.

I threw my force wall the second he moved, and his attack slammed into mine before it could hit the emotion mage. The boom as our powers collided echoed through the woodlands.

Levi yanked out the sword he kept strapped along his

spine instead and advanced on Grant. His chest rose and fell rapidly, as if he was terrified, and his eyes darted back and forth like he was seeing something the rest of us couldn't. I quickly launched myself between them, blocking Levi's path to Grant.

"You're attacking me?" Levi ground out between gritted teeth. "I just saved your asses, and you're fucking attacking me?"

"I'm not attacking you," Grant said in a calm voice somewhere behind my back. "I'm simply not protecting you anymore. And if this is what it feels like when I'm no longer offering you the courtesy of shielding you from the effects inside these gardens, imagine what it would feel like if I *was* actively attacking you."

"Grant," I snapped over my shoulder. "Enough."

Levi was gripping his sword so hard that his knuckles were white, and panic flashed in his eyes as he blinked repeatedly while he also tried to move around me. Behind him, all of his people were in similar states.

Then the faint violet mist shifted back around them again, and they all sucked in a collective breath.

Shaking his head, Levi blinked again while dragging in a deep breath and raising his sword to point at Grant. "You—"

"Levi," I interrupted. Staying silent, I waited until his furious eyes locked on mine. "I know asking for a blood oath is rude. But we have a deal. That's all there is to it."

And the King of Metal never broke a deal.

Rage crackled in his eyes like lightning. But in the end, he forced out a long breath and raked a hand through his black hair. Steel sang into the warm afternoon air as he spun his sword around and rammed it back into its sheath.

"I fucking hate emotion mages," he ground out.

Grant said nothing. And when I turned around, I found

him just watching Levi with a pleasant smile on his lips. I shook my head.

Heaving a deep sigh, I stepped back to my previous position next to Audrey while Levi pulled out a small knife and drew it across his palm. Audrey was staring at him with raised eyebrows as he spoke the words of the blood oath. She didn't know Levi like I did. Didn't know that he really was one of those people who always followed through on his deals and promises. So it didn't surprise me that she was shocked to see him swear a blood oath like this.

Sam drifted over to me and began healing my arm again while Levi gave the order for the rest of his people to swear the blood oath as well.

When all of them were finally done, Sam had finished his work and I had at last regained control over my left arm. Flexing my fingers, I relished in the fact that it no longer felt as though they were being pricked by thousands of needles.

"There," Levi snapped once the last of his people were finished. "Done."

Grant gave him a nod. "Thank you."

Surprise flitted across Levi's features, as if he had expected Grant to gloat rather than express gratitude. Drawing his eyebrows down, he studied the emotion mage. But before he could say anything else, Malcolm spoke up.

"We need to make a plan for how to proceed." His intelligent brown eyes moved from face to face. "However, tensions are running high because we were just ambushed by Quill, and we're angry about that, and now you are angry about Grant's need for caution. And we are all just... too angry right now. If we all were to sit down right now and discuss next steps, I am fairly certain that several of us would be dead before the day is over. So, I suggest that we get Arden and his people settled, and then we pick this up in the morning. Any objections?"

Silence fell over the woodlands as we all just looked at each other.

"Excellent," Malcolm said. "In the morning then."

And with that, he turned around and started towards Grant's mansion.

I watched as the rest of them began walking as well.

Fucking hell, I couldn't wait until this war was over. Getting dark mages to cooperate was like trying to herd a flock of vicious cats into a pond against their will.

Dragging a hand through my hair, I shook my head.

If Quill didn't kill us before this was over, we might just end up killing each other instead.

Chapter 14

I slammed the door to our room shut behind me. Callan whirled around at the noise and blinked at me in surprise. In *surprise*. As if he didn't already know exactly why I was pissed at him.

"What the hell was that?" I snapped before he could get a word out.

He glanced from side to side, as if the correct answer would magically appear out of thin air. "What was what?"

"You know exactly what!"

Stalking up to him, I gave his chest an angry shove. It did nothing to actually push him back, which just pissed me off more, so I placed my palms on his chest and tried again. That time he did take a step back, but then his hands shot up and wrapped around my wrists.

"Audrey, what the hell are you talking about?"

I yanked against his grip on my wrists while glaring up at him. "Have you already forgotten what we talked about in Malgrave?"

His brows scrunched up in confusion. "Which part?"

"Fucking hell, you are unbelievable!"

My left hand finally slipped free of his grip, and I whirled sideways to make him release the other one too. But I wasn't fast enough. He spun me around, twisting my trapped hand up behind my back while his fingers closed around my throat. A snarl tore from my chest as he used his grip on me to push my back harder against his chest, keeping me pressed against him.

"Just tell me why you're angry," he said into my ear.

Grant had made us take our shoes off before we went upstairs, so I lifted my foot and tried to stomp my heel down onto Callan's bare foot. Since his hand around my throat prevented me from being able to look down, I missed and instead slammed my heel into the pale wooden floorboards with a thud that echoed around the room.

Callan tightened his grip on my throat while also raising his hand higher, forcing me up onto my toes.

"Stop," he said, his voice infuriatingly calm. "Why are you angry?"

"Because you were going to sacrifice yourself!"

Deafening silence descended on the room. However, Callan kept me balancing on my toes and trapped against his chest.

"I told you in Malgrave that I'm not some fucking damsel that needs protecting," I growled and yanked against his iron grip. "So why the hell would you try to sacrifice yourself for me? I'm not some weak—"

"That's not why I did it."

"We're equals!"

"I know."

"Then why did you…" I trailed off as he finally released me.

Not wasting a second, I slapped my palms together and whirled around right before placing my hand against his thigh. Thankfully, the magic worked, and poison flooded his pain receptors.

He sucked in a sharp breath between his teeth as his leg

buckled, sending him crashing down on his knees. Using his moment of surprise and pain, I planted my foot on his shoulder and shoved him backwards. He landed back first on the spotless floorboards while I ripped out the knife I had strapped to my thigh, and flashed down. Straddling his chest, I pressed the edge of the knife against his throat.

Anger crackled through my veins as I held his surprised stare.

"We do not sacrifice ourselves," I ground out between gritted teeth. "*Heroes* sacrifice themselves. We are villains. Merciless villains. We don't give up and accept defeat. We fight and torture and kill our way out of dangerous situations. Together. Do you hear me?"

His face softened. Blowing out a deep sigh, he let his head fall back the final bit to rest on the floor. "Yeah, I hear you."

"Good. So then why the hell did you try to sacrifice yourself?"

He slid his gaze from mine and instead stared up at the glittering chandelier in the ceiling above.

I wrapped my free hand around his strong jaw, forcing his eyes back to mine. "Answer me."

Something flashed in his eyes. He wasn't used to someone ordering him around like this. *Good*. I wanted him to snap out of whatever this was and to make him actually tell me what he was feeling instead of just remaining this infuriatingly calm.

Pressing the blade harder against his throat, I ordered, "Answer."

"Because I'm terrified!"

That stunned me enough that I loosened my grip on the knife. Callan used that moment of inattention to push himself into a sitting position. The move made me slide down from his chest so that I was straddling his lap instead. I kept the blade against his throat as he reached up, but he only raked his fingers through his messy hair. Letting his hands drop back down to the floor, he shook his head at me while a hint of vulnerability swirled in his dark eyes.

"I'm terrified, Audrey. I don't know if it's different for you because you had Paige for so long, but I... Even before I left Eldar, I didn't really have anyone. And then after I left, I didn't get close to anyone either. I killed colleagues and casual friends on Levi's orders without a second thought. I've never really cared about anyone." He shook his head again, desperation bleeding into his voice. "It wasn't until Malcolm kidnapped Henry that I even realized that I cared about him. And then *you*... I love you. I didn't even know I was capable of an emotion like that, but I *love* you. And now, I can't breathe, Audrey. I can't breathe because I'm so fucking terrified that you or Henry will get hurt in this war. And I don't know how to handle it!"

For a few seconds, I just stared back at him. My heart squeezed painfully at the genuine dread swimming in his eyes. I hadn't realized just how foreign these feelings were to him. While it had shocked me beyond belief that I had fallen in love with Callan, caring about someone in general wasn't a new concept to me. Because Callan was right, I'd had my amazing friendship with Paige all throughout our academy years. But he had never had that.

"Oh," I managed to press out.

Embarrassment blew across his face. "Yeah."

Removing the knife from his throat, I set it down beside us and instead placed both my hands on his cheeks. "Look, we all worry. It's normal. I panic at the thought of someone hurting you too."

"Really?"

"Yes."

"So how do you deal with it?"

I let out a soft laugh. "By remembering that you're a

fucking lethal bastard who has somehow managed to survive five years of war against *me*. You're deadly. And hard to kill. And if I haven't been able to kill you, how the hell would someone like Godric Quill manage it?"

A smile spread across his lips. It chased away the haunted look in his eyes. Reaching up, he brushed a hand along the side of my face and hooked a few loose strands behind my ear. "That's actually a very good point, my vicious little poisoner."

"I know." A sly smile played over my lips. "And you seem to have forgotten just how vicious I can really be." Taking my hands from his face, I slowly touched them together. "Let me remind you."

Glittering green mist rose up between us and swirled down Callan's throat. He coughed and blinked as it moved through his windpipe and down towards his lungs. I wrapped my hand around the back of his neck. While letting the poison slide through his body, I leaned forward and slanted my lips over his.

"I love you for worrying about me," I breathed against his mouth while he choked on my poison. "But you don't need to. Because I am lethal too."

I claimed his lips in a sensual kiss. His chest shook with the effects of the poison, and he braced his hands on my hips to keep from toppling backwards as he answered with equally heart-wrenching passion.

Keeping my grip on the back of his neck, I deepened the kiss and then sucked some of the poison from his body in a long inhale.

His hands tightened on my hips.

The poison disappeared from his chest, making the trembling in his muscles stop.

With my mouth still locked on his, I inhaled again.

My magic obeyed immediately, sliding out of his lungs and up his throat until I had sucked every single drop from him.

Tearing my lips from his, I leaned back slightly and tilted my head back. Then I blew out a long breath.

Glittering green mist swirled out of my mouth and twisted above us before fading into nothing.

Callan sucked in a deep breath.

"Never forget that," I finished as I looked back down to meet his gaze.

His brown eyes glittered in the golden light falling in through the windows. "By all hell, you're fucking glorious, have I told you that?"

"Yes." A wicked smile tugged at my lips. "But I could stand to hear it again."

He curled his fingers under the hem of my shirt and pulled it up and over my head. I raised my arms to help navigate them out of the fabric before Callan tossed the garment to the pale wooden floor. My nipples hardened as he removed my brassiere as well.

Both lust and admiration burned in his eyes as he raked them up and down my body. Then he met my gaze again and held it. "You're glorious."

Heat spread through my core.

I grabbed the edge of his shirt and yanked it over his head as well. It had barely joined my garments on the floor before he wrapped an arm around my back and leaned forward to kiss his way down my chest.

The change in position made me slide up so that I was sitting directly on top of his hard cock. A moan tore from my chest.

Callan sucked my nipple into his mouth and rolled it between his lips.

It made a shiver course through my body, and I slid my hands up his muscular arms while grinding my pussy against his cock. He groaned, making his warm breath dance over my breast. I let out a small whimper as he nipped at my nipple with his teeth before swirling his tongue around it.

My clit throbbed with need.

Fuck, I needed his cock inside me right now.

Bracing myself on his shoulders, I scooted backwards until I could reach the top of his pants. Metal clinked faintly as I unbuckled Callan's belt while his very distracting tongue made lazy circles around my nipple.

My fingers fumbled as he flicked it with his tongue.

While dragging in a steadying breath, I renewed my efforts with his pants. The belt finally fell open, and I quickly undid the buttons as well before wrapping my fingers around the edge of both his pants and underwear.

Callan leaned back on his elbows and lifted his hips, allowing me to push both garments down to his mid thighs. His thick cock sprang free. The sight, combined with the impressive abs currently on display, made heat ripple through me.

Deciding that halfway would have to do, I left his pants where they were on his thighs and instead made quick work of my own.

After tossing them aside, I swung my leg back over Callan again and then placed my palms against his chest. With a firm push, I shoved him the final bit down towards the floor. He wrapped his hands around my wrists, keeping them trapped against his hard chest, while I slid down onto his cock.

Deep groans tore from both of us.

Curling my fingers against his heated skin, I lifted my hips and then moved down his shaft again. He tightened his grip on my wrists while his eyes fluttered. I shifted my position so that my clit ground against his cock as I started up a steady rhythm.

Callan released my wrists and slid his hands up my arms and then down along my sides instead. I leaned forward and stole a savage kiss while continuing my movements. He answered by pinching my nipple and then twisting it hard. I gasped into his mouth.

His strong hands cupped my tits and kneaded them while I rode his cock. Pleasure built inside me.

He alternated between massaging them and playing with my nipples in a way that made my brain flicker. Shifting my hips slightly, I moved into the perfect position while raising and lowering my body. The friction of his thick cock against my pussy made a shudder roll through my body as I soared towards the coming orgasm.

Callan rolled my nipple between his fingers right at the same time as his cock hit the perfect spot inside me.

Release shot through my body.

My thighs shook on either side of him as the wave of pleasure swept through me. Callan shifted his hands from my tits and wrapped a hand around my throat, moving my face down so that he could see it properly. And instead of chasing his own release, he stopped moving and just watched me. As if searing the image of me coming on top of him into his mind forever.

When the last of the tremors had died down, he used his grip on my throat to move my face all the way down to his and steal a deep kiss from my mouth. Then he released me and gently lifted me off his cock.

I rolled to the side and collapsed on the floor.

My chest heaved.

Lying there, I just stared up at the white marble ceiling above. Light from the golden afternoon sun fell in through the windows and hit the crystal chandelier. It made the glittering light fracture in the glassy stones, which cast a million shifting shapes over the walls and ceiling.

"Satisfied already?"

I pushed myself up on one elbow and raised my head.

Callan was watching me where he sat next to me on the floor, his pants still only halfway down his thighs and his cock still stiff from the release that he never claimed.

After glancing down at his thick shaft, I met his gaze and smirked. "Satisfied? Never."

"Good." A villainous grin curled his lips. "Because we're just getting started."

Excitement rippled through me as he twisted around so that he was on his knees instead. Reaching forward, he grabbed me by the hips and did the same to me. Sparkles skittered across my skin as he drew his hands over my ribs before positioning me on my knees in front of him. I glanced over my shoulder and was met with a wicked smile.

"Eyes front," he ordered.

I flashed him another smirk before obeying his command.

Behind me, a slow sliding sound began. Then it ended abruptly in the snap of a leather belt.

A thrill raced through me.

Callan stroked gentle fingers down my spine before drawing his belt around my throat. I sucked in a short breath as he tightened it. A moment later, he placed his large hand between my shoulder blades and pushed my chest down towards the floor. I followed his directions, raising my ass up into the air as I did. His hand trailed down my back and caressed the curve of my ass before adjusting my hips to his liking.

With my hands flat on the floor, I arched my back farther as Callan moved into position behind me.

Desire rippled through me as he dragged his cock through my wetness and towards my entrance.

Then he shoved inside.

A moan tore from my chest as his cock slid in all the way to the hilt until it filled my pussy completely. Callan must have rolled the leather belt around his hand because it tightened against my throat. I pushed my ass harder against him.

He slowly pulled out and then pushed back in again. I curled my fingers on the wooden floorboards. A low groan rolled from Callan's throat. He increased the pace.

My body rocked forward as he shoved harder inside me before drawing out and then slamming into me again. He jerked me back towards him using the belt around my throat for leverage. Pleasure crackled through my veins as he pounded into me.

Then his hand disappeared from my hip.

A few seconds later, he brushed two vibrating fingers against my clit.

I let out a strangled cry of pleasure.

Callan rolled his hand around the belt again, tightening it over my throat while his force magic pulsed into my already throbbing clit. Keeping my back arched, I pressed my forehead against the cool floor as Callan fucked me with brutal strength.

The pressure inside me kept mounting until my body was screaming for release.

His vibrations drew a garbled plea from my lips as they pulsed against my sensitive skin. Callan kept slamming into me.

White light flickered in front of my closed lids.

My whole body was trembling with the pent-up orgasm.

I sucked in strained breaths underneath the tight belt around my throat.

Just when I thought that I was going to lose my mind, Callan shoved into me at the same time as his vibrations sent me over the edge.

Violent release exploded through my body.

All of my limbs shook, and I almost collapsed to the floor. Callan kept my body steady with his belt while he rode the orgasm with me until release crashed over him as well.

My pussy still trembled around his cock as he came inside me.

I sucked in desperate breaths while my heart slammed against my ribs. Heat radiated from my cheeks.

When Callan at last pulled out and slid the belt off my neck, I just collapsed onto the floor chest first. I swore that the room below could hear the loud thumping of my heart through the floorboards.

A thud sounded next to me.

Tilting my head to the side, I rested my cheek against the floor and looked over at Callan.

He was lying on his back beside me, and his broad chest rose and fell with rapid breaths. Light from the windows cast gilded streaks across the sharp ridges of his abs. I let a smirk slide home on my lips as I dragged my gaze up to his eyes.

"Satisfied already?" I taunted.

His eyes glittered with mischief as he turned his head to face me. "Never."

Chapter 15

Callan

"Get a lot of rest last night?"

I glanced over at Henry, who kept his face suspiciously blank. "I have no idea what you're talking about."

"Uh-huh." Amusement pulled at his lips. "Must've been the wind then. Rattling the walls like that."

Letting out a snort, I rammed my elbow into the side of his ribs. "Watch your mouth."

He huffed out a laugh but bit back his retort as we crossed the threshold and entered Grant's dining room.

Morning sunlight shone in through the windows and illuminated the grand paintings of forest scenes that covered the walls. We had already eaten breakfast separately earlier, so the massive table in the middle was bare except for the unlit candleholders placed down the middle. I scanned the people seated around it.

The only person who hadn't arrived yet was Sienna. Everyone else was already seated. Grant sat in the lone chair at the head of the table, which I could tell irked Levi to no end. As if to make a point, he had taken a seat far down the side that

Audrey and Paige were on. Malcolm and Sam sat on Grant's other side, so Henry and I rounded the table and dropped down in the empty chairs beside them. It put me right opposite the King of Metal. He dragged his gaze to me but said nothing as I leaned back and crossed my arms.

A moment later, Sienna sauntered into the room. We all watched her as she strolled over to the windows and promptly took a seat on the windowsill. I resisted the urge to groan.

"Sienna," Grant said. "Why don't you come and join us at the table instead?"

She frowned at him. "Because I don't want to. Honestly, if I had wanted to sit by the table, I would have sat there. But I don't, so I'm not."

"Please," Henry interrupted before Malcolm could strangle her with his shadows. Meeting her gaze, he waved a hand around his ear. "You know my hearing is busted, so I can't hear you properly when you're all the way over there."

It took great effort not to raise my eyebrows. There was absolutely nothing wrong with Henry's hearing.

Sienna rolled her eyes, but then forced out a sigh. "Fine."

Jumping down from the windowsill, she strode over to the table and plopped down in the empty chair next to me.

I glanced over at my friend, who just lifted his massive shoulders in a shrug. Damn, I really had to give him a raise.

"Excellent," Malcolm began, and straightened the cuffs of his suit. "Now that we're all here, and seated properly, we need to make a plan for how to proceed."

"Look, I've agreed to help you out," Levi began before anyone could so much as open their mouth. "But I don't plan on getting my people killed needlessly in a war that frankly doesn't concern me at all."

Malcolm's brown eyes sharpened as they locked on the

metal mage. "Then why did you agree to come in the first place?"

He shrugged. "Because Callan and Audrey gave me something I wanted in exchange."

"But you are still not willing to risk your people?"

"Needlessly? No."

"How am I supposed to go into battle when I can't even be sure that the people I fight with will have my back when the time comes? If you—"

"I agree with Arden," Grant interrupted.

Anger flashed across Malcolm's face as he snapped his gaze to the emotion mage. "I was not done speaking."

"I don't—"

"Guys," Sam cut in. There was a pleading look in his gray eyes as he looked from face to face. "Please, enough with the fighting. We're all on the same side."

Malcolm clicked his tongue, but said nothing more. Grant only gave the shadow mage a slow smile. Opposite me, Levi flicked an assessing gaze over our healer.

When no one protested further, Sam went on. "Can we at least agree that open war is a bad idea?"

We all exchanged a glance, and then nodded in unison.

"Two armies facing off on an open battlefield is for people who have to play by the rules," Audrey said. Flicking her long black hair behind her shoulder, she shrugged. "We don't have to play fair."

"Exactly." Sam nodded vigorously. "So we do this in a way that minimizes casualties."

Sienna's citrine eyes burned like yellow flames in the morning sunlight as she grinned. "On our side, at least."

From across the table, Levi let out a dark chuckle. "Agreed."

I leaned forward in my seat. "And we also need to get the

Blade of Equilibrium from the academy so that you, Levi, can destroy it."

"And how do you propose we do that?" Malcolm asked, while arching a dark brow. "The academy is impenetrable. Not to mention that there is an army of constables currently standing between us and the city of Eldar."

"What we need to do is to take out Quill and his parliament," Audrey countered. Raising a hand, she waved it in the direction of the windows. "Not all of these constables."

"Except all those constables are standing between us and Quill."

"I know, but..." Blowing out a sigh, she fell silent.

I studied her while the others began arguing about the best way to get through the army and to reach Quill. With her head tilted slightly to the side, she drummed her fingers on the smooth wooden tabletop. I recognized that glint in her eyes. She was scheming.

While Malcolm tried to talk Sienna out of setting half the grasslands on fire, Audrey leaned closer to Paige and whispered something in her ear. The blond forger considered for a few seconds, then nodded. Then Audrey went back to tapping her fingers on the table again while staring out into nothingness.

"Careful with that tongue," Levi said, a lethal edge to his voice. "I don't appreciate you trying to give me orders."

"I'm not trying to give you orders," Sienna snapped back. "I'm just saying that if you're here, you might as well do something useful."

"He is doing something useful," Malcolm cut in. "He has a hundred dark mages on the other side of this mansion, just waiting for his orders."

Sienna stabbed her arm towards the windows. "Then give them the order to follow me out there and we can burn Quill to ashes before the end of the day."

"Which part of 'avoiding needless casualties among my people' was difficult for you to understand?" Levi retorted in a voice that I knew meant that he was close to losing his cool any second.

Anger flashed in Sienna's eyes. "Don't talk to me as if I'm stupid."

"Then don't make suggestions that—"

"I have a plan."

We all turned to look at Audrey. Her green eyes moved from face to face, meeting everyone's gaze until the threat of violence had begun fading from the air.

"I have a plan," she repeated when the tension in the room was gone. "We need to split into two teams. One small team will go into Eldar to get the Blade of Equilibrium while the rest stay here to keep Quill and his army occupied so that they won't know what we're doing until it's too late."

Grant arched an eyebrow at her. "And what exactly *are* we doing?"

"I'm getting to that part."

Looks of skepticism were replaced by approval by the time that Audrey reached the end of her plan. I studied her as she at last leaned back in her seat again. Damn, she really was brilliant.

From her place next to me, Sienna grinned while her eyes glittered in the sun. "I like it." Her long red hair rippled as she shrugged. "Well, as long as I get to be on the team that stays here and kills people while you go into Eldar to do all that."

"I will stay here too," Grant said. Amusement blew across his face as he shot a pointed look at the people around the table. "I don't trust you degenerates in my home unsupervised."

I snorted. "Fair."

Sam sat up straighter. "I should also stay here. Since this is where the bulk of the fighting will take place, my skills will be most needed here."

"That sounds good," Audrey said before nodding towards Paige. "Paige and I will go to Eldar, since this is my plan and she has a lot of contacts in the criminal underworld."

"Henry and I are coming too," I announced.

A small smile played over her lips. "I suspected as much."

I slid my gaze to Levi. "And you obviously need to come too, since you're the one who's gonna destroy the blade. But what about your people? Will you leave them all here to help with the fighting?"

For a few seconds, he said nothing. His calculating eyes only moved from face to face. "Do you need them?"

"Honestly? Yes." Malcolm met his gaze with a frank expression on his features. "You saw what we will be facing out there. And losing Callan and Audrey cuts our battle strength quite drastically."

Levi nodded to himself a couple of times and then sucked his teeth. "Alright. They'll all stay here then." His eyes locked on Malcolm again. "I'll leave them under your command."

The shadow mage blinked in surprise.

To be honest, shock flickered through my chest as well. Levi wasn't exactly known for sharing command.

Leaning back nonchalantly in his chair, the King of Metal shrugged as if it was no big deal. "There needs to be one clear leader in a war, and from what I've seen since we arrived yesterday, you're by far the most qualified one here."

A lot of the previous hostility bled out of Malcolm's eyes as he instead gave Levi a slow nod.

Levi dipped his chin briefly in acknowledgement too. "Remember what I said about needless casualties among my people, though."

"Noted."

"Alright," Audrey said. "It's settled then." She turned to our host. "Grant, we're going to need to borrow some horses. You have some here on your property, right?"

"Of course I do." He raised his eyebrows and scoffed. "What kind of amateur do you take me for?"

She just waved off the comment. "Good. Then Paige, Callan, Henry, and Levi, get ready to leave. We'll head out as soon as possible."

"Careful with that tongue, poisonous snake." Levi flashed her a sharp smile. "Wouldn't want to catch you trying to give me orders, now would we?"

She just shot him an answering smile dripping with poison.

Huffing out something between a sigh and a chuckle, I shook my head and then pushed to my feet.

This had gone better than expected. No blood had been spilled during the meeting, and we had a plan to take down Quill and his whole parliament.

We were finally taking the fight to them.

Chapter 16

My muscles groaned as I slid down from my horse and landed on the dry grass. Almost two days in the saddle was nothing compared to what we had endured while traveling from the dark mage mountain in Castlebourne and all the way to Malgrave, but my body was somehow still sore after this short trip. While rolling my shoulders back and stretching out my arms, I glanced back at my borrowed mount. I had probably spent more time on horseback these past few months than the entire rest of my life combined.

Loud pounding echoed through the night.

I slid my gaze back to the area ahead. Callan was standing in front of a door to a wide one-story building that looked to have seen better days. Even with only the moonlight providing illumination, I could make out the shifting hues on the roof where moss speckled the tiles. Henry was holding the reins of Callan's horse where he stood a couple of steps behind with Paige. Next to me, Levi Arden was watching the rundown stable with suspicious eyes.

"The entrance is in here?" he said.

"Yeah," Callan answered without turning around.

Candlelight flickered in the windows of the building. He pounded his fist against the door again in a demand for the person inside to hurry up. Locks clicked on the other side. Then the door was opened and a muscular man in his forties became visible.

"Take it easy with the door, you..." He trailed off and his eyes went wide as he took us all in.

Both Callan and I flashed him a wicked grin.

Dread washed over his face, and he stumbled a step back. "Oh no, not again."

"Hello, John." Pushing the door all the way open, Callan strode across the threshold while John backed away. "You know the drill by now, right?"

His gaze flicked over the rest of us again. "Y-yeah."

"Five horses. Make sure they're still here when we return. We'll help ourselves to the trapdoor. Any objections?"

"No."

"Smart man."

"So..." Paige began, drawing out the word, as she handed the reins to John and followed Callan through the door. "You know each other then?"

Callan and I chuckled.

Handing my own reins to John, I gave him another villainous smile. "Yeah, you could say that."

John just cleared his throat and hurriedly began leading our horses into his stable.

The smell of hay enveloped us as we all filed in through the door and started down the narrow path towards the other end of the building. A few horses lifted their heads and snorted when we disturbed their peace by bustling past. Candles burned on a wooden table up ahead.

"You said *trapdoor*," Levi said as we closed the final distance to said building feature. There was an edge to his voice when he spoke. "Exactly what kind of entrance is this?"

"It's used by smugglers," Callan replied vaguely.

"That's not what I asked."

Confusion flitted through me. It deepened even more when Callan didn't respond. Instead, he just crouched down and shoved aside the bale of hay that covered the trapdoor. I glanced between him and Levi while he slid the metal bar aside and then grabbed the handle.

The trapdoor groaned faintly as Callan lifted it to reveal the hole and the narrow ladder that led into the cramped space below.

Panic flashed across Levi's face.

It was there and then disappeared so quickly that I wasn't even sure that I had actually seen it. Frowning, I studied the King of Metal as he stared down into the hole. He slowly dragged his gaze back up to Callan.

"No," he simply said.

Callan spread his hands. "It's the only way into the city."

"I don't give a shit."

"Look, it's just a short tunnel under the wall. It's not that—"

One second, Levi was standing in front of Callan. The next, he had lunged straight for him. I slapped my palms together and called up my magic, but Levi already had his fist buried in Callan's collar and a vicious-looking knife pressed to his throat. Beside me, Henry and Paige had summoned wind and water magic too. However, with the blade to Callan's throat, none of us dared to move farther.

"You." Power and incredible danger pulsed from Levi's whole being as he yanked Callan closer to growl the words in his face. "You're doing this on purpose, aren't you? You fucking traitor. Payback for the beating, huh?"

Callan just looked back at him unflinchingly. "Which one? You do love to go overboard, so I've lost count at this point."

"So this *is* payback?"

"No."

Levi's fingers tightened around the knife. It sent a flare of alarm down my spine, and I took a step forward while my poison cloud expanded.

Callan met my gaze over Levi's shoulder. "Don't." His eyes slid to Henry. "That goes for you too."

I frowned at him in confusion, but let my magic fade out again. Henry and Paige did the same.

"Look..." Callan began, and heaved a deep sigh while shifting his attention back to Levi. "As much as I'd love to beat your arrogant ass into the ground..."

Levi snorted, as if the mere thought of Callan beating him was absolutely ridiculous.

"The truth is that we need you," Callan finished. "Alright? We need you to destroy the Blade of Equilibrium, so me doing something just to piss you off would be the height of stupidity."

"You've done stupid shit before."

Holding his gaze, Callan said nothing. Only kept looking back at him.

After another few seconds, Levi let out something between a snarl and a sigh. While still keeping the knife to Callan's throat, he glanced down at the hole again. "How long?"

"It's just under the wall. It connects to a building right on the other side."

Silence descended on the stable. Back by the front door, John was still moving our horses inside and unsaddling them. The faint clopping of hooves against the ground was the only sound to break the stillness while Levi and Callan stared each other down.

At last, Levi took the blade from Callan's throat and gave

him a shove backwards while releasing his collar. Threats pulsed in his eyes as he used the knife to point towards Callan. "If I find out that you lied about this being the only way in, I'll fucking skin you alive."

"I know."

Spinning around, he rammed the knife back into its sheath and stalked over to the trapdoor. I watched him with furrowed brows. Was crawling through a dusty tunnel beneath the high and mighty King of Metal, or what?

I opened my mouth to say as much, but before I could, Callan's fingers wrapped around my wrist and gave it a small squeeze. Glancing up, I found him shaking his head discreetly. And no matter how much I wished it were otherwise, Callan was right that we did need Levi, so I swallowed my snide remark and instead just shifted my attention back to the object of my confusion.

Without so much as a glance at the rest of us, Levi climbed down the ladder and jumped into the hole.

Callan released me and motioned towards the trapdoor. "Well then, after you."

A sly smile blew across my lips as I arched an eyebrow at him. "So that you can stare at my ass again?"

Smirking, he drew his hand along my jaw and stole a kiss from my mouth. "You bet."

I huffed out a laugh and slapped his chest with the back of my hand. Then I turned towards Paige. "Ready?"

"Yep." She grinned and adjusted the straps on her pack. "But I'll go after Callan."

My brows furrowed. "Why?"

With that mischievous smile still on her lips, she hiked a thumb in Henry's direction. "So that *he* can stare at *my* ass."

Red flashed into Henry's cheeks, and he jerked back slightly, which brought on a sudden coughing fit. Paige just wiggled her eyebrows and let out a cackle. Chuckling, I shook my head at the two of them and then swung myself down onto the ladder.

I had never seen Henry this flustered before. Usually, he was just standing behind Callan's shoulder with that annoying scowl on his face. But ever since Paige joined our group, he seemed to be experiencing all sorts of emotions. Or rather, she seemed to be forcefully dragging those emotions out of him whether he wanted to or not.

Dust rose up in a small cloud as I jumped the final distance and landed on the ground before the tunnel. Immediately dropping to my knees, I started forward.

Leather creaked behind me, informing me that Callan was making his way down the ladder too.

His dark laugh echoed between the stone walls behind me. "I still love watching you crawl."

"Shut up," I muttered while hiding a satisfied smirk.

Those white gems that were set into the walls illuminated my path as I made my way towards the other side of the tunnel. And I may or may not have swayed my ass more than strictly necessary while I moved.

When I at last reached the other side and climbed up the waiting ladder, I found the King of Metal leaning against the outer wall with his arms crossed. Moonlight streamed in through the grimy windows and fell across half of his face. No trace of the rage or that brief hint of panic remained on his handsome features. Now, he just looked bored.

"Took you long enough," he remarked.

Dusting off my black riding clothes, I shot him a smile dripping with sweet poison. "I wasn't the one holding up the descent by throwing a temper tantrum."

His gray eyes flashed. Pushing off from the wall, he took a threatening step towards me. "Careful."

"*You* be careful. This is my city. And if you ever put a knife to Callan's throat again, I'll lead you down a dark alley that you won't return from."

"Was that a threat?"

"Yes."

"Do you know what happens to people who threaten me?"

"The same thing that happens to those who threaten me or the people I love, I'd imagine. So I'd suggest you keep your pointy sticks clear of our throats in the future."

A wolfish smile spread across his lips. It was tinged with a hint of insanity that sent an involuntary chill down my spine. But I refused to let him see that, so I just kept glaring at him with hard eyes.

"What's going on?" Callan's voice drifted through the gloomy room.

Levi and I only kept staring each other down while Callan climbed out of the hole and straightened on the floor.

At last breaking eye contact, I let out a light chuckle and turned to Callan. "Just a friendly chat."

He didn't look convinced. But when Levi only shrugged his agreement that it was nothing, he gave us a slow nod and then moved over to the door. We checked that the street was clear while Paige and Henry emerged from the smugglers tunnel as well.

"We need a place to stay," Henry said once we were all gathered. "A safe house to use as our base."

"I'd offer my house, but the constables seized it when they arrested me," Paige replied with a shrug.

"That's alright," I said.

Callan and I exchanged a knowing look.

"We've already taken care of that."

Chapter 17

Callan

We stopped outside the low fence. On the other side was a small garden, and then a grand two-story house made of white marble. Moonlight fell across the red-painted door and glinted against the tall windows beside it.

"How do you know that no one lives here?" Paige asked. "Look." She jerked her chin towards the building. "There are curtains in those windows. If a house is unoccupied, it doesn't usually have curtains."

Next to me, Henry chuckled. "So, you've got burglary on that already rather extensive resume of yours too?"

"Says the guy working for a dark mage."

"Deflecting, huh? Suspicious."

"I'm a *forger*." She raised her chin and tried to give Henry an offended look. It worked terribly when she had to crane her neck to look up at him. "Not a burglar."

"So how did you know about the curtains?"

"I usually hire a thief when I need to... *acquire* an original. But sometimes when it's a document I don't want others to know about, I carry out the acquisition myself."

Amusement pulled at his lips as he raised his eyebrows at her. "By burgling the place?"

"I..." Drawing her eyebrows down in a mock scowl, she slapped his ribs with the back of her hand. "Shut up. My point is, that's usually what a house looks like from the outside when there are people inside." She turned back to me and Audrey. "So how do you know that it's empty?"

"We stayed here when we came to kidnap Lance last time," I said. "The people who owned the house were renting it out because they'd moved to Malgrave."

"They might have come back."

"They haven't."

"When we were in Malgrave, we tracked them down," Audrey picked up. She paused for a few seconds and then cleared her throat. "And bought the house from them."

Both Henry and Paige's eyebrows shot up. Levi only watched us with cunning eyes, his expression betraying nothing.

"You've bought this house?" Paige blurted out, and swung an arm towards the building. "Why?"

Audrey and I exchanged a long look.

Then she lifted her shoulders in a light shrug. "For the future."

For a moment, no one said anything. Then it was as if a candle was lit behind both Henry and Paige's eyes when they finally connected the dots. Matching grins bloomed on their faces.

"Aww," Paige began. "That's so—"

Embarrassment flickered across Audrey's face, and she held up a hand. "Do not finish that sentence."

"I agree," Henry said. His damn eyes practically glittered as he turned to grin at me. "That's so—"

"If you say *cute*, I'm gonna kick your ass."

He snorted. "Yeah, 'cause that's worked out so well for you before."

"There won't be a future for any of you," Levi drawled before I could retort. Cocking his head, he shot a pointed look between us and the house. "Unless you stop this insufferable bickering and go unlock that door right now."

Audrey gave him a lethal smile. "Careful now. Or I might make you sleep out here on the street instead."

My whole body tensed, and I snapped my gaze to Levi. But he only watched her with a matching lethal smile on his own lips while she breezed past him and sauntered up to the door.

It still shocked me that he didn't retaliate when she said things like that. If anyone, literally anyone else, had spoken to him with such blatant disrespect, he would've made them crawl at his feet and grovel for mercy. But for some reason, he tolerated Audrey's sharp tongue. It made me wonder what his wife was like. Whether she possessed an equally sharp tongue and if that was why Levi tolerated Audrey's too.

The faint jasmine scent that had hung in the night air outside disappeared when we all stepped across the threshold and closed the red front door behind us. I scanned the hallway ahead. It looked exactly the same as last time we'd been here.

Emotions crashed over me. They were so intense that I had to brace myself on the smooth marble wall. There were so many memories in this house.

This was the place where I had locked Audrey into that empty third room for almost half a day. It was where she had almost poisoned me to death when I asked her about her family. The place where I had told her about *my* childhood. Where I had ripped open her dress and then washed her hair and body for her after she had helped me bury a dead body in the parliament gardens. It was the place where we had kissed for the first time. And fucked for the first time.

My heart squeezed almost painfully when I swept my gaze over the darkened hall and the rooms visible beyond.

This house, right here, was where I had begun falling in love with Audrey Sable.

A slim hand slid into mine. I blinked, pulled out of my memories, and glanced down to find Audrey standing next to me. There was a soft smile on her lips as she looked up at me, as if she had been thinking the exact same thing. I squeezed her hand.

"So..." Henry began a bit awkwardly. "Sleeping arrangements?"

Realizing that the silence had begun to stretch, I cleared my throat while Audrey released my hand again. "There are three rooms upstairs, but only two of them have a bed."

"Since this is your house, I'm assuming you two will be taking the master bedroom?"

"Yeah."

"I'll take the other room then," Levi announced.

I shifted my gaze to him and said carefully, "It's a double bed."

He just looked back at me, challenge dancing over his sharp cheekbones. "Good."

"Wouldn't it be better if—"

"I'll take the couch," Henry interrupted. Dragging a hand through his brown hair, he shrugged. "We should be able to get another bed delivered here sometime tomorrow, so it's just for one night."

"I'll join you," Paige said in a surprisingly cheerful voice, and nodded at Henry.

A satisfied smirk slid home on Levi's mouth. *Bastard.* Given how friendly Henry and Paige had become these past few weeks, I was pretty sure they wouldn't have minded sharing the double bed. That would've meant that only one person had to sleep on the couch. But because the arrogant King of Metal would never lower himself to such a thing, two people now had to take the couch while he commandeered the bed. Hell, I couldn't wait for us to finish this mission so that he could go back to his damn kingdom in Malgrave.

"Excellent," Levi said, that smug expression still on his face. "Now that that's settled, what's the plan for tomorrow?"

"As Audrey said back at Grant's mansion, we can't break into the academy to get the blade," Paige said. "It's impenetrable."

I nodded. "Which is why the plan is to get them to take it to us."

"Correct," Audrey filled in. "And for that, we'll need leverage." She ran a hand along her jaw before shrugging one shoulder. "As I said earlier, a few loved ones usually does the trick."

Levi gave her an approving nod.

"Only problem is," Henry began. "How do we find them?"

"Or rather, how do we find the most effective ones?" Audrey continued. "Kidnapping someone's wife and threatening her life won't matter if the husband doesn't actually care about her. We need to know exactly which loved one's safety will make the members of parliament come crawling to the negotiating table."

"Uhm, excuse me." Paige flapped her hands in the air and raised her eyebrows while looking from face to face. "Did you forget the part where I've been *the* most sought-after forger in Eldar's entire criminal underworld for the past six years?"

Audrey chuckled. "Humble too."

"Shut it, Miss-oh-tremble-before-your-dark-mage-queen." She failed pretty spectacularly at keeping the amusement from her face as she tried to glower at Audrey. "You're not exactly the epitome of humility yourself."

While trying to suppress her own smile, Audrey lifted her hands in surrender.

"Thank you." Paige flicked her wavy blond hair behind her shoulder. "Now, where was I? Oh, right. I'm a very well-connected person in the underworld, which means that I have contacts who can find out what we need."

"Alright then, problem solved." I gave her an appreciative nod. "Let's pay them a visit tomorrow."

Everyone murmured agreement and nodded back.

Hoisting my pack up onto my shoulders again, I started towards the staircase farther down the hall. Behind me, Henry and Paige talked softly while drifting over to check out the dining room and the other large room meant for socializing that was located across the hall from it. Both Audrey and Levi followed me.

"Your room is on the right," I spoke over my shoulder to Levi as we ascended the steps.

He didn't answer, but I hadn't really been expecting him to either. Instead, he just branched off as soon as we reached the upper floor and disappeared into his room. The door shut with a click behind him.

I set course for the master bedroom, but to my surprise, Audrey just walked right past it. Trailing to a halt outside the door, I blinked at her as she sauntered down the corridor.

"Where are you going?" I asked.

"To take a bath." Turning around, she flashed me a sly smile while continuing to walk backwards. "You coming?"

Warmth flooded my chest.

With a wide smile on my lips, I followed my brilliant poison mage towards the bathroom and the luxurious sunken bath that had just been waiting for us to return and relive some old memories.

Chapter 18

Audrey

Cheerful chatter drifted through the warm morning air as people strolled along the street a short distance away. All of them were completely oblivious to the fact that three dark mages, a forger, and whatever the hell Henry was, snuck through the deserted alley just a few steps from them.

Paige leaned around the edge and scanned the next road before waving us forward.

"This is absurd," Levi said as we all followed her and rounded the corner. Raising his arm, he stabbed a hand towards the unwitting citizens strolling in the morning sunlight. "We could slaughter every single person on that street if we wanted to. Without even breaking a sweat. They should be backing up and bowing down as we pass. But instead, we're... skulking in the shadows like rats."

I glanced over at the metal mage. Annoyance and indignation swirled in his sharp gray eyes, and his muscular body seemed taut with pent-up frustration. My gaze glided over his broad chest. At least Callan had managed to convince him to leave his metal shoulder plates and bracers back at the house. That sort of thing drew far too much attention in Eldar.

"This ain't Malgrave," Callan said in response. "Dark mages can't just walk the street openly here."

A villainous smile slid across Levi's lips. "Yet."

Callan chuckled and shot him a knowing look. It was so casual. Like it was something that they had done a thousand times.

Then, as if remembering themselves, both of them snapped their gazes away while masks of indifference descended on their features.

We continued sneaking through the deserted alleys in silence. The scent of baking bread drifted out from an open window that we passed. It made my stomach rumble and reminded me that we needed to pick up some food before we went back to our house. I was just about to say as much when Paige suddenly jerked to a halt and gasped.

Panic shot up my spine.

Touching my hands together, I called up a tendril of poison while whipping my head from left to right. On either side of me, Callan, Levi, and Henry had also summoned magic and fallen into a battle stance.

"What is it?" I demanded, my pulse thrumming in my ears.

Paige pointed towards the pale stone wall while a scowl marred her brows. "They've made me look ugly."

Confusion flitted through my chest. Twisting around, I glanced towards where she was pointing.

Our own faces stared back at us.

An exasperated laugh tore from my throat.

There were three large sheets of paper hanging side by side on the wall. The one on the left depicted a scowling Callan. In the middle was a drawing of me, while the one on the right had Paige's face painted on it. At the top of each paper, one word had been written in massive letters using red ink. *WANTED*.

"What the hell," Callan grumbled, letting his force magic fade out. "I thought we were under attack."

"I *am* under attack," Paige protested. With her brows still furrowed, she waved a hand towards the honestly rather bad drawing of her face. "Or my public image is, anyway. Now people are going to start thinking that I actually look like that."

"This is what you stopped for?" Levi interrupted. Disbelief lined his features as he shook his head at the rest of us. "How you people get anything done is beyond me. Now, let's get a move on."

Paige muttered something under her breath that I hoped to hell that Levi hadn't heard. Since he didn't throw a sheet of metal at her, it seemed as though he thankfully hadn't. I suppressed my smile as we started up again.

We had only made it another street down when Paige began chuckling softly.

"What now?" Callan said with a sigh.

A wicked smile shone on her lips as she looked up at Henry. "I just realized that you didn't have a wanted poster." There was a sly expression on her features as she flicked her hair over her shoulder. "I guess that means I'm more important, more *infamous*, than you."

He huffed out a laugh. "Or it just means that I'm better at being sneaky and remaining unnoticed." Shooting her a pointed look, he gave her shoulder a soft push. "Despite being *eight feet tall*."

Her answering laugh warmed something deep inside my chest.

"I didn't say..." She trailed off and abruptly swung towards a pale wooden door on the right. "Oh, we're here."

As if on some unspoken signal, Callan, Henry, Levi, and I

all began checking our weapons and brushing our hands together in anticipation.

"To talk," Paige stressed. "We're here *to talk*. Remember?" Raising an accusing finger, she pointed it at all of us while continuing to walk backwards towards the door. "And I'll do the talking."

The four of us exchanged a glance, but we didn't summon any magic or draw any weapons as we followed her to the door. She rolled her eyes at us. But in the end, she just twirled back around and placed her hand on the handle. Without bothering to knock, she simply shoved it down and flung the door open wide before strolling across the threshold.

"What's up, Kenny?" she said.

We followed her into the room beyond and closed the door behind us while a man jerked up from the counter he had been leaning against. The four of us moved up so that we were standing side by side behind Paige as she strolled up to the man. I swept my gaze around the room.

Even though it was a bright summer morning, the room was gloomy because the wooden shutters still covered the windows. It made the wooden walls and floor look darker than they probably were. Shelves lined the walls, but I couldn't make out what exactly was on them all. It was just a jumble of books and papers and scrolls and maps. Due to the presence of the counter that Kenny was leaning against, this looked almost like a shop. But for what, I had no idea.

"Paige," Kenny blurted out.

I shifted my attention back to him. Surprise washed over his narrow face as he stared at Paige with wide brown eyes. His brown hair fell down to his jaw, and he pushed it back behind his ears as he straightened.

"I didn't know that you were…" He began but then trailed off, as if he didn't know how to finish the sentence.

"Out of prison?" Paige supplied. Stopping before the counter, she leaned her elbow on it in a casual move. "Alive? All-around unharmed?"

Kenny flicked a nervous gaze over the rest of us before he returned it to her. He licked his lips. "All of the above, I suppose."

"Hmm." Paige poked at a cluster of pens that had been shoved into a glass jar on the tall counter. They clanked faintly, disrupting the tense silence. Dropping her hand again, she looked up to meet his gaze once more. "I've got a job for you."

"I, uhm..."

She straightened suddenly, and a harshness bled into her voice that I had rarely heard before. "You *owe* me."

"Well, I—"

"How many documents have I forged for you over the years? Huh? How many?"

"I—"

"And yet, when the constables came for me, you disappeared into your little hole like a rat."

"I had to protect my own business." Holding up his hands, he shook his head. "You know what it's like. I couldn't risk them finding me too."

"Uh-huh." She crossed her arms. "Well, you didn't help me then, but you can make up for that now. I need a list of names. A rather long list. And very specific names."

Kenny's brown eyes flicked across the four of us again, and suspicion shone on his face. Clearing his throat, he glanced back at Paige. "Look, Paige. Last I saw you, you were being hauled away in handcuffs by an entire squad of constables. And now you're suddenly here, free again. That doesn't usually happen for people like us."

"Are you suggesting that I'm a snitch? That I turned and

traded my underworld connections to the constables for my own freedom?"

"I'm just saying... How do I know you're not setting me up right now?"

Without even having to say anything, all four of us touched our palms together. A massive metal blade grew from Levi's hand while a spinning arc of force magic appeared above our heads and glittering green poison mist swirled around me, showing Kenny that we were dark mages and clearly not on the side of the righteous. On Callan's other side, Henry had summoned wind magic too.

Fear crackled across Kenny's features, and he stumbled back from the counter. The sudden move made him trip over something on the floor, and he went sprawling down on top of whatever else was down there. Clangs and thuds echoed through the room.

Paige glanced back over her shoulder to see what had caused his sudden fear. When she noticed our magic, she rolled her eyes at us. But there was a grateful smile on her lips too.

She turned back to Kenny. "You were saying?"

More clanking sounded as he no doubt pushed stuff aside while he climbed back to his feet. Clearing his throat, he dragged a hand through his hair to smoothen it down again. "What do you need?"

We let our magic fade out again.

"I need the names of the people that the parliament members care about the most," Paige said, once more leaning casually against the counter. "One loved one per parliament member should suffice, but it has to be the one they care about the most. No kids, though."

Kenny snatched up a pen and jotted down notes on a piece of paper while nodding to himself. Then he looked up again. "Alright. I can have that ready for you in a week."

Brushing our palms together again, we all filled the room with our lethal magic once more.

Panic flickered in Kenny's eyes as his gaze darted between the four of us and Paige. He cleared his throat. "I mean, by the end of the day."

"Excellent," Paige said. "You can leave it in our usual spot."

With his eyes still darting between her and us, he nodded distractedly. She just pushed off from the desk and spun around. A grin played over her lips as she started back towards us. We led our magic fade out again.

Well, everyone except Henry. His gray eyes were locked on Kenny, and wind magic swirled around his massive frame as he took a threatening step towards the counter.

"You," Henry began in a low and dangerous voice. It was the voice that he had used on me when he had threatened to kill me if I hurt Callan. "You left her to hang last time."

Kenny edged a step back.

Wind magic twisted around Henry's arms. "If you do anything to endanger her now, I will be back."

"I... I won't. I swear it."

From where she had trailed to a halt on the floor, Paige was staring at Henry with both surprise and a sort of sparkling joy on her face. I glanced over at the mountain of a man too.

I might not have liked Henry very much before. He had threatened to torture and kill me. And I might have planned to kill him too along with Callan when that damn force mage took me captive. Suffice it to say that we'd had a rocky start. But since Paige joined our group, I had started to see different sides of him.

And now, as I watched him threaten to kill a man if he did anything to hurt Paige, I had to admit that I was rather starting to like him.

Chapter 19

Callan

The scent of fried eggs, spiced chicken, and herbs hung over the whole kitchen. Standing in front of the circular countertop in the middle of the room, I shoveled another forkful of the delicious omelet into my mouth before looking up at Paige. Damn, she was a good cook.

My gaze slid to Audrey, and I couldn't help raising my eyebrows in a teasing gesture. Narrowing her eyes, she shot me a vicious glare as if saying, *don't even think about it*. I let out a silent chuckle. At our mansions, both of us had had people who cooked for us and cleaned and did all the things that we had no interest in doing. When we moved into this house together, properly moved in, we should probably hire some staff too.

A plummeting sensation rippled through my stomach at that thought, and my heart did a backflip in my chest. When we moved in together. When all this was over, Audrey and I were actually going to move in here together. Start a life here. Together. Energy crackled through my body and I had to suppress the urge to inhale the rest of my food and run out the door to make that future happen faster.

It was followed by a sudden flash of embarrassment. When

the hell had I become this pathetic? I was supposed to be a dark mage. But ever since I met Audrey, I had started to feel more and more like some infatuated schoolboy. It was absolutely ridiculous.

A wicked smile threatened to spread across my lips. Tonight, I was going to have to show that infuriating little poisoner exactly what she did to me, and subject her to some excruciatingly pleasurable payback.

"And what are you grinning about?" Henry's teasing voice echoed through the kitchen, pulling me out of my thoughts.

Shaking my head, I shoved the enticing thoughts aside and stabbed into my omelet again. "Nothing."

From across the smooth wooden counter, Audrey was watching me with glittering green eyes, as if she could see right through me.

"You said the list of names from your contact arrived last night," Levi thankfully said before either Audrey or Henry could call me on the lie. His penetrating gaze slid to Paige. "Can we trust the intel?"

Paige paused with her fork halfway to her mouth. Raising her eyebrows, she swept her gaze over all of us and then waved the fork around, making a few pieces of omelet fly through the air and land on the counter below. "After that little dark mage obey-or-die show you all put on, yeah, I'm pretty sure he wouldn't dare to so much as sneeze unless we gave him permission."

Villainous smiles spread across all of our faces. "Good."

Rolling her eyes, she waved her fork around again. "By the way, didn't I tell you that I would do the talking?"

"You did do the talking," Audrey reasoned with an innocent shrug. "We just... backed you up."

She shot her friend a flat stare. "Uh-huh. Anyway, yes, we have the list and we can trust that it's accurate. So, now what?"

"We need a way to take them all at the same time," Levi said. A knowing look passed over his features as he slid his gaze to me and Henry. "You know what prey is like when it knows that it's being hunted. If we take one of these people, the rest will go to ground immediately."

"Yeah," I said while Henry grunted his agreement too.

Audrey looked over at Paige. "Wait, all of the people on the list, they're involved in the social circles, right?"

"They're all spouses or family of parliament members, so yeah they're involved in some form or other," she replied.

"I think I know how to get them all to come to the same place at the same time." Schemes glittered in her eyes as she turned to meet my gaze. "But for that, we need some leverage."

The midday sun shone down on the outdoor market. People talked softly while drifting through the stalls or stopping to peer at different products. The colorful awnings that provided shade for the owners of the stalls fluttered slightly as a gentle breeze whirled through the open square. I kept to the shadows as I stalked our prey through it.

A short distance away, Henry and Levi were doing the same. However, since neither of them had their face plastered on wanted posters, they didn't have to skulk around as much as I did. Audrey and Paige had remained back at the house in order to minimize the risk of detection, but we needed at least one person who actually knew what our target looked like, which was why I had gone with Levi and Henry.

Two women came strolling down the path right towards me. Keeping my head slightly bowed, I pretended to study a table of freshly baked pies until they had passed. Then I started forward again.

Our target was still moving in areas that were far too crowded. We needed him to branch off towards the alleys on the right. I scanned the square again.

The small trees that had been planted at regular intervals on the pale cobblestones rustled their branches as another warm summer wind stroked their leaves. Everywhere, people chatted and laughed as if there wasn't a war happening in the hills outside their precious city right at this very moment. And not a single constable to be seen.

By pulling everyone out for the war, they had left their city practically undefended. I wondered how the regular criminals in here had reacted to that.

I snuck down the path and then turned right as my prey finally began making his way towards the edge of the market. Raising my head, I met Henry's eyes and then jerked my chin. He nodded back. Levi was with him, but I wasn't stupid enough to give the King of Metal such an obvious order so I just hoped that he would follow Henry. Amusement played over Levi's features, as if he saw right through me. But thankfully, he followed Henry towards another side street.

Making sure to stay a short distance behind, I casually walked towards the edge of the market too. Anticipation thrummed inside me. After the way our prey had behaved last time Audrey and I had spent time with him, I found that I was rather looking forward to this.

Bright sunlight painted his brown hair in an almost golden color, and made the crisp white dress shirt he wore look even paler in comparison to his black pants. I picked up the pace as he neared the mouth of the alley.

Once he had reached it, I silently jogged the final distance to catch up.

The buildings here were so tall that they shrouded the

narrow alleyway in gloomy shadows. I blinked against the change, trying to get my eyes to adjust quickly.

My target was so close now.

All it would take was a few long strides, and then I'd be able to grab him.

As if the bastard had eyes in the back of his head, he suddenly whirled around to face me. "What's..." He trailed off, and his brown eyes went wide as they took me in. "You."

"Carl Dawson." I flashed him a wolfish grin. "Long time no see."

He slapped his palms together and threw a blast of wind at me, probably to knock me backwards. But it didn't matter. I was faster.

Using a force shield, I shoved his attack into the pale stone wall of the building on my left. Dust and a few pieces of gravel rained down as it hit. I raised my eyebrows. Panic flashed across Carl's face, and he shot a lightning bolt towards me.

It wasn't even aimed that well, so all it took was a slight push with another force shield and it cracked into the wall instead.

Damn, I had almost forgotten how bad ordinary people were at battle magic. Constables were weaker than us because they had to rely on the Great Current, but they had at least gotten combat training. These normal citizens, they really had no idea how to effectively attack someone with magic.

Shaking my head, I tutted, "Oh come now, Carl. None of that."

He seemed to realize that he would never be able to beat me, so he dropped his next water magic attack and instead whirled around and sprinted towards the other end of the alley.

I heaved a deep sigh. Letting my force shield fade out, I strode after the fleeing man.

When he had almost reached the end, two people suddenly appeared around the corner and stalked into the alley.

"Oh, thank the Current," Carl blurted out as he skidded to a halt a couple of steps in front of them. Raising a hand, he pointed back towards me. "There's a dark mage here and he's trying to kill me."

"A dark mage?" A predatory smile spread across Levi's lips as he brushed his palms together and summoned a wicked-looking metal blade out of thin air. "You don't say?"

I couldn't see Carl's expression from this angle, but he jerked back as if in fear and panic. Henry didn't even bother to call up his magic, his physical presence was threatening enough as it was.

Stumbling backwards, Carl whipped his head back and forth, trying to keep both them and me in view. I used the opportunity when he was looking in the wrong direction to quickly close the distance between us.

A gasp tore from his throat as he turned his head and suddenly found me right in front of him.

Taking a firm grip on his impeccable white shirt, I swung him around and shoved him back first up against the wall. Air exploded from his lungs in a huff. With my hand still buried in the collar of his shirt, I held him pinned against the wall while Henry and Levi flanked me.

"P-please," Carl managed to press out, and raised his hands in surrender. "Look, I'm sorry for telling the constables what we knew about you. But we had to cooperate. Chancellor Quill himself supervised the interviews. We had to tell them. Please."

"Oh we're not here about that." I cocked my head and let a vicious smile curl my lips. "But thanks for telling me that you ratted us out too. I'll keep that in mind for later."

A whimper escaped his throat.

"No, we're here about something else entirely," I continued.

"What?"

Pulling him away from the wall, I swung an arm around his shoulders as if we were old pals. By the way he cringed, it was very obvious that we weren't. But he was going to have to learn to pretend until we got where we were going.

"Come on, let's take a walk."

Chapter 20

Audrey

Lounging on the blue and gold sofa, I sipped at the expensive wine in my crystal glass. The afternoon sun shone in through the windows and filled the elegant living room with wonderful natural light. With one arm draped over the backrest, I stretched out my legs and shifted my weight on the soft cushions. As far as ambushes went, this one was definitely one of the more comfortable ones.

"Where do you buy your wine from?" I asked.

Carl looked up at me from his place on the floor and blinked in surprise. "I, uhm... I don't know."

I raised my eyebrows.

"It's the cook who orders all the wine," he added hurriedly.

Saying nothing, I just looked him over for a few seconds. He was handcuffed and on his knees in the middle of the room while Callan prowled back and forth behind him like a restless wolf. His gaze darted between me and Callan. Cocking my head, I continued watching him. He looked decidedly nervous. I couldn't fathom why. We weren't going to start threatening him until *after* his wife had showed up.

"Huh," I said at last. After lifting one shoulder in a shrug, I swirled the wine in my glass and took another sip. "I might need to have a chat with your cook later then."

Carl looked like he couldn't decide whether he was worried for his cook's safety or relieved that I had found someone else to threaten besides him.

From across the room, Callan met my gaze and raised his eyebrows in silent question.

"What?" I gave him my most innocent look. "I'm just getting a few friendly tips from the locals."

He snorted and shook his head at me while amusement danced across his face.

A tapping sound came from the window.

Glancing towards it, I found Paige's face staring back at me. She waved her hands around in front of her and then pointed in the direction of the door. I nodded.

"Well then," I said. "I guess it's showtime."

Swinging my legs back down from the couch, I set my glass of wine down on the table with a soft thud and then pushed to my feet. The flowing dark green skirt rippled around my legs as I straightened. I smoothened it down while Callan touched his palms together and summoned a force blade.

Fear washed over Carl's face. "No, wait, what are you—"

"Unless I give you permission to speak, you'll keep your mouth shut," Callan said, and leveled the force blade at his neck. "Understood?"

He flicked a glance towards me.

I just raised my eyebrows expectantly and jerked my chin towards Callan. "I'd suggest answering him."

Snapping his gaze back to Callan, he swallowed and then said, "I understand."

Before Callan could say anything else, a lock clicked. A moment later, the sound of the front door being opened and closed echoed through the silent house. It was followed by a feminine voice.

"Honey?"

Callan kept his vibrating blade steady next to Carl's neck and said in a quiet voice, "Tell her to come in here."

"I'm in here," Carl called in a surprisingly strong voice.

Footsteps sounded from the corridor outside the living room. I used the time to move over to the white marble wall halfway between the open doorway and where Callan and Carl were waiting. Leaning back against it in a casual pose, I brushed my palms together and called up a tendril of poison that snaked lazily around my forearm.

"You won't believe who I saw on my way back." The voice was coming from right outside the living room now. "And what they were doing. By the Current, when people find out that she..."

A gorgeous woman with loose blond curls and blue eyes walked around the corner and then screeched to a halt a couple of steps inside the room. Shock and terror flashed across her beautiful face as she stared in open-mouthed disbelief at Carl and Callan.

"Hello, Elise," I said.

Elise Dawson jumped in surprise, making the small package she had been carrying slide from her hands and hit the hard floor before her. The sound of shattering glass filled the room while she whirled towards me.

Raising my hand, I curled my fingers in a mocking wave while the green poison tendril continued slithering around my wrist. She flinched. I just flashed her a wicked smile.

Her gaze darted between me and Callan and her husband while she edged a step back.

"Please, I'm sorry," she blurted out. "We didn't want to tell the constables about you, but we had to. We had to tell them everything. The Chancellor himself was there, and he insisted. Please."

Disapproval swirled through me, and I drew my eyebrows down in a scowl. "You ratted us out to the constables?"

"I, uhm..." Surprise, hesitation, and then regret flickered in her eyes. "Well..."

"Yes, they did," Callan said.

I turned towards him and raised my eyebrows. "How do you know?"

He jerked his chin towards Carl. "He said the same thing when we ambushed him up by the market." Meeting my gaze, he shrugged. "I was gonna tell you when we got back."

"Huh." I slid my gaze back to Elise. "Well, now I feel a bit less bad about blackmailing you."

"Blackmail?" she stammered.

"Oh, who am I kidding? I never felt bad about that at all."

Callan chuckled. It made the force blade shift closer to Carl's exposed throat. He flinched, trying to discreetly lean sideways. Worry washed over Elise's face, and she took a couple of steps towards her husband before Callan stopped her with a commanding stare.

"Are you okay?" Elise asked, her eyes on Carl. "Did they hurt you?"

Still on his knees, Carl looked up at Callan, silently asking for permission to speak.

Callan clicked his tongue. "You can answer her."

Tilting his head back down, he met his wife's gaze and said, "I'm okay. They haven't hurt me."

A sigh of relief whooshed out of her lungs. She had been twisting her fingers in her pale blue skirt, but now she forced her hands away and let her arms hang by her sides while she straightened her spine and looked between me and Callan. "What do you want?"

"You're going to host a charity event," I said.

Shock bounced across her features as she jerked back a little and blinked at me. Whatever she had been expecting me to say, that had apparently not been it. "Why?"

"Because we said so."

She raised her chin. "And if we refuse?"

"I don't think you want us to answer that, Elise."

Her gaze drifted towards Carl again. Callan shifted the force blade closer to his neck.

"And don't even think about trying to contact what remains of the constables in Eldar," I continued. Then I paused, waiting for her to drag her eyes back to me. When she did, I held her gaze to let her know that I truly meant what I was about to say. "If you make one single move that we don't like, anything at all that we think looks suspicious, we'll make you watch as we kill all of your friends. One by one. And then we will kill you."

Her face drained completely of color.

"Am I making myself clear?" I demanded.

"Yes," she breathed.

Pushing off from the wall, I started towards her while pulling out a folded-up paper. Elise flinched and made as if to back away. But when I cocked my head slightly, she froze in her tracks again and just stood there while I closed the final distance between us.

"Here's the list of people you're going to invite." I shoved the paper into her hand. "Make it happen in two days."

"In... two days?"

"Yes. Problem?"

She shook her head vehemently.

"Good." I stabbed a finger against the paper she was now clutching in her hand. "Make sure every single person on this list is there. If even one person is missing, I will hold you personally responsible."

"I'll... I'll make sure they're all here."

"Excellent." I slid my gaze to Callan. "Shall we?"

He gave me a nod and then let his force blade fade out. Both Carl and Elise heaved a sigh of relief. Bending down, Callan unlocked the manacles around Carl's wrists and then strode towards me without another word.

Our footsteps echoed into the crackling silence as we made our way towards the front door.

Elise Dawson was at the top of the social hierarchy in Eldar. If anyone could throw a party and make sure that all of the parliament members' loved ones were there, it was her. Then, we just had to grab them all.

Sunlight washed over me as we stepped back out into the small garden, and I had to shield my eyes with my hand until we reached the street and turned away in the other direction. Three people fell in beside us.

"So," Paige began from where she strolled next to Henry. "It went well then?"

"Yeah," I said, and flashed her a smile. "Thanks for being the lookouts."

"Anytime."

"She's gonna invite them all?" Henry asked, looking between me and Callan.

Callan nodded. "Yeah. In two days. So now we just need to find a way to keep them all compliant once we make our move."

On my other side, Levi slid his hands into his pockets and then lifted his broad shoulders in a casual shrug. "I can take care of that."

I turned to face him and raised my eyebrows. "Really?"

"Yeah. Just get me some metal."

Chapter 21

Callan

The shed creaked in distress as I used my force magic to saw through the metal, splitting two of the walls at the joint. I glanced over my shoulder to make sure that no nosy neighbors were peeking over the hedge, but it was the middle of a weekday morning so everyone was presumably at work. Once I was sure that no one was spying on us, I slid my gaze back to the man standing on the other side of the shed, holding up the wall until I could cut through it completely.

"So," I began, a teasing smirk on my mouth. "You and Paige, huh?"

Henry, who had been focused on the metal wall, snapped his gaze up to me and blinked. Then he cleared his throat. "I don't know what that means. Paige and me, what?"

"Oh come on, Henry. I've got eyes, you know."

"Then they're blind as fuck because there's nothing going on between me and Paige."

"Really? That why you threatened to kill that Kenny guy earlier?"

Drawing his eyebrows down, he kept his face carefully

blank. "I was just looking out for her, that's all. Since she's not used to running with dark mages, and all that."

"Uh-huh."

My force magic severed the last bit, and the two final walls came free as well. Releasing my grip on the magic, I yanked my hand up to brace the wall closest to me before it could crash right into my chest. Henry kept his grip on the perpendicular wall.

Once I had gotten a hold on mine, he began slowly lowering the long flat sheet of metal to the ground. It clanked in annoyance as he dragged it up and then dropped it on top of the other two walls we had already taken down. I swept my gaze over the small garden.

It was a rather beautiful place. Both the jasmine and the rose bushes were in full bloom, and the tall hedges that framed the area provided almost complete privacy. Most of the ground was covered in soft grass, but there was also a small area made of stone where outdoor furniture could be placed.

My gaze returned to the butchered shed. Audrey and I would have to replace that at some point, but right now, Levi needed the metal.

"It would be okay, you know," I said as I dragged the final wall up onto the pile, and then straightened to meet Henry's gaze. "If there was something going on between you and Paige."

Hesitation flickered briefly in Henry's usually calm gray eyes. But instead of answering, he just bent down and grabbed the side of the walls. I did the same on my end.

Metallic clanging drowned out the soft rustling of leaves as we hauled the pile towards the back door.

"It's just…" There was a hint of desperation on Henry's face as he looked up and met my gaze from across the sheets of metal. "She terrifies me."

I couldn't stop a surprised laugh from escaping my throat.

The thought of that skinny blond scaring the seven-foot-one mountain of muscle that was Henry was straight up hilarious.

Henry shot me a disapproving scowl, and I quickly wiped the grin from my face and cleared my throat instead.

"I'm serious," Henry said while we maneuvered into position in front of the open door. "She makes me... *feel* things. And it's fucking terrifying."

Understanding flooded my chest. I knew that feeling well. After all, I had gone through the exact same thing with my vicious little poisoner.

Henry shook his head at me while we tilted the metal sheets to the side to get them through the door. "She can make me laugh when I'm really not supposed to be laughing. And she can make me blush. Blush!" He shook his head again while he backed across the threshold. "I don't *blush*. And yet, she can draw those emotions from me."

"I know what you mean. It terrified me when Audrey began affecting me like that too."

"Yeah, but you could cover those feelings behind threats since you were literally trying to kill her." Light and shadows shifted across his face as we made it into the hallway and continued moving past the windows and towards the living room. "I can't do that with Paige. Because as opposed to Audrey, Paige is actually kind and sweet and just... a nice person."

Another laugh ripped from my throat as I shot him a mock warning glare. "Hey, careful."

"Sorry." He cleared his throat and gave me a sheepish look. "But you know what I mean, right? You and Audrey were trying to kill each other while you were falling in love, but Paige isn't hostile like that and since I really do like her—"

"Ha!" I interrupted, flashing him a smug grin. "So you *do* like her?"

He let out a groan. "Fuck."

"Like who?" Levi's voice filled the air as we at last made it into the living room.

Instead of answering, we just carried the metal walls over to the long dining room table and set them down on top of it. Levi tracked us with sharp gray eyes, still waiting for an answer. From across the table, Henry gave me an almost imperceptible shake of the head.

"Don't tell me," Levi said, a knowing smirk on his lips. "It's Paige, isn't it? Anyone with eyes can see how you bumble about around her."

Henry shot a panicked glance around the room, as if Paige would suddenly pop up from behind one of the red armchairs even though she and Audrey were scouting out a building for us to use and wouldn't be back for at least another few hours.

Flicking his gaze between me and Levi, he cleared his throat and hiked his thumb towards the doorway while backing towards it. "I'm gonna go... put the things away... from the... shed."

A smug laugh echoed into the room as Levi watched Henry disappear around the corner. I scowled at him.

The King of Metal snapped his gaze to me. "And what are you scowling about?"

"You know exactly what."

"Enlighten me."

Walking around the table, I moved until I was standing right in front of him. We were about the same height, so I locked hard eyes on him before answering. "You might be the one running the show in Malgrave, but this ain't Malgrave."

"Really? I hadn't noticed."

"This is Eldar," I continued as if he hadn't interrupted. Holding his gaze, I spread my arms wide to motion at the building around us. "And this is my home. You don't just come in here and start acting like you're in charge, and you don't disrespect my people. Because guess what? Henry doesn't work for you anymore. He works for me."

Barely before the final word had even left my tongue, pain pulsed through my stomach and chest as a round metal pole suddenly slammed into it. It happened so fast that I couldn't bring my arms back together in time. In fact, I hadn't even seen Levi brush his palms together.

The strike sent waves of pain shooting down my legs and throughout my whole body, and I crashed down on one knee. Before I could manage to push myself up or get my own hands together, Levi's knee slammed into the side of my head. Another jolt of pain shot through my shoulder as I hit the floor hard.

Black spots swam in my vision.

While sucking in a desperate breath, I blinked furiously to clear my head while rolling over on my back.

Before I could get my wits about me again, a boot appeared across my throat.

A strangle gurgle ripped from me as Levi leaned forward, putting more of his weight right on top of my windpipe.

His gray eyes were brimming with threats and there was a lethal edge to his voice as he spoke. "Let's get one thing straight—"

Slapping my palms together, I shot a concentrated force blast at him. Since his feet weren't planted firmly on the ground, it was powerful enough to throw him off balance and push him back a couple of steps.

I used the opportunity to roll away from him and leap to my feet.

Air exploded from my lungs as one of the metal walls from the shed smacked into me, making me collide back first with the marble wall. A second later, the metal sheet twisted and shifted into bands that wrapped around my whole body. They hardened instantly against the wall.

Fury and dread washed over me as I glanced down at my body. Bands of metal wrapped around my arms and legs, pinning them to the wall, while two of them spanned my chest and a third was locked in place over my throat. I stifled an annoyed snarl.

In hindsight, picking a fight with Levi next to a giant pile of metal was a dumb fucking move. But oh well.

Steel sang into the silence as a sword was drawn from its sheath.

Clenching my jaw, I dragged my gaze back up to Levi.

"Let's get one thing straight." Power and authority rippled off his muscular frame as he leveled his sword at my throat. "I might be helping you because of that deal we made, but that doesn't mean that I'll tolerate any insolence from you. Is that clear?"

I glared back at him while discreetly yanking against my restraints. They only tightened more until I had to grit my teeth against the pain.

Levi pushed the tip of his sword harder against the base of my throat. "Answer."

"Yes," I ground out.

"Yes, what?"

Hell damn it all. If I'd been able to move my arms, I would've punched his teeth down his fucking throat. But I couldn't. So I swallowed my pride and averted my gaze. "Yes, sir."

For a while, he just stood there. Staring me down. I kept my eyes on the ground, waiting for him to finish feeding off the power and control he held over me in that moment. Fucking bastard.

The fact that I craved the exact same power and control as

he did was of course entirely beside the point. After all, this time, I was on the receiving end of it.

Abruptly, the metal bands disappeared. The sudden loss of support made my legs buckle, and I crashed down on the floor.

Levi only turned around and strode back to the table. Clanking metal echoed between the marble walls as he returned the bands to the dining room table and the rest of the pile Henry and I had brought in.

"Get over here and put these away as I finish them," he ordered.

Grinding my teeth, I pushed to my feet while trying to smother the urge to run a force blade through the asshole's back when he wasn't looking. I shook out my arms and drew in a few deep breaths before I managed to get my rage under control.

By the table, Levi was molding the metal from the shed into manacles that we were going to use on our hostages later. Since we needed such a large amount, and on such short notice, we hadn't been able to rely on my usual shop to provide everything in time. But thankfully, Levi was good at more than just threatening people. I grabbed each pair of stiff handcuffs and lined them up on the floor by the windows while he continued with the next one.

A comfortable rhythm set in, and for a while, we just worked in silence.

Pausing on my way back from the window, I studied him as he manipulated the metal in the air between his hands.

"Why did you let me live?" The question was out of my mouth before I could stop it.

While continuing to craft the manacles, Levi looked up and met my gaze. He knew very well that I didn't mean when he attacked me just now. I meant before that. After I had betrayed him.

"I sent assassins to kill you for three years," he replied eventually.

"Yeah, but then I went back to Malgrave. And we both know you could've killed me the moment I set foot inside the city."

"Maybe I should have."

"But you didn't. Instead, you beat me within an inch of my life and then you let me and Henry pay off our financial debt and then work off our blood debt."

"Is this going anywhere?"

"I worked for you for years, Levi. In all that time, you never let anyone live who betrayed you."

There was a sharp gleam in his eyes as he looked back at me. "If you're saying that you think I made a mistake, we can always rectify that right now."

Ignoring his taunt, I just blew out a breath and repeated, "Why did you let me live?"

For quite a while, he said nothing. Morning sunlight glinted against metal as he continued twisting it into handcuffs and then set them down on the table before pulling up another piece from the shed walls. I didn't move. Only kept watching him.

Just when I thought that he wasn't going to answer, he heaved a deep sigh and set his newest pair of manacles down before dragging a hand through his hair.

"Because I liked you, Callan."

His words shocked me enough that I just blinked back at him in stunned silence.

"You were smart, skilled, and ballsy as hell. You were almost like a... little brother." A hardness crept into his eyes. "Do you have any idea the kind of bloody retribution I rained down on the house you framed for your supposed death?"

"I, uhm... I guess I never apologized for that."

"No, you didn't."

"I'm sorry."

Holding my gaze, he nodded.

For a while, no one said anything. We only looked at each other.

"When you and Henry came crawling back to Malgrave after all those years, I had every intention of slaughtering you where you stood. But then I just..." He heaved a deep sigh, and his eyes softened a fraction. "You remind me of me."

My mouth dropped open slightly.

"And if I'd been in your shoes," he went on, "I would've left too. I wouldn't have been satisfied serving someone else. I'd want my own kingdom. So I understood why you left. And... yeah, you remind me so much of me sometimes. So I guess that's why I let you live."

The silence that descended on the room was so thick that I could've cut it with a knife. For a few seconds, I could only stare at him because I had no idea what to say. I knew that *I* had seen Levi as a sort of brother back when I worked for him, but I hadn't known whether he truly felt the same. Now, I guess I did.

"Thank you," I said at last, as if that would somehow settle the gigantic debt that I actually owed this man before me. And not just for my life, but for everything that he had taught me over the years.

But he seemed to understand the full meaning behind those words, because he nodded. "Yeah."

We watched each other in silence for another few seconds.

Then he huffed out a short chuckle and shot me a knowing look before returning his attention to the pile of metal before him.

"Don't make me regret it."

Chapter 22

Audrey

Half of our dining room floor was covered in handcuffs. Trailing to a halt, I raised my eyebrows as I stared down at the mass of restraints before me. Damn, they really had been busy.

"Damn, you really have been busy," Paige said, echoing my exact thought, as she stopped and stared at the floor too.

I let out a surprised laugh.

Turning to me, she arched an eyebrow in confusion. I just waved a hand in front of my face.

"Yeah, he has," Callan said, and jerked his chin towards Levi.

The King of Metal was sitting in one of the plush red armchairs while Callan and Henry lounged on a couch each. Slouching back against the cushions, he raised his glass of whiskey in a kind of salute.

"You made all of these?" Paige asked. "In just the few short hours that we were gone?"

Levi shrugged and took a sip from his whiskey. "Yeah."

"Have a lot of practice creating handcuffs, do you?"

"As a matter of fact, yes, I have." A devilish smile played over his lips. "And lots of other types of restraints too."

I raised my eyebrows. Well, I supposed now I knew who had influenced Callan into developing certain sexual preferences.

As if he could hear my thoughts, Callan slid his gaze to me. The intensity of his stare made a pulse of desire shoot through me.

"How did your mission go?" Henry suddenly asked, trying to change the topic. "Did you find a place?"

Callan and I only kept our eyes on each other.

"Yeah," Paige replied while strolling towards the couch. After pushing her hair back behind her shoulders, she unceremoniously plopped down on the couch next to Henry. "We found the perfect building. It's near the academy too, so we can use that to add more weight to our threats. We've cleared it out, so it's all done and ready."

While keeping my eyes locked on Callan, I slowly bent down and picked up a pair of handcuffs from the floor. Fire surged to life in his eyes. I straightened and spun the handcuffs around my finger.

Levi's sharp gaze zeroed in on me. "And what exactly do you think you're doing?"

"I'm going to test them out." Throwing a smirk in Callan's direction, I turned around and sauntered into the corridor while speaking over my shoulder, "You know, to make sure that they won't break."

Wood groaned as Callan pushed himself up from the couch and cleared his throat. A thrill of anticipation made my spine tingle as he started after me. From her place on the sofa, Paige cackled and then whistled suggestively.

"Anyone who comes into our room in the next few hours will get a force wall in the face," Callan announced while metallic clanking drifted through the air, informing me that he had also picked up some handcuffs.

As I reached the stairs, I glanced over my shoulder to find Callan striding after me with dark eyes. A satisfied grin spread across my lips, and I hurried up the steps.

"Just keep the damn noise down," Levi called after us. "Or I swear to hell, I'll barge in there and fucking gag both of you myself."

Ignoring the annoying metal mage, I slipped into our bedroom and brushed my palms together while drawing myself up against the wall right inside the door. Callan's footsteps echoed against the floorboards outside. Wicked anticipation swirled through my chest as I readied my attack.

The moment Callan stepped across the threshold, I threw a small poison cloud at his face.

It slammed right into his force shield.

Amusement danced across his cheekbones as he turned to me with raised eyebrows while pushing the door shut behind him with his heel. "Did you really think that would work?"

I snorted. "Of course not. I was just testing out your reflexes."

"My reflexes, huh? And how—"

I lunged at him. Whipping up the manacles, I dove forward to snap them shut around his wrist. I almost made it. Almost.

Just before I could push them closed the final bit, his strong hand wrapped around my forearm, stopping my movements. The handcuffs slipped off his wrist and landed on the floor with a clank. I tried to yank my arm back, but before I could, the damn bastard snapped his own borrowed manacles shut around my left hand.

With a wicked grin on his face, he kept his iron grip on my arm while backing me towards the four-poster bed. "When will you learn that, physically, you will always be outmatched against me?"

"Physically, maybe. But in terms of magic..."

I whipped up my right hand, getting ready to slap it against my trapped left and summon more poison. Callan saw the move coming and yanked my arm upwards, high enough to force me up onto my toes. The back of my hand connected with the wooden bedpost a second before a soft click sounded. Then Callan stepped back.

Disbelief flitted through me. *Oh he did not...*

Reaching up with my right hand, I tried to get it high enough to touch my left one. It didn't work. Since I was standing on my toes, and my left hand was trapped so far above my head, I couldn't balance out my weight enough to reach it. All it did was make me spin slightly in place.

A smug laugh drifted through the air.

Narrowing my eyes, I dragged my gaze back to the smirking force mage. "Seriously?"

"Need I remind you that *you*, my troublesome little poisoner..." He took a step closer and trailed light fingers up my throat. "Attacked *me* first."

His touch made sparkles dance across my skin, and I suppressed the urge to moan.

Faint clinking of metal filled the room again. I snapped my gaze down as Callan removed his hand from my throat and instead pulled out another couple of handcuffs. My eyebrows rose as he moved back over to the ones I had already dropped and picked them up as well.

"What are you doing?" I asked as he began linking up the manacles with each other.

"I thought you wanted to test these out."

"I was actually planning to test them on *you*."

With that lethal smirk on his lips, he walked back over to me and brushed his lips along my jaw. "Sure you were."

Pleasure pulsed through my body as he stole a deep kiss from my lips. While I was still lost in it, he snapped a manacle shut around my right hand and then pulled back.

"That's so not fair," I muttered.

He trailed his fingers over my collarbones while a villainous expression settled on his face. "When have I ever played fair, sweetheart?"

Grabbing my right hand, he spun me around so that I was facing the bed and the marble wall behind it instead. While remaining behind my back, he lifted my arm towards the other bedpost. Suddenly, I realized why he had linked three handcuffs together. They would never have been able to reach the other side if he hadn't.

With another faint click, Callan locked my right hand to the top of the post, leaving me standing spreadeagled before the bed with him at my back. I pulled slightly against my restraints, but they didn't give. Behind me, I could feel Callan's hungry gaze searing into my body. It made my pussy throb with need.

"Well," I pressed out. "Are you just going to stand there?"

A dark chuckle sounded right behind me. Gripping my long unbound hair, he wrapped it around his hand and then pulled down, forcing my head back while his lips skimmed the side of my neck. "Always so impatient."

Lightning skittered across my skin as his fingers suddenly appeared between my shoulder blades. He draped my hair over my shoulder instead and then released it before both of his hands slid down to the laces at the back of my dress. I arched my back as he began unlacing it. My body jerked slightly as he pulled at the strings.

Just when I was about to tease him for being inefficient, the pressure around my ribcage disappeared and the dress fluttered down around my waist. I drew in a short breath as Callan slid his hands down my sides and then pushed the dress fully off my hips. It landed on the floor around me in a rippling pool of dark green fabric. This kind of dress didn't require me to wear a brassiere underneath, so I was left standing there in only a pair of panties. My skin prickled and my nipples hardened at the exposure.

Callan hooked his fingers over the edge of my panties and slowly slid them over my ass and then my thighs. A moan slipped past my lips, and I arched my back even more.

When the fabric finally dropped down to land on the floor, my whole body was pulsing with need. I drew in a deep breath, waiting for his hands to return to my skin.

They didn't.

Twisting my head, I tried to see over my shoulder to figure out what he was doing, but with the tight restraints keeping me firmly locked in place, I couldn't make anything out.

"Callan," I breathed when the waiting was starting to drive me insane.

Cold steel kissed my skin. I sucked in a gasp as the point of a blade scraped lightly against my back.

"What did I say about being impatient?" Callan murmured while tracing the knife down my spine.

A shudder of pleasure rolled through my body. I wiggled my ass slightly as the blade reached my lower back. Immediately, a strong hand appeared on my hip. Digging his fingers into my skin, he forced me to stop moving.

"Careful," he whispered.

My pussy throbbed and I desperately wanted to grind my clit against something, but I forced myself to remain perfectly still as Callan trailed the point of the blade around the curve of my ass. I drew in rapid breaths as the pressure inside me grew. Still standing on my toes, I tried to keep my legs from trembling as Callan drew the knife down my inner thigh and then up the other.

"Fuck, you really are beautiful."

His rough voice made my heart thump in my chest.

The knife disappeared from my skin. A few seconds later, his firm body pressed against me. It was only then I realized that he must have taken his clothes off earlier, because his naked skin was warm against mine and his hard cock pressed into my back.

My mind flickered with pent-up need as he slid one hand down my stomach. Stopping right before he reached my pussy, he traced his fingers around the spot where I really wanted them. They vibrated slightly with magic. Teasing me. Torturing me. I ground my ass against him.

"Beautiful," Callan repeated. His hot breath caressed the shell of my ear, sending another shiver down my spine. "Wicked. Lethal." In one smooth motion, he yanked up his other hand and positioned the knife across my throat. "And *mine*."

Another moan escaped my lips as I pushed my body harder against his.

He teased the inside of my thigh with his fingers, almost brushing against my pussy but not quite. Placing the flat of the blade underneath my chin, he pushed upwards and used it to tilt my head back.

"Say it." He spoke directly into my ear while his fingers continued torturing me.

"Yours," I gasped out.

"Good girl."

At last, he slid his fingers up to my aching pussy and swirled them around my clit.

I threw my head back against his shoulder and sucked in a desperate breath of relief as the vibrations pulsed into my sensitive skin. Callan shifted the knife with my move so that it was once more pressed firmly underneath my chin, keeping my head against his shoulder like that.

Tremors rippled through my body as he rolled my clit between his fingers while increasing the strength of his magic. I careened towards the edge. Sparkling tension built at my core, making my heart slam against my ribs.

Callan brushed his lips over my jaw, and it almost made my brain shut down right there.

A pitiful sound slipped past my lips as I rolled my hips, trying to grind my pussy harder against his fingers. He let out a dark chuckle but answered by increasing his vibrations once more.

Release crackled through my body.

I gasped as my inner walls trembled and pleasure rushed through my every limb. My legs shook, and if it hadn't been for the handcuffs locking me to the bedposts, I don't think I would have been able to remain on my feet.

Callan kept his magic pulsing against my clit, prolonging the orgasm until garbled mumbling fell from my lips.

Metal rattled as I yanked against the manacles.

My heart was beating so hard that I thought it would break through my ribcage. I sucked in deep breaths while the last waves of release rolled through me.

"Mine," Callan whispered into my ear.

Then he at last removed the knife from underneath my chin. Taking his fingers from my soaked pussy, he stepped back. The sudden absence of his warm body against mine was disorienting.

"Wait," I protested, my mind still scrambled from the intense orgasm. "Where are you going?"

His wicked laugh filled the room. "Oh, don't you worry. I'm not done with you yet."

Soft clicks sounded, and then the metal around my right

wrist disappeared. I wasn't at all prepared for it, so my legs buckled and I almost crashed to the floor. But before I could, Callan's muscular arm wrapped around my middle, stopping my fall. He transferred my weight to his other arm before reaching up to unlock the other manacle.

My arms just dropped down by my sides.

Callan remained standing behind me, one arm around my waist and the other hand pushing my hair out of my face and hooking it behind my ear. I swore I could feel his heartbeat thrumming against my back.

"You okay?" he asked.

I nodded. "Yes."

His grip on me loosened slightly, as if he was checking to make sure that I could stand on my own before he released me fully. When I remained firmly on my feet, he withdrew his arm.

Turning around, I raised my eyebrows expectantly and flashed him a wicked smirk. "I thought you said you weren't done with me yet."

Both amusement and lust swirled in his eyes as he shook his head at me. "I swear, that impatience of yours is gonna be the death of me."

I shot a pointed look at his cock. "If you can't keep up, you could just say so."

The fact that his cock was rock hard was kind of rendering my jab moot, but Callan took the bait anyway. Taking a step forward, he locked a hand around my jaw and claimed my mouth with a possessive kiss.

"Turn around," he ordered, speaking directly against my lips.

After stealing one more kiss, he released his grip on me. I looked up at him and bit my lip. His eyes darkened like thunderstorms.

Grabbing my hips, he spun me around before planting a

hand between my shoulder blades. With a firm push, he bent me over the foot of the bed.

"Hold on to the frame," he commanded.

A thrill raced down my spine.

With my body bent forward like that, I wrapped my fingers around the wooden bedframe.

Callan drew his hands down the side of my ribs, making lightning dance over my skin, before he repositioned my hips. I arched my back and lifted my ass slightly.

"You know, you never did manage to break that table in Malgrave," I said, letting him hear the teasing smirk in my voice. "Maybe we could give it another shot with this bed? Unless you think you're too weak to—"

He rammed his cock deep into my soaked pussy.

"Hell fucking damn it, Audrey Sable," he began while pulling out and then shoving back in again. It tore a moan from my chest, and I tightened my grip on the wooden frame. "Even after all this time, I still can't decide whether I want to fuck you or kill you every time you open that pretty mouth of yours."

I let out a dark laugh.

He pounded into me again. "Maybe I really will gag you this time."

"Come try it, pretty boy."

"Or I might just find some other use for your wicked mouth."

Before I could retort, he increased the speed of his thrusts. My body jerked forward as he slammed into me, setting a rough pace that had pleasure rising inside my body once more. I held on to the wooden frame hard as he railed me with furious passion and utter command.

His grip on my hips tightened, helping to keep me steady against his forceful thrusts.

Shifting my weight slightly, I angled my ass a bit to give him better access.

The change in position made his cock slide even deeper with his next thrust, and a moan ripped from my lungs as waves of pleasure pulsed through me. Squeezing my eyes shut, I tried to hold off the orgasm a little longer while I slipped rapidly towards the edge.

But with every thrust of his thick cock, the friction sent me sliding closer to it.

He slammed into me again.

Pleasure ricocheted through my body as I came hard. More moans dripped from my lips as my clit throbbed while my pussy clenched around his cock. Callan kept up his brutal pace, riding the orgasm with me until a satisfied groan tore from his throat as well.

With my fingers still gripping the bed, I sucked in deep breaths that didn't seem to contain enough oxygen while my whole body thrummed with the crashing release still washing through me.

Lifting my head slightly, I glanced up at the poor bed that we had probably traumatized by now.

A small smile drifted over my lips.

Well, to be fair, given the future that Callan and I had planned together, the bed was about to see a whole lot worse.

Chapter 23

Callan

Footsteps sounded on the stairs. Henry and I stopped talking and instead turned towards them while Levi just remained leaning against the front door with his arms crossed over his chest. My eyebrows rose in surprise. Next to me, Henry openly gaped.

Paige was walking down the steps with Audrey behind her. Her wavy blond hair had been swept up before it curled down her back, and she was wearing an incredibly well-tailored red dress that matched her red-painted lips. Since the day I met her, I had practically only seen her in those brown pants and the loose white shirt she had been wearing when she fled from Quill's constables on horseback. She was objectively good-looking, but when she dressed up like this, it was taken to a whole other level.

"Well, what do you think?" Paige asked once she reached the hallway floor. Paper rustled as she unfolded a wanted poster and held it up next to her face. "Not much of a resemblance, right?"

"You're gorgeous," Henry blurted out.

Surprise flitted across her face, and a blush crept into her cheeks as she blinked at him.

He cleared his throat. "I mean, uhm... You look nothing like your wanted poster, which looks terrible, so you look... uhm. Well, I mean..."

It took all of my self-control not to laugh. Henry looked like he wanted to punch his way out through the wall as he awkwardly trailed off.

A brilliant smile spread across Paige's lips. "Thank you."

"You've got some new clothes too," I said, and jerked my chin at Audrey in a, in my opinion, very generous act of mercy to save Henry from trying to figure out what to say next.

Audrey ran her hands down the metal corset before smoothing down the flowing black skirt. It was one of those half armor dresses complete with metal bracers that she always used to wear before we went on several consecutive secret missions that required less conspicuous clothes.

"Yes," she replied. A hint of fury sparked in her eyes. "Since Quill made the incredibly ill-advised decision to burn my mansion to the ground, I need to start restocking my closet."

"Where did you even get it?"

"From the same shop that I custom-ordered all my other ones."

"If you're quite finished gawking at each other," Levi interrupted from where he was still draped against the door. "Let's get this done already."

Audrey rolled her eyes, but both of them started for the door. I turned around as well. Another wave of amusement rolled over me. Both Henry and Levi were wearing stylish black suits with a dress shirt underneath. It was such an odd sight on the King of Metal, who always favored tight black shirts and metal shoulder plates and bracers, that I had to fight hard to keep from grinning.

Pushing off from the door, Levi straightened and shot me a sharp look that I knew meant that he would break every bone in my body if I made a single comment about it. Mission and deal be damned. So I swallowed my mocking words and instead cleared my throat.

Apparently satisfied, Levi turned and opened the door.

Warm evening air smelling of roses and jasmine drifted into the hallway. I let Levi, Henry, and Paige exit before I followed Audrey out the door. We were going to take different routes to our target, so we needed to split into two groups.

"Alright," I began while locking the front door behind us. "Once Elise Dawson confirms that everyone has arrived, give us the signal. Then all hell breaks loose."

Henry and Paige nodded agreement. Levi only turned on his heel and stalked down the street. Shaking my head at his retreating back, I gave the others one final nod before Audrey and I slipped away in the other direction.

Thick clouds blanketed the already darkened heavens and blotted out the moonlight. Thankfully, the areas we passed through were all wealthy ones, which meant that the streetlamps had already been lit. Flickering pools of warm yellow light broke up the darkness as Audrey and I made our way towards the Dawsons' house.

Music and laughter spilled out of the bright windows when we at last crept up to the gardens. Even with only two days of preparation, it looked like Elise could put together one hell of a party.

Audrey and I snuck over to one of the thick bushes in the small garden that we had marked earlier. It was dense enough to hide us from view, but still close enough to the living room windows that we would be able to see when Levi gave the signal.

My leather armor groaned softly as I lowered myself to the ground. Audrey scowled at the grass as if she would rather not ruin her new dress, but she sat down next to me in the end anyway.

For a while, we just sat there next to one another, watching the party from the outside.

Since we took the long way around, Henry, Paige, and Levi had already arrived by the time we got to the garden. Through the window, I could see Paige and Henry dancing. There was a wide smile on Paige's lips, and Henry looked absolutely mesmerized by it. I couldn't see Levi from this angle, so I just had to hope that he wasn't blowing their cover by glaring people to death.

Footsteps sounded on the street.

Audrey and I remained completely still as a man and a woman strolled up to the front door and rapped the metal knocker against it. A few moments later, Elise became visible in the doorway. Against the darkness outside, the brilliant light from the candles in the room beyond created a glowing halo around her body. She kept a smile on her face as she waved them inside.

If she was nervous about tonight, she didn't show it. Though I supposed that people who were high up on the social ladder had to be incredibly accomplished liars to even get that far.

Leaves rustled around us as a warm evening breeze swept through the garden. It brought with it the scent of blooming night flowers and rain. I glanced up at the dark clouds. Hopefully, we could get this done before the skies opened.

Tipping my head back down, I returned my gaze to the windows. In the glowing candlelight, Carl Dawson was laughing while putting a casual hand on a dark-haired woman's shoulder. Memories flickered to life inside me.

"Did you know," I began, keeping my eyes on the scene inside the living room. "That when Carl was showing you around that time we went to their soirée, the only thing I could think about was that he needed to get his hands off my wife."

I could feel Audrey turning to look at me. "Really?"

"Yeah. Why do you think I ditched Elise and stalked up the stairs to find you?"

"Well, at the time, you said that it was because you were worried that I was going to blow our cover and poison the whole house."

A chuckle drifted from my throat. "I lied."

"Shocker."

Huffing out another laugh, I continued watching the windows. No signal yet. But it should come any second now.

"Maybe we should make that official sometime."

While still scanning the building, I replied, "Make what official?"

She said nothing.

For a few seconds, everything was silent and still while my mind finished processing her words. *My wife.*

I whipped around and met her gaze head on. There was an open and almost a bit vulnerable expression on her face.

My stomach lurched and my heart seemed to skip several beats and then thump twice as hard to make up for it.

She was dead serious about this.

An absolutely ridiculous sense of giddiness swept through my whole body, and my face split into an idiotic grin.

"Yes," I said, holding her gaze. "I think so too."

A smile spread across her lips, and her eyes sparkled even in the dark.

Something moved in the corner of my eye.

Both of us snapped our gazes back to the windows. Levi was standing right in front of the one in the middle, and he lifted his glass of wine in a small salute.

"Showtime," Audrey said. "I'll take the back."

I gave her a nod and squeezed her arm before I darted towards the front door. My mind was still reeling from our conversation, and it took every ounce of strength I possessed to push that aside for now and focus on the mission.

Stopping briefly in front of the door, I drew in a deep breath to gather my wits. Once I felt calm and in control again, I opened the door and snuck inside without knocking.

The sounds of music and happy chatter washed over me as I stepped into the elegant hallway. Since Levi had given the go-ahead, it not only meant that everyone was present, but also that Elise and Carl had gathered everyone in the living room for their fake welcome speech. Remaining where I was, I waited for Audrey to appear on the other side of the corridor.

At last, I caught a hint of candlelight glinting against her metal corset. I waited until I could see the soft green glow of her poison before I started forward. Brushing my palms together, I called up my magic as well while rounding the corner into the living room.

And then I hurled a wide force blast straight into the ceiling.

Chapter 24

Screams erupted throughout the elegant living room. While everyone whirled towards the main doorway and summoned magic to defend themselves, I slipped in through the side door that Elise had so helpfully told us about.

Callan was standing in the doorway, providing them with a clear target. Water and wind and lightning magic twisted around several people's hands, but he easily parried their attacks. Another large portion of the crowd tried to bolt. I swept my gaze over them.

Paige, Henry, and Levi had spread out around the room so that the five of us circled the whole crowd. We exchanged a glance.

As one, the four of them shot their magic towards their side of the group. Force magic, a large sheet of metal, and wind blasts from Paige and Henry slammed into the panicked guests and shoved them all back towards the center of the room.

While they were too shocked, and too focused on the others, to see it coming, I hurled a massive poison cloud into the room.

Within seconds, glittering green mist enveloped the entire

cluster of people. I increased the poison levels enough to make sure that even the strongest members lost their grip on their magic. It made the weaker half crash to their knees. To my surprise, Elise Dawson was one of the people who managed to remain standing.

"Sorry to crash your party," Callan said over the sound of choking people. "But we're gonna need you to come with us."

Fear washed over their faces as they looked between the five of us. Carl was on his knees, dry heaving on the rich blue carpet, while Elise squeezed his shoulder where she stood next to him.

"Here's what's going to happen," I said. "I'm going to remove this poison cloud and then we're going to give you a series of instructions. Obey them without question, and you'll live to see another sunrise."

It was difficult to tell since most of them were coughing their lungs up, but I was pretty sure that they nodded.

I let my mist dissipate.

Lightning zapped through the air. I only had time to blink in surprise as the white bolt shot straight towards my chest.

Right before it could hit, it crashed into a thick sheet of metal.

The resounding boom it created echoed throughout the white marble room.

I dragged my gaze to Levi as the metal shield disappeared. My pulse thrummed in my ears. If Levi hadn't blocked it for me, that lightning strike, aimed straight at my heart from close up, might actually have killed me. I gave the King of Metal a slow nod.

Out on the floor, people had drawn back from a short man with a thick mustache, as if they were afraid that just standing near him would make them guilty too. The man in question shot a panicked look between me and Levi while raising his hands.

"I'm... I'm sorry," he stammered.

"Elise," I said, keeping my eyes locked on the man. "Who is he? Is he on the list or is he a plus one?"

"He's a plus one," she replied.

"Good."

A thin tendril of poison shot through the room and forced its way down the man's throat within seconds. He collapsed to the ground immediately. Shock still twisted his features while his lifeless eyes stared up at the pale ceiling.

Two steps away, a woman let out a raw scream. Presumably the person who had brought him as her plus one.

I spread my arms wide. "Anyone else want to try their luck?"

They shook their heads desperately and edged a few steps back. That only put them closer to Levi, which they realized when they glanced over their shoulders, so they tried to shift again only to run into the same problem on Callan's side. It created a weird shuffling motion that only stopped when Henry pulled out a large bag that we had stashed inside the house before the guests arrived. Metallic clanking filled the air as he tossed it onto the floor a short distance from the group.

"Elise," I said, meeting the blond woman's eyes from across the room. "Separate them into list people and plus ones. Put the plus ones on their knees by that wall." I pointed towards the one that Levi was standing in front of.

"No, please," another woman blurted out. "Please, we don't want to die."

"Have you already forgotten what I said earlier?" I shook my head at her in exasperation. "Do as you're told, and you'll live."

She didn't look convinced, but I didn't particularly care so I just slid my gaze to Elise and spun my hand in the air. Elise held my gaze for a few seconds before she turned around and began steering people away from the group and towards the wall.

Most of them outright trembled as they staggered over to their place and then dropped to their knees. We made them face the wall and leave their unprotected backs to us in order to discourage any other futile attempts to be heroes.

When Elise at last nodded in confirmation, thirty-five people were left standing huddled together in the middle of the room.

Callan, who was still blocking the doorway, slid his gaze to Henry before returning it to the group and announcing, "Now, you're gonna put on some handcuffs. Walk up to him," he nodded towards Henry and then to Paige, "when she calls your name. Don't try anything stupid because it won't work. All it will do is get you hurt. Understood?"

No one dared answer.

The faint rustling of paper sounded almost deafening in the dead silent room as Paige pulled out the list and began reading names off it. A few steps away, Henry bent down and pulled out manacles from the bag before snapping them shut around the approaching people's wrists. Callan, Levi, and I watched them all with sharp eyes. Thankfully, no one was dumb enough to try another attack.

Once they were all restrained, we separated them into groups of five.

Elise and Carl remained standing on the floor next to one of their expensive blue couches. Dread and regret swirled in their eyes, but all they could do was watch as we rounded everyone up.

"You five," Callan snapped, and jerked his chin at the closest group. "Let's go."

They cast worried looks back at the others, but followed Callan into the corridor. Levi and Henry joined them too.

Hope sparkled in several people's eyes when the three of

them had disappeared out the front door with their captives. I blew out a sigh and brushed my palms together.

Glittering green magic immediately shot through the air above their heads.

"Don't even think about it," I warned. "You can either be conscious or unconscious while you wait. It's all the same to me, so it's your choice."

No one moved. They all just stared up at the poison mist with wide eyes. All except the people still kneeling by the wall, since they couldn't see what was happening behind their backs. But a lot of them hunched forward as if trying to make themselves smaller.

"Excellent," I said when the silence had stretched for a while.

While letting my magic fade out again, I walked around the dark blue and golden couch and sat down in the middle of it. By the other wall, Paige pulled out a chair and sat down as well. This was going to take a while, after all.

Since we couldn't very well transport thirty-five handcuffed prisoners through the streets of Eldar without drawing attention, we had to walk them over to our secure location in smaller groups. Callan and Henry would remain at the target building to watch the groups as they arrived while Paige and I kept an eye on the people still here. Levi, whose face was not plastered on wanted posters and who was lethal enough on his own, would walk the groups between this house and the other one.

It was going to take longer than I would have liked, but it was still the most efficient method to get everyone where we wanted them without risking our mission.

I slid my gaze to our two hosts. Elise and Carl were standing side by side in the exact same spot as before. Carl had wrapped his arm around Elise's back and was holding her close to him, while she only stared unseeing at the gilded painting on the opposite wall.

"You can sit down," I said.

They snapped their gazes to me. I nodded towards the couch positioned perpendicular to mine.

For a few seconds, they didn't move. Then they exchanged a glance and carefully moved over to the indicated sofa. Sitting down, they positioned themselves as far away from me as they could get.

"Are you going to kill them?" Elise asked.

Light from the oil lamps danced across her beautiful features and glittered in the expensive-looking gold jewelry around her neck and wrists. She kept her back straight and her chin slightly raised as she looked back at me.

"As long as we get what we want, all of them will be released unharmed," I answered.

Out on the floor, about a dozen people let out shaky breaths of relief.

"And if you don't?" she pushed.

Saying nothing, I simply looked back at her.

She swallowed. Her hands were trembling a little, so she shook them out and then clasped them in her lap.

Silence descended on the room again. It was only broken by the occasional whimper or sniffle from the people kneeling by the wall. I studied Elise and Carl while they tried their best to pretend that they didn't notice.

Amusement bubbled up inside me. Damn, they must be bitterly regretting the day that they invited us into their home and offered us tickets to the ball. I wondered how much trouble they had gotten into for that. After all, they were the reason that Callan and I had even been able to get into the ball and kidnap Lance in the first place.

"Why are you doing this?" Elise asked suddenly, pulling me from my musings.

I cocked my head and watched her in silence for another few seconds before replying. "Because people like you refuse to even consider that the way you live your lives is not the only way to live."

"And that justifies kidnapping? Blackmail?" She stabbed a hand towards the body of the man I had killed earlier. "Murder?"

"It does to me."

"There is something seriously wrong with you."

"If you truly can't understand why we dark mages are fighting back when you people declare war on us, then I would say the same to you."

Pressing her lips together, she tore her gaze from me and went back to staring at the painting across the room. I rolled my eyes. Why did almost every single person in this entire city only see the world in terms of black and white?

After a while, the front door was opened. It was forceful enough that it could only be Levi, so I remained where I was.

Just as I thought, a moment later, the metal mage stalked into the living room. Dragging his hand through his black hair, he met my gaze. I nodded to confirm that everything was under control. He barely dipped his chin in response before snapping his gaze to the next group and twitching his fingers.

"Let's go," he commanded in a voice that left no room for argument.

Clothes rustled and shoes thudded against the polished floor as they shuffled after him.

I settled back against the cushions again. Across the room, Paige stretched her arms above her head and then leaned back in her chair as well.

The rest of the time passed in silence as both Elise and the other people with us kept their mouths shut while Levi appeared and disappeared several times.

When there was only one group of five people remaining on the floor, Levi paused before ordering them forward. His gray eyes slid to me but he jerked his chin towards Elise and Carl.

"And the hosts?" he said.

The Dawsons tensed. Carl's worried gaze flicked between me and Levi, and after a few seconds Elise dragged hers to me as well. I let the silence stretch because I was a vicious bastard and I enjoyed making them nervous.

"They kept their end of the bargain." I lifted my shoulders in a nonchalant shrug. "So I say we let them live."

Levi shrugged too. "Fine by me."

On the couch, Carl let out a shuddering breath while Elise sucked one in.

I pushed up from the cushions and strode towards the other wall. Wood groaned faintly as Paige rose to her feet as well. The people on their knees next to her whimpered and crouched down even more as I approached them from behind.

"After we leave, you are going to stay here in this room for one hour," I began. "Once an hour has passed, you're going to take the fastest horses you can find and ride straight to Chancellor Quill's army and tell them exactly what we did tonight."

Several heads snapped up. A few of them even turned to stare at me over their shoulders. Disbelief shone on their faces.

"No, this is not some kind of trick," I said. "One hour. Then you ride for Quill's camp."

Some of them nodded while others just continued staring into the wall.

Since their response was rather underwhelming, I added, "If you don't, we'll track you down and kill you. Got it?"

"Got it," half of them mumbled while the rest nodded.

"Great." I turned back to the Dawsons. "Elise. Carl. Thanks for hosting. I knew we could count on you."

Both of them stiffened and cast panicked looks towards the remaining guests, who now shot a few accusatory glances at them. I let out a dark chuckle under my breath. This was going to damage their social standing quite a bit.

Was it a dick move? Yes.

Was I a petty bitch who just wanted to watch their world burn? Also yes.

After giving them a mocking wave, I sauntered towards the doorway. Paige fell in beside me while Levi took the lead, the five hostages stumbling after him.

This had gone surprisingly well. We had our leverage.

Now, all we needed to do was to wait for our blackmail victims to show up.

Chapter 25

Callan

After five days of captivity, I had expected our hostages to look haunted and exhausted. To stare unseeing into a wall while defeat hung in the air like acid. But instead, the opposite had happened.

The first two days, they had been terrified to even breathe too loudly. But after that, when they realized that we weren't going to hurt them just for the hell of it, they started to relax ever so slightly. We gave them enough food and water since we couldn't have them dying on us before Quill and his parliament got here, and the building we kept them in was an old athletics hall that had been abandoned when the academy built a new one inside their walls. There were no beds for them to sleep in, but because of the building layout, they had plenty of space to move around and also access to bathrooms whenever they needed them.

As far as kidnappings went, it could have been a lot worse. And I was pretty sure that they realized that too, which was why our thirty-five captives were in relatively good spirits, all things considered.

"You're certain that your sources saw the Chancellor and his people arrived last night?" Levi asked, arching an eyebrow at Paige.

"Yes," she replied.

"And they can be trusted?"

"Yes."

Levi shot a pointed look towards the morning sunlight falling in through the windows. "And yet, we've been sitting here all night, and they still haven't shown up."

"They'll be here," I cut in.

The rickety chair creaked as I turned slightly and swept my gaze over the room. Our hostages were all sitting on the wooden floor, their backs resting against the wall behind and their shackled hands either on their knees or in their laps. Since we had told them to be ready, they knew that their saviors were close now, and hope shone on many faces as they stared towards the door on the other side.

We had taken turns watching them, but when Paige's contacts had sent word yesterday evening that Quill and his people had arrived in Eldar, we'd had a messenger inform the Chancellor and his parliament where to meet us, and to come alone. And then we had all gathered in here to wait for them. Despite what I had just told Levi, I found it odd that they hadn't come here straight away.

"I'm just saying," Levi continued. "If someone was holding my wife hostage, I wouldn't be dragging my feet."

"He's probably plotting something," Audrey replied. Looking between the four of us, she shrugged. "Trying to figure out a way to get them back without having to deal with us. So be ready."

As if on cue, a rapid series of knocks in a strange pattern echoed from the front door. We all whipped our heads towards it.

When it stopped, we turned to Paige, who was the only one

who could decode the messages from her underworld contacts. There was a determined set to her jaw when she looked back at us and nodded.

"It's time," she said. Placing her palms on the table, she pushed to her feet. "Quill and his parliament, plus Lance and his friends, are coming. Five minutes out."

Gasps and sighs of relief came from our hostages.

"And they're alone?" I asked while standing up as well.

Paige nodded again. "No other constables."

"Alright." I gave her a nod back before turning towards our captives. "On your feet and form a line."

Clothes rustled and shoes scraped against the floor as they all maneuvered themselves into a standing position and then rearranged themselves so that they formed one long line that faced the door. Glittering hope shone in their eyes now.

"You've survived this long, so don't throw it all away now at the finish line by doing something stupid." I swept a hard stare over them. "Once we get what we want, you'll be able to go home to your families. So keep your mouths shut and do as you're told. Clear?"

They nodded.

"Good. Let's go."

A warm morning breeze whirled through the street as we exited the abandoned athletics hall and took up position outside. We made our captives kneel in a long row a few steps away from the building while we stood behind them, keeping them between us and the rest of the street while the wall behind protected our backs.

The street we were on was made of smooth cobblestones, and a few small trees had been planted farther to our right. Their delicate branches trembled slightly as another breeze swept along the road, bringing with it the scent of wet stones and damp soil from the rain that fell yesterday. A few streets to our left, the massive walls that protected the academy rose over the rooftops.

I glanced from side to side. Audrey was standing on my left, with Paige on her other side, while Levi and Henry were positioned on my right. All of them had calm and confident expressions on their faces. I did too, but in my chest, my heart was thumping.

If we played this right, we might be able to win at least half of the war today. And once that half was taken care of, the other part would be much easier. The only problem was of course that Godric Quill, for all his talk of heroism, was a damn shrewd bastard. He no doubt had something planned for our meeting. We just needed to figure out what.

Footsteps echoed into the air. They were coming towards us along the street to our right, and it wasn't just one pair. It sounded like a large group.

"They're coming," Henry said in a low voice.

"Yeah. Stay alert." I flicked a glance to my left. "Audrey?"

"I know," she replied.

Touching her palms together, she called up a wide poison cloud. Our hostages sucked in sharp breaths between their teeth and cast panicked glances upwards while some ducked slightly.

"Calm down," I snapped.

Audrey moved her green mist so that it hovered right above their heads, ready to drop down and choke them at a moment's notice if Quill and his people did anything even remotely threatening.

When our captives realized that the poison would stay above their heads for now, they blew out small sighs of relief and returned their gazes to the street.

A few moments later, a large group became visible.

Chancellor Godric Quill, wearing an impeccable charcoal suit, marched at the front. Sunlight fell across his features, making his hair appear the color of steel. His sharp blue eyes snapped straight to me and Audrey as he drew closer.

On either side of him, flanking him like bodyguards, were Lance, Darren, Jessica, and Leoni. Jessica cast worried glances at our hostages while both Lance and Darren kept their features blank. Leoni, on the other hand, was glaring at us with unbridled rage.

The other thirty-five members of Quill's parliament trailed behind them.

Crackling tension hung over the whole street as they came to a halt and positioned themselves right opposite us while still keeping almost the entirety of the wide street as a buffer between our two groups. The parliament members shot worried glances between their captured loved ones and the poison cloud that swirled above their heads. Since the hostages were on their knees, the glittering mist was only chest level with us, allowing us to meet their eyes properly.

As if on some unspoken signal, Audrey, Levi and I gave our enemies a slow and vicious smile. It was the cold and psychotic smile of a killer, and it made several members of parliament flinch. I had to suppress the urge to laugh at the fact that the three of us had had the exact same thought. Were we dark mages really all the same after all?

"You have gone too far this time," Chancellor Quill announced in a voice filled with barely restrained anger. "Kidnapping civilians. This is unforgivable."

"Aww." Audrey pressed a hand to her chest in a mock show of regret. "And here I was, desperate for your forgiveness."

Next to me, Levi chuckled under his breath.

Rage flashed in Quill's eyes as he locked them on Audrey. "Do you know why I despise *you* most of all?"

"Because of my charming personality?"

"Because you had it all."

From the corner of my eye, I could see Audrey furrow her brows slightly in confusion.

"I was born without magic in one of the poorest parts of this city," Quill continued. "I had to work my fingers to the bone to rise all the way to the top. But you... You were born into a wealthy family in a nice neighborhood. You had magic and, from what I've heard from your former teachers, you were also naturally gifted, allowing you to breeze through school without effort."

The poison cloud before us whipped faster as Audrey squeezed her hand into a fist.

Quill jerked his chin towards me. "In some ways, I understand people like him. Born into a poor family with seven other siblings. I can understand resentment in people like that, in people who are forced to make do with less. But you... You had *everything*. You've never had to work for anything in your entire life. And still you weren't satisfied. You became a dark mage because you wanted *more*. More. When you already had everything!"

"You know nothing about me," Audrey said, her voice flat.

Ice skittered down my spine at the sound of it. If Quill didn't stop talking soon, she was going to start poisoning everything and everyone in sight.

He raised his eyebrows. "Don't I?"

Right then, footsteps sounded from the street to our left. Magic flashed to life in our hands as we whipped towards it, expecting to see constables rushing towards us. But it wasn't constables. I squinted. It was four civilians. Two older women, and one younger, and one older man.

Surprise slammed into me as their faces came into view.

Next to me, shock and dread washed across Audrey's face for a second, and she actually stumbled a half step back.

Audrey's parents, along with her sister Jenny, came to a halt next to Leoni, who was guarding Quill's right flank. But my eyes were not on the black-haired trio who stared at Audrey from across the street. No, my gaze was on the fourth person. The other older woman. My mother.

Her hair had been a dark brown color when I left. It was gray now. Faint wrinkles were etched into the skin around her eyes and mouth, but her brown eyes had lost none of their sharpness. She squinted towards me.

"Is that Callan?" she asked, pointing at me while looking towards the Chancellor.

I wished I was surprised, but I wasn't. She had never paid me much attention, even when I was living in her house, so it didn't surprise me that she didn't recognize me.

"Yes," Quill replied.

"Are you sure? I don't recognize him at all." Her eyes returned to me. "Young man, regardless of who you are, anyone who does something like this..." She pointed towards our hostages. "Is no son of mine."

Her words didn't even sting. I hadn't cared about her opinion of me for almost fifteen years. I didn't know what Quill was thinking, bringing her here. It didn't affect me at all, so why...

Dread surged up inside me as a sudden realization struck. I flicked a quick glance down at Audrey.

Oh, shit. This was Quill's plan. To rattle us by bringing our families here. To rattle *her*.

And based on the pain that flickered across Audrey's stunned face as she stared at her family, it was working.

Chapter 26

"I am so ashamed of you."

It took every ounce of my self-control not to flinch at my father's words. At the look on his face. On my mother's face. On Jenny's face. They were all staring at me with such utter disappointment that I felt like I was fourteen years old again, being scolded for performing a too vulgar dance at the midyear exams. It made cold acid spread through my whole chest, and I didn't know whether I wanted to scream or bawl my eyes out.

"I don't understand where we went wrong." He shook his head at me. "How could you turn out like this? You're a... a villain. A murderer. How could our sweet and well-mannered little girl turn into... into *this*?"

It felt as though everything was suspended in time. I could hear Callan's voice gently say my name on my right, and a hand brush over my arm in a comforting gesture on my left, but I couldn't focus on any of it. All I could do was stare at my family while the next second seemed to drag by in slow motion.

I hadn't spoken to my family since before I ran away six years ago. Not one word in six years. And this was the first thing they said to me? No statements about how worried they had been about me or relief to see me alive and well after so long? No, the first thing out of their mouths was, *I am so ashamed of you.*

That broken little girl inside me that was desperate to please people in order to prove that she deserved love rose up to the surface inside me, and her first instinct was to apologize. The words were right there on my tongue. Like a reflex. A behavior so ingrained in me that I barely needed to think about it.

Disappointment was etched into every line of my father's strong jaw and brimming in my mother's green eyes. And Jenny, she looked at me with... pity.

I couldn't breathe.

Barely a second had passed since my father stopped speaking, but I didn't know how to make time start moving again. I couldn't concentrate, and my poison cloud wavered before me.

Why were they here? Now? They shouldn't have been here. I wasn't prepared for this. I—

A lightning storm shot towards me.

Jerking back, I tried to snap myself out of the cold black ocean I was currently drowning in. But I wasn't fast enough. The white bolts of lightning barreled towards me straight from Quill, Leoni, and at least five more members of parliament.

Deafening booms ripped through the morning air, loud enough to shatter the stunned haze covering my brain like spiderwebs. I snapped back into the present right as the storm of lightning crashed into Callan and Levi's layered wall of force and metal.

Shouts echoed between the buildings, and more attacks zapped through the air. Next to me, Paige threw up a water shield to turn a yellow fireball into hissing mist while Henry shoved aside a water blast with a gust of wind. Darren and

Jessica and Leoni were pelting Callan and Levi's shields with their dark mage level powers.

On the ground before us, the hostages were screaming.

The hostages.

My mind finally caught up, and I yanked the poison cloud down.

Fury, the likes of which could have set the whole world aflame, seared through my body and burned out the last of those broken feelings until all that remained was rage and hatred. The strength of my poison increased in a heartbeat, and every single person on the ground doubled over. Panicked noises came from their throats as they choked and gagged and clawed at their necks.

"Quill," I bellowed across the booms of colliding magic. "Stand the fuck down. Right now. Or they die."

From across the street, Quill's hard blue eyes locked on me. I stared back at him, letting him see every wicked, every depraved, every blackened piece of my soul and the gigantic hole where my missing morals should have been. If he didn't stand down, I was going to kill every single one of these thirty-five completely innocent people. And even if he did stand down, I was going to kill him. Because he brought my family into this. And that had just bought him a guaranteed death sentence.

"Stand down!" Quill called.

All the members of parliament, as well as Lance's three friends, ceased attacking and spread their hands. Lance, who was the one person present who didn't have long-distance magic, just looked at me with pleading eyes. It did nothing to affect my stone-cold heart.

I kept the poison around our hostages, making them writhe on the ground in fear and pain and panic.

"Enough," Quill snapped. "We've already ceased fire."

For another few seconds, I just stared at him with hard eyes.

Then I at last raised the poison cloud so that it hovered above their heads again. They all sucked in desperate breaths and coughed against the pale cobblestones.

"What do you want?" the Chancellor ground out.

Callan discreetly brushed the back of his hand against mine, as if to make sure that I was okay, before replying, "We want the Blade of Equilibrium."

"Never."

"Hand over the blade, and abolish the laws that forces mages to complete the graduation ceremony," Callan continued. "And we'll stop this whole war right now."

Confused murmuring spread through the group of parliament members. On Quill's right, Lance blinked at us in genuine surprise.

"What do you mean *stop the whole war*?" Lance blurted out.

"I meant exactly what I said. We won't attack you. None of the dark mages will. We will just keep going about our lives the way we did before you decided to declare war on us."

His pale brows creased slightly. "You would actually do that? Just back off?"

"Yes. Despite what you've been told, we don't actually want to kill people just for sport. We just want you all to stop trying to steal our magic."

A sneer twisted Quill's features as he interrupted, "Those hostages would disagree."

I gave him a smile dripping with poison. "You attacked first."

"Give us the Blade of Equilibrium," Callan cut in before he could retort. "And abolish those laws, and you can have your people back. No more war. No more destruction. No more death."

Well, apart from Quill, who we were definitely going to slaughter anyway. But he didn't need to know that.

Another wave of murmuring washed over the parliament members while Lance looked questioningly over at his Chancellor. I had no idea how my family was reacting, because I refused to look at them.

Quill held up a hand, silencing his people. Steel crept into his eyes as he looked between me and Callan. "No."

I raised my eyebrows. "No?"

"No." He jutted out his chin. "We do not negotiate with dark mages."

"And that, right there, is the root of all your problems."

His furious gaze snapped to me while he stabbed a hand towards the still gasping people kneeling before me. "You have committed a war crime."

"I'm sorry, a what?"

"A war crime."

I snorted and flicked my hair behind my shoulder. "Darling, there are no crimes in war. Only winners... and losers."

"Look, Quill," Callan began before the Chancellor could pop a blood vessel. "I know you're a smart man, so let me spell it out for you. Either you do what we want, or we will execute all of these people, and then we'll just attack the academy and take the Blade of Equilibrium anyway."

For a few seconds, no one said anything. Leoni looked like she was ready to fry us with lightning any second. But both Jessica and Lance glanced between us and Quill as if they desperately wanted him to take the deal.

Some kind of owl hooted from a street on our left.

A smirk curled Quill's lips. "Funny you should say that."

He jerked his hand forward in a cutting motion.

Battle cries split the air.

I whipped my head towards the left to find a horde of... teenagers barreling towards us. Shock and confusion rippled through me.

Black shadows and orange fire and massive lightning bolts shot towards us. Callan and the others threw their own magic towards them, blocking the attacks, but the teenagers just kept coming. Conviction shone in their eyes and they were screaming at the top of their lungs as they sprinted towards us while slapping their hands together and calling up more magic.

They were students. Students from the academy who had snuck up to ambush us. It took me another second to realize that they weren't there randomly. Based on the satisfaction flashing across Quill's face, *he* had set this up earlier and brought them here to attack us.

I snapped my gaze between my friends while a sudden pulse of dread shot through me.

Since they were from the academy, they all had the power levels of dark mages, which would be difficult for us to deal with when there were so damn many of them. But that wasn't why alarm crackled through me.

Some of the students looked to be close to graduating, but at least half of them were under fifteen.

There weren't a lot of lines that I was unwilling to cross at this point, but killing thirteen-year-olds was one of them. No matter how delusional and misguided they were, I wasn't so far gone that I could justify the slaughter of children.

"I'm not killing kids," Paige said, echoing my thoughts, while she used her magic to parry attacks from the parliament members.

"Agreed," Callan said as he shoved a force wall to block the twisting mass of shadows and fire coming from the students. "We make a run for the building behind us. Henry, blow the windows. We need to split up."

Henry grunted in acknowledgement.

"Levi," Callan continued. "Can you find your way back through the city?"

The King of Metal slammed up a wall that blocked Leoni and Darren's combined strike of lightning and wind. "I'll manage."

"Audrey," he said without turning to look at me. "Get your magic ready."

The hostages had thrown themselves flat on the ground, trying to duck the hail of attacks shooting through the air above them. I could use my poison magic to follow through on my threat and kill them all right now, but it wouldn't accomplish anything other than to make sure that every member of parliament dedicated their entire life to hunting us down. And that would make it harder for us to get what we wanted. So instead, I shifted the poison cloud towards the left.

"Now!" Callan called.

While he used his force magic to clear a path for me, I hurled the glittering mist towards the first ranks of students. They collapsed immediately.

"NO!" Lance screamed.

"They're not dead," I yelled across the chaos while Callan and the others whirled around and darted for the door behind us. While shooting another poison cloud towards Lance's friends, I held the Binder's gaze and called, "They'll wake up in half an hour. Because as opposed to your Chancellor, I don't kill children by sending them into an adult dark mage battle."

Emotions rippled across Lance's features, but I couldn't spare any more time so I whipped around and sprinted into the doorway while Callan and Levi covered my escape.

Shattering glass exploded through the athletics hall while I slammed the door shut behind me. Henry's wind blast had blown out every window on the ground floor.

"Go!" Callan yelled.

Without a second glance at each other, we all raced towards the windows on opposite sides of the building.

The door banged open behind us right as I leaped up and dove through the broken window.

Fabric ripped as part of my shirt sleeve got caught in the shards that still remained on the frame. I tucked in my head and landed on my shoulder as I rolled across the ground outside. Pain pulsed through my body at the rough landing, but I shot to my feet and sprinted down the nearest side street. A short distance to my right, I caught sight of Paige's blond ponytail whipping through the air before she disappeared down another street.

Grabbing the edge of the building, I swung myself onto the next road while shouted orders echoed through the bright morning behind us. It was followed by the pounding of feet as they no doubt tried to round the building and follow us.

Wind ripped through my hair and clothes as I hurtled down the alley. There were people strolling past on the next cross street, but I couldn't slow down because I had to put more distance between me and my pursuers, so I just skidded around the corner and kept running.

Two women leaped out of the way as I almost mowed them down, and several more people gasped in shock and outrage. I was drawing attention, which wasn't good, but right now speed was more important than stealth.

I sprinted through the streets, angry grumblings following in my wake.

My heart slammed against my ribs. I didn't dare look behind me since it would slow me down, so I had no idea how much distance I had managed to put between me and my hunters. Darting through another cluster of stunned morning shoppers, I threw myself around the next corner.

And screeched to a halt.

Constables were marching up the street, coming right towards me.

I whipped my head from side to side.

There were constables in *every* direction.

Dread pulsed through my chest like cold waves.

Shit. All of the people who had been fighting us in the hills were now returning to Eldar, which meant that the entire city would be crawling with constables.

Slowing to a walk, I forced myself to move at a leisurely pace so that I wouldn't attract too much attention. Blood rushed in my ears. I had to get off the streets. There was no way I would be able to make it all the way back to our house while an entire army trickled through the streets. I had to find somewhere to lie low until they had all gotten back to their headquarters.

The squad of constables up ahead was getting closer. Keeping my head lowered, I moved along the edge of the road. My heart hammered in my chest and my lungs begged me to suck in deep breaths after my mad dash across the city, but I forced myself to breathe normally.

By all hell, if those constables looked in my direction right now, they would spot me. They would see exactly who I was. *Fuck.* I needed to get out of sight.

A tavern appeared on my right.

Making a split-second decision, I yanked the door open and slipped inside.

The gloomy light in the building was a stark contrast to the bright morning sunlight outside, and I had to blink furiously to get my eyes to adjust enough to make out the faces inside. While staying close to one of the walls, I moved farther into the building.

The patrons inside were a mix of customers who looked to be enjoying a hearty breakfast before work, and people who still hadn't stopped drinking from the night before. There weren't any good seats left so I was forced to sit with my back halfway facing the door, which made my skin crawl with unease, but I drew in a bracing breath just as the tavern keeper wandered over.

Rage and panic and frustration crackled inside me like a lightning storm. I didn't usually drink strong spirits like whiskey, but after staying awake all night and then seeing my family and then dealing with that damn ambush and the students and the constables, my nerves were raw and my whole soul felt frazzled. So when the tavern keeper asked me what I wanted, I ordered a double shot of whiskey.

A muted sense of amusement pulled at my lips as he returned with the large glass and set it down in front of me. Callan would've been proud.

It wasn't until I reached forward to pick up the glass that I realized that my hands were shaking. Gripping the glass tightly, I took a large gulp.

Hell fucking damn it all. What an absolute fiasco this had turned into. After all of our scheming and careful preparations, Quill had managed to walk out the victor. Not only had they managed to get their loved ones back without handing over the Blade of Equilibrium, but Quill had also managed to rattle me. And I hated it.

His bloody stunt with my family had thrown me off my game, and because of that, I had almost messed up our entire plan. Guilt wormed its way through my chest. And now Quill and Lance and all the other constables were back in Eldar, which meant that we had lost the element of surprise.

Four of the most cunning people I knew had helped me come up with this plan, and we had still been outsmarted. Or rather, outplayed. Using the students to attack us... I really hadn't seen that coming. And that turned out to be our downfall.

Fuck. I was going to kill Quill. As long as we took him out, the rest of his parliament should be easy to threaten into submission.

Raising my glass, I took another large gulp of whiskey while considering.

We needed to figure out a way to—

Fire flickered in the corner of my eye, but I was still holding my whiskey glass so I didn't manage to slap my hands together fast enough.

My stomach lurched as I was yanked up from my chair and shoved back first up against the wall.

"I thought it was you," a man growled in my face. He was alone, but he was wearing the telltale uniform of a constable. "I would recognize you anywhere after you poisoned my best friend out in the hills."

Yellow flames danced around his hand as he held it up in front of my face and leaned closer to me while his other hand tightened around my trapped wrist. Rage flickered in his brown eyes.

"Now, you and I are gonna—"

I spit out the whiskey in my mouth.

The amber liquid sprayed straight into his flames, making them blow right into his face. Since he wasn't fireproof in the way a real fire mage was, he was forced to jerk up his other hand to shield his eyes and protect his face. The move made him release his grip on my wrist, and I slapped my palms together. Glittering green poison shot straight into his throat before he could finish screaming from the flames that licked his skin.

His legs gave out and he toppled over. Wood clanked as he crashed into my table, knocking my chair over in the process, before the body hit the floor with a series of loud thuds.

Deafening silence hung over the whole tavern as everyone turned to gape at me.

Crap.

Slamming my palms together, I called up my biggest and fastest attack. Poison mist exploded across the dimly lit room. A few people had begun to summon magic of their own, but my cloud hit them before they could finish.

While every single person in the tavern slumped down, unconscious, I darted towards the door. My heart pounded in my chest as I glanced out through the small gap.

No constables in sight.

Yanking the door open, I sprinted across the threshold and took off down the street.

Hopefully, the others were having an easier time.

Chapter 27

Callan

My heart pounded against my ribs and worry twisted through my insides like snakes. The whole fucking city had been crawling with constables, so I'd had to hide out in an abandoned building until they had all finished filing in through the main gates. That meant that I still didn't know if Audrey and Henry were okay. The constables might not recognize Henry on sight, but Audrey was another matter.

Trying to block out the terrible fear that threatened to drown me, I leaped over a low hedge and then jogged onto our street. From a distance, our house looked deserted. I tried to persuade myself that that didn't mean anything. It was still only afternoon, so there was no need to light any candles or oil lamps. They could all be in there. Safe. Waiting. They had to be.

I opened the small gate in the fence and then ran the final distance to the door before yanking it open.

Three people whipped around to face me.

Relief, so intense that I almost sagged to the floor, crashed over me.

Henry and Audrey were standing in the middle of the hall

with Levi a few steps away. My own relief was mirrored in both Audrey and Henry's faces as they hurried over to me. Glancing over their shoulders, I found Levi giving me a small nod. I nodded back.

"You okay, boss?" Henry asked as he clapped me on the shoulder.

Reaching up, I squeezed his muscled arm. "Yeah."

"Thank hell," Audrey said before giving my bicep a hard slap. "Don't you dare make me worry like that again."

A smile pulled at my lips as I raised my eyebrows at her. "I thought you didn't worry about me."

She just shot me a withering glare in reply. Then a serious expression washed over her features, and she leaned sideways to peer around me. "Paige isn't with you?"

"No." Frowning, I glanced around the hall. "She's not back yet?"

Worry flickered in both Audrey and Henry's eyes.

"No," she replied.

I looked between the two of them. "She knows this city better than any of us, and she has lots of contacts in secret places. I'm sure she's fine. Just waiting out the constables like I was."

Neither of them looked fully convinced, but they nodded.

For the next half hour, the two of them anxiously paced back and forth across the hallway floor while Levi and I took up position by the wall. There was so much tension in the room that the very air seemed to vibrate with it.

"We should go out after her," Audrey said eventually.

Henry nodded. "Yeah, if she—"

The door was yanked open.

All of us whirled towards it in time to see a blond woman stroll across the threshold. Both Audrey and Henry let out deep sighs. Paige just flashed them a brilliant smile.

"Look who I ran into," she said, and hiked a thumb over her shoulder.

My eyebrows rose as I watched Malcolm Griffith, Sienna Hall, Harvey Grant, and Sam Foster walk through the door and into our hallway.

"They were hiding by the smugglers tunnel," Paige explained while Sam closed the door behind them.

Malcolm drew his dark brows down in an affronted scowl. "We were not *hiding*."

She chuckled and shot him a knowing look. "Uh-huh."

"We were waiting until we were sure that all the constables had passed."

"Potato, potahto." Waving a hand in the air, she sauntered farther into the room. "Anyway, I found them *not hiding* by the smugglers tunnel, so I brought them all here."

"Which is very much appreciated," Sam interjected before Malcolm could say anything else.

Paige stabbed a hand towards him while throwing a pointed look at Malcolm. "See? At least someone has manners."

Malcolm closed his eyes and massaged his temples while blowing out an exasperated sigh.

"She also explained what happened at your meeting with Quill," Grant picked up.

Opening his eyes again, the shadow mage drew his eyebrows down and looked from face to face. "Yes, that it didn't work."

"He truly used the students as soldiers... and shields?" Grant asked. When we nodded, he clicked his tongue and shook his head. "I disapprove of that very much."

"Yeah, he—"

"Can we go and sit down or something?" Sienna interrupted. Raising her eyebrows, she stared at us all and flicked her wrist. "Or are we seriously going to have this conversation right here in the hallway? I just rode two days from Grant's mansion on the heels of an army and then crawled through a dirt tunnel to get inside the city. I want to sit down and I want a glass of wine."

"I thought you didn't care for sitting down," Malcolm said, a smug look on his face.

"Yes, let's go and sit down," Audrey thankfully managed to say before Sienna could burn down our new house.

After bringing in some wine and whiskey along with a bunch of glasses from the kitchen, we all claimed the couches and armchairs in the second living room across the hall. It had a larger arrangement of sofas and armchairs than the other one since the dining room table took up half of that room.

Leaning back against the dark red cushions, I blew out a long sigh and then drank deeply from my glass of whiskey.

"So, the hostages didn't work," Sienna said as she crossed her ankles and rested her feet on the low wooden table in the middle. "Which means that we need a new plan."

"And now we have lost the element of surprise," Malcolm added in a disapproving tone.

"What were we supposed to do?" I snapped. "Slaughter a bunch of thirteen-year-olds?"

"I'm not saying that I disagree with your actions. I'm just stating a fact."

"Well, here's a fact for—"

"By all hell," Levi interrupted. Lounging on the couch opposite me, he shook his head at all of us. "Enough bickering. How do you people get anything done?"

"I don't bicker," Malcolm and I said in unison.

Surprise flitted through my chest. It was mirrored in Malcolm's eyes too as he blinked at me. For another second, no one said anything.

Then we both let out a low chuckle.

It dispelled the tension in the room immediately. Furniture groaned as we all settled more comfortably in our seats and drank a bit more from our preferred choice of alcohol.

"So, to summarize," Grant said eventually while tracing the rim of his glass with his finger. "We have two objectives. Get a hold of the Blade of Equilibrium so that you," he nodded towards Levi, "can destroy it. And we need to kill Chancellor Quill."

"Speaking of," Levi began while shifting his penetrating gaze to Malcolm. "Where are my people?"

"Hiding in the hills right outside the city," the shadow mage replied without hesitation. "Waiting for us to find a way to sneak all one hundred of them inside."

"All one hundred?"

"Yes. There have been no casualties."

A satisfied smile spread across Levi's lips, and he raised his glass in a salute.

"If we're going to launch another attack, his people won't be enough," Henry said. "We need more."

Everyone fell silent for a while. A cloud passed over the sun, temporarily blocking out the light that had previously been filling the room with a golden glow.

"There are a lot of resentful mages in the city's underworld." Paige swept her gaze over the rest of us and then shrugged. "We could probably persuade a lot of them to join us in taking down Quill. They hate the current parliament for forcing them to give up their magic."

"Alright, that would give us the numbers," I said, giving her an appreciative nod.

Sienna blew out a sigh and swigged from her glass of wine. "It still doesn't solve our problem with the blade. Getting into the academy to steal it is next to impossible. Trust me, I barely managed to escape the graduation ceremony myself. I had surprise on my side and I was trying to get out, not in. And I still had to burn down two whole city blocks to do it."

"What if we get them to move the blade?" Malcolm said.

Several pairs of eyebrows rose as we all turned to look at him.

He shrugged. "Let's say we discreetly let slip that we're going to attack the academy with a massive force. Quill will try to outmaneuver us by moving the dagger before we can hit it."

"Move it where?" Sam asked.

"I don't know. But anywhere is better than the academy."

"And how do we let our plans slip without him knowing that it's us?"

"I can take care of that," Paige said. "A few words to the right people in the underworld, and the news will get back to Quill without him knowing that it came from us. He'll think that his sources have managed to uncover a great secret."

"Sneaky." Grant gave her a nod. "I approve."

"So, we need to split into teams then," I said, already running through options in my head. "Some of us need to get Levi's people into the city and get them, and you, set up in temporary safe houses since we can't fit a hundred and nine people in this house. And some of us need to start convincing the resentful mages to join our fight." I glanced towards the blond forger. "We'll leave the discreet sharing of our plans to you."

She waved a hand in front of her face. "Oh, that's an easy one. I can help with convincing people once I'm done."

"Alright." I gave her a nod. "As for the rest of us..."

The clouds blew clear again while we began dividing up the work between us.

Our first plan might have gone to hell because Quill had

pulled a stunt we hadn't seen coming. But that wouldn't happen again.

We didn't have to play by the same rules as they did.

And it was time that we started using that to our advantage.

Chapter 28

Murmurs of agreement swept through the tavern. When Paige and I had first arrived, we had been met with suspicion, if not outright hostility. But the mood had shifted the moment that I had shown them my poison magic. It was the same thing that had happened at all the other bars and taverns that Paige had brought us to. Places where people, particularly people who had been full mages before being forced to give up their powers to the Great Current, gathered to curse their lot in life and drown their anger in alcohol.

"It's time to take a stand," I continued, delivering the same speech I'd given at all the taverns. "To fight back. If you could change the past, don't you wish that you could've fought back *before* you allowed them to strip you of your magic?"

Resentment and anger blew through the candlelit room as they nodded and grunted in agreement.

"We can't give you your magic back, but we can make sure that they don't steal your children's magic too." A vicious smile curled my lips as I swept my gaze over them. "And we can make Chancellor Quill pay for what he's done."

Several people let out calls of agreement while others thumped their wooden tankards against the worn tabletops.

"Good." I nodded. "We're going after the Blade of Equilibrium so that we can destroy it once and for all. When the attack happens, Quill and his constables will try to stop us. That's when we'll need your help to fight. Against all of us, they won't stand a chance."

The cheers and thumping of mugs grew louder.

"Spread the word to likeminded friends," Paige called across the noise. "But make sure the constables don't find out. We need the element of surprise."

To be honest, it didn't really matter if word got back to Quill that we were recruiting people for an attack. In fact, it would just help lend more credibility to our ruse if it did. Quill would just believe that we were planning on attacking the academy, since we had told him that we would do that during our failed hostage negotiation, and since Paige had purposely let that slip to her carefully selected contacts. If he heard rumors that we were trying to recruit people from the underworld, it would just strengthen his belief that we were amassing an army to launch at the academy.

However, we still told everyone we recruited to keep it quiet because if they started blabbering about it too much, we would look like amateurs. And that would make Quill suspicious.

Paige and I exchanged a satisfied glance while the tavern's patrons grinned excitedly.

"Be ready," I said.

And with that, we turned around and walked back out into the night.

The smell of urine and spilled alcohol hung over the darkened alley, so I made sure not to breathe too deeply while we made our way back to the wider road ahead. The moment we reached it, I drew in that deep breath and felt the clear air swirl into my lungs. This street was one of the more neutral ones in Eldar. Nothing too fancy, and nothing too shabby either. But it connected to several alleys where many of the less reputable citizens spent their evenings, which was why we used it as our main path while we worked our way through the seedy taverns.

I glanced up and down the road. It was thankfully empty, which was a relief since I didn't feel like slaughtering people right now. Callan, Henry, and Levi were also sneaking through the city relatively close to our position while trying to get all of Levi's people through the smugglers tunnel and into the different inns that Paige had suggested. Poisoning people in the middle of the street would draw attention both to us and to them, and I didn't want to risk that.

"The next one is about a five-minute walk from here," Paige said as we passed through the small pool of light provided by one of the streetlamps. "But this one's fifty-fifty. There might be people who don't share our view there, so let me finish checking the whole room before you start breaking out your lethal glitter."

I chuckled. "Of course."

We walked in silence for another minute. I glanced over at her as we continued down the street. Her wavy blond hair was pulled up in a ponytail, and she had slid her hands into the pockets of her brown pants while she strolled along with carefree steps. She looked utterly at ease. Utterly at home.

"You're pretty incredible, you know that?" I said.

I had been thinking about it all evening. In fact, I had been thinking about it for days now, but for some reason, I hadn't said anything yet.

Mischief glittered in her eyes as she twisted to meet my gaze while a grin slid home on her lips. "Oh, I always think I'm incredible. But just out of curiosity, what brought this on?"

"This." I motioned up and down the street, and then shook my head in amazement. "The insane amount of knowledge that you have about every little aspect of Eldar's underworld. You do realize that none of our plans would've worked if it wasn't for you, right?"

She blinked at me in surprise, as if she hadn't been expecting such a serious answer. Clearing her throat, she scratched the back of her neck while flicking a glance towards the street ahead. "Thanks. I, uhm... I have to admit, I was feeling pretty useless during those weeks in Malcolm's mansion. But here, in Eldar, I guess I do feel like I can contribute."

I was just about to protest that she had never been useless, but she suddenly changed the topic.

"Are you and Callan really going to stay here?" A guarded flicker of hope shone in her eyes. "In the city?"

Smiling, I gave her a nod. "That's the plan."

Relief, and joy, washed over her features as she beamed at me. "Good. Because I want to live here in the city too. I don't think I'm cut out to live isolated in a mansion in the hills. I feel much more at home here. And besides, this is where all of my clients live."

"You wouldn't have had to move out there with us if you didn't want to."

"No, I know. But I want to live close to you."

I arched a teasing eyebrow at her. "You mean close to Henry."

A wicked laugh rolled off her tongue. "Well, I won't deny—"

Slapping my palms together, I called up a cloud of poison as water magic suddenly sloshed a short distance from us. Two people had rounded the corner, coming from another cross street, and had screeched to a halt when they saw us.

Two pairs of blue eyes stared at us in shock.

I blinked as the same stunned surprise pulsed through me as well.

Lance and Jessica stood frozen on the dark cobblestones while Jessica's water magic floated like a shield before their chests.

Keeping my eyes locked on them, I pushed Paige backwards while I let the green mist twist before me. "Go. I'll hold them off."

"No!" Paige protested.

"It's not up for discussion."

"I—"

"Paige, please!"

"Fine." She shot me a pointed glare. "But you'd better be right behind me."

"I am."

Without another word, she turned around and sprinted down the street. Relief flashed through me. Paige wasn't a battle mage, and if she had stayed, she would have been in serious trouble facing off against people like Lance and Jessica.

"How did you find us?" I called to the two blond mages up ahead.

Lance scrunched up his eyebrows. "How did we find you? How did you find *us*?"

Confusion swept through my chest. Weren't they here to ambush us and capture us?

Now that the initial shock of their sudden appearance had worn off, I looked at them. Really looked at them. Lance was wearing a white dress shirt, and his golden blond hair had been combed and swept back from his face. Jessica looked equally stunning in a dark blue dress and red-painted lips. My frown deepened.

"Are you on a date?" I asked, utter disbelief crackling in my veins.

Neither one of them answered.

I raised my eyebrows in shock. "You *are*." Shaking my head, I stabbed a hand to the left to indicate the city. "We're in the middle of a war!"

Something snapped in Lance's eyes. Holding my gaze, he threw his arms out in an exasperated gesture while all but yelling, "Maybe we're tired of war! Maybe we just wanted to go out and have *one* normal evening without people trying to kidnap us and kill us and torture us."

"Then maybe you shouldn't have started the war in the first place."

For a moment, it looked like Lance was going to retort, but then he just ground his teeth together instead. His gaze slid to the spot where Paige had been standing earlier before he lifted his eyes to stare down the now empty street.

"You told her to run," he said. "Which means that you didn't come here to ambush us either." His eyes were serious when they met mine again. "So, are you going to try to kill us now?"

"I haven't decided yet."

He held my stare unflinchingly. "If you come one step closer to us, I'm going to bind your magic and never give it back."

A cold smile, the smile of a predator, curled my lips as I cocked my head slightly. "We both know that I don't need to get close in order to kill you."

"Except my water magic will block your poison," Jessica said, and raised her chin.

"Because you accomplished that so well when we fought on that mountain in Castlebourne."

"I can't figure you out," Lance interrupted before she could press out her flustered reply. "On the one hand, you torture me and threaten to kill my friends and slaughter anyone who stands in your way without an ounce of regret. But then you give up your leverage and your only shot at getting the Blade of Equilibrium because you don't want to kill the students who attacked you."

Looking back at him, I said nothing.

"We both know that you could have killed them," he pressed. "Or at least killed all the hostages. But you didn't. You just ran instead and left everyone alive."

"Just because my morals are different from yours, doesn't mean that I don't also have lines that I'm not prepared to cross."

"But I don't understand. It's like you're two different people. The one who slaughters and tortures without remorse, and the one who gives up everything just so she won't have to hurt a bunch of teenagers. Which one are you?"

"Both."

"It doesn't—"

"Look, we meant what we said during that negotiation. We want the blade and we want you to stop forcing people to give up their magic and to just let us dark mages live in peace. We don't *want* to slaughter Eldar's entire constable force and burn the city to the ground. But we will. If you keep forcing our hand, we will rain down death and destruction on everything and everyone."

"Chancellor Quill would never agree to that deal."

"I know. Which is why we need to kill him. He is going to bring Eldar to the brink of ruin with his stubborn refusal to even negotiate with dark mages. Trust me when I tell you, this war will decimate the city. Homes will burn. People will die. And not just constables. Innocent citizens will be caught in the crossfire too."

Desperation flooded his eyes, and he threw his arms out

again. "Then just stop the war! Just stop fighting and we can avoid all that."

"Why can't *your* side be the one to stop the war?" I held his gaze. "You've spent time with us, so you know how we feel about our magic, right?"

"Well, yes."

"Then you know that we would rather die than give up our powers." I paused for a few seconds to make sure that the words I was about to say would truly sink in. "So the question you need to ask yourselves is, are *you* prepared to die for your right to steal our magic from us against our will?"

Silence fell across the street. It was so thick that I could almost see it hanging in the air like smoke.

Jessica looked up at Lance, but the Binder only kept his eyes on me. I stared back at him. None of us said anything.

Footsteps and voices suddenly came from farther up the street, behind Lance and Jessica. It shattered the strange standstill that we had come to. While keeping her water shield floating before them, Jessica cast a quick look over her shoulder.

"I'm going to leave now," I said, shifting my attention between the two of them. "If you try to attack me or pursue me, I will kill both of you without hesitation. So, you need to make a choice right now if that is something you're willing to risk just to capture me."

The voices were drawing closer as we watched each other in silence for another couple of seconds. When neither of them made any move to attack, I nodded.

"Smart choice." I flicked a glance up and down their fancy clothes while backing down the street. "Have a nice date."

Both of them remained standing firmly where they were while I disappeared back into the darkness in search of Paige.

Chapter 29

Callan

"I still can't believe that they haven't raided this building yet."

"Hey," Audrey interrupted, and shot Henry a sharp look. "Don't jinx it."

He raised his hands. "I'm just saying, if this is the house you stayed in last time, it should've been Quill's first target."

"He probably thinks that we won't be stupid enough to use a busted safe house a second time," I said. "And besides, this house is no longer for rent."

"Exactly." Audrey smirked and held out her glass of wine towards me. "Because it's now owned by a very well-respected couple from Malgrave."

A low chuckle rolled from my chest, and I clinked my glass against hers. "Indeed."

Henry raised his eyebrows. "You faked your ownership certificate?"

"Obviously." Audrey lifted one shoulder in a shrug. "We couldn't very well tell the couple we bought it from who we really were." After taking another sip, she waved her hand in front of her face. "I'll just ask Paige to forge us a real certificate later."

"It's not a real certificate if it's forged."

"Don't let Paige hear you say that."

A click sounded from the front door as someone unlocked it, and then Paige strolled into the dining room as if us merely speaking her name had summoned her from the night. Stopping a few steps from the couches we were currently occupying, she flashed us a grin that looked like trouble. Hopefully, though, it was the good kind.

"I've just heard from my sources and..." Trailing off, she looked around the candlelit dining room. "Where's Levi?" Before any of us could reply, she sucked in a breath and bellowed, "Oi! Levi! Get down here. I have news."

I cringed slightly. Levi didn't exactly like being summoned. What was it with these people? First Audrey, and now Paige too. Did they really not have any sense of self-preservation at all?

A door banged shut somewhere upstairs. It was followed by slow thumping footsteps coming down the stairs. I steeled myself and got ready to intervene before things could get out of hand.

In the armchair next to me, Henry stiffened slightly too. Draped across the couch, Audrey just sipped from her glass of wine again. Golden light from the mass of candles throughout the room reflected against the dark windows and glittered in her eyes as she looked towards the doorway.

Two seconds later, Levi prowled around the corner. He looked about as happy as I had expected him to be. His dark brows were drawn down, and his eyes were sharp as he locked them on Paige. The sleeves on his black shirt had been rolled up, exposing his forearms, and the muscles there shifted slightly as he brushed his hands together.

My whole body tensed, ready to leap up from the cushions at a moment's notice.

A wicked-looking blade materialized in Levi's palm. With his eyes still locked on Paige, he moved towards her while twirling the blade in his hand.

"If you want to speak to me, you ask politely," he said, his voice low and dangerous.

Paige just looked back at him, entirely unfazed. "I *was* being polite. I could've just told everyone else the news without bothering to let you know."

He held her gaze as he continued towards her. But then he just walked right past her without doing anything. Letting the blade in his hand disappear, he threw himself down on the couch next to me and raised his eyebrows expectantly.

"So, as I was saying," Paige began as if she hadn't just narrowly avoided Levi's wrath. "I've just heard from my sources and Quill has moved the Blade of Equilibrium from the academy."

We all sat forward in our seats.

"You're sure?" I asked.

She nodded. "Yes. They moved it this afternoon." With a smirk on her face, she flicked her hair back behind her shoulder. "They thought they were being sneaky, but we're better. The underworld sees everything."

"Where did they move it?" Audrey asked.

"Yeah, uhm, that's the thing... They moved it to the parliament building."

Silence fell over the room. Paige, who had been standing this whole time, finally wandered over to the couch and dropped down next to Audrey.

"I take it that's not a good thing," Levi said when the silence began to stretch.

I sucked my teeth. "No. Well, it's easier than the academy at least. But it's still gonna take one hell of a plan to breach it."

"Isn't that the same building you kidnapped Lance from?"

"Yeah."

"So how did you get in then?"

Audrey and I exchanged a look, and amusement pulled at her lips at the memory.

"We just walked right up to the front doors and handed them our invitations," I replied, sliding my gaze back to Levi. Then I shrugged. "I doubt it will work a second time."

Another short silence descended over our cozy living room as we all no doubt considered our situation. Outside the windows, the night was dark and quiet.

"I hate to say it," Henry began. "But we should probably get the others here too. I know that Malcolm is an insufferable prick, but he's smart. And so are the others. None of them would've survived this long if they weren't."

"Another dark mage gathering, huh?" I chuckled. "I wonder how many more of those we can manage before someone finally snaps and takes that first shot."

Audrey let out a low laugh. "Yeah." Then she tipped her head towards Henry. "But you're right, we do need them."

We let out a collective sigh as we all pushed to our feet.

"Alright." Audrey gave us all a nod. "Let's go get them. It's time to plot the very last stage of this war."

Chapter 30

Audrey

Restlessness flitted through my chest like erratic butterflies. I tried to finish undressing, but I couldn't concentrate. My dress, along with the metal corset, lay draped over the chair next to the unlit fireplace in our bedroom, leaving me standing there in only my underwear and my metal bracers. I fumbled slightly with the leather strings on the bracers, and then just ended up yanking at them in frustration.

A snarl ripped from my throat.

On the other side of the room, Callan looked over at me while he finished hanging up his leather armor. His gaze dipped down to my hands. After drawing a hand over his armor, he strode towards me.

"Here," he offered, reaching out as if to take my arm.

"I don't need your help," I growled.

Callan slapped my hand away from the leather strings and then wrapped strong fingers around my wrist. "Yes, you do."

I tried to yank my arm back, but his iron grip didn't budge. Without even commenting on it, he just lifted his other hand

and began undoing the strings on the bracer that was wrapped around my trapped forearm.

Another annoyed noise came from my chest, but I stopped struggling and let him help me. He easily got it open. After sliding it off my arm, he placed it on the chair next to my dress and then turned back to me. Raising his eyebrows, he snapped his fingers and pointed towards the air in front of him. I narrowed my eyes at him but held out my other arm.

"What's wrong?" he asked while he started undoing the strings on the other one.

"What's wrong? Are you fucking serious?"

His hand shot up and wrapped around my jaw. While holding it in a tight grip, he leveled a commanding stare at me. "I already know how talented you are with that sharp tongue of yours, so I would suggest using it to answer my question."

Dark amusement trickled through my annoyance, and a half smirk slid across my lips. "Or you'll gag me?"

Leaning closer, he slanted his lips over mine. "Oh I'll do far worse than gag you, sweetheart." After stealing a kiss, he pulled back and released my jaw. Then he went back to untying the leather strings. "So, what is it?"

I heaved a deep sigh and stared up at the pale ceiling for a few seconds before meeting his gaze again. "This is it, Callan. We've made all the plans and plotted all the schemes and moved all the pieces into position. There's nothing more we can do now. Tomorrow, we bet *everything* on an outcome that we can't control. I hate it."

"Yeah, me too."

"I hate that we can't control what happens. What if something goes wrong? What if *everything* goes wrong? There are too many unknown factors. Too much we can't control."

Callan pulled off my other bracer and placed it next to the

first one. "I know. I feel the same way." Straightening, he met my gaze again. "But you said it yourself. We've done everything we can to prepare. There's nothing more to be done now, and worrying about what might happen tomorrow won't make it better."

"Except I can't make my brain shut up."

"So what you're saying is..." He drew light fingers up my arms and across my collarbones, making my skin tingle. "You need a distraction."

I dragged my gaze up and down his body. He was also only wearing underwear, leaving his lethal body on full display. My heartbeat quickened at just the thought of having those hard muscles pressed against my naked body. A sly smile curled my lips as I forced my eyes back up to his face.

"Yes, I do," I replied.

Wickedness glittered in his eyes as he trailed two fingers down the center of my chest while he leaned forward and placed his lips next to my ear. "Well then, allow me to fuck you until the only thought left inside your head is my name."

Excitement shot down my spine. Locking my hands around the back of his neck, I yanked his mouth to mine in a violent kiss. He chuckled against my lips. Then his tongue slid in, claiming my mouth with commanding strokes, while he grabbed my ass and lifted me up. I wrapped my legs around his waist.

A moan rumbled from deep within his chest as I ground my pussy against him while he carried me towards the bed.

I let out a small yelp as he tossed me down on the mattress.

His eyes were dark with desire as he ran them over my body before locking them on mine again. He jerked his chin.

"Strip," he ordered.

Heat pooled inside me. Licking my lips, I maneuvered myself up onto my knees and then lifted my hands to undo the fastenings on my brassiere. On the floor beside the bed, Callan bent down and stripped out of his own underwear. I dropped my brassiere on the floor before lying down on my back and starting on my panties.

To my left, Callan watched me intently.

While slowly sliding the panties over my ass and down my thighs, I bit my lip.

His eyes flashed. With a few quick strides, he had rounded the bed so that he was standing at the foot of it instead. Reaching forward, he grabbed my ankles and then yanked me towards him.

I slid across the cream-colored sheets with my panties still bunched around my knees. Kicking my legs, I tried to get his hands off. They remained firmly locked around my ankles. I raised myself up on my elbows and narrowed my eyes at him.

He shot me a deliciously lethal smile. "You vicious little poisoner. Always playing dangerous games that you have no hope of winning."

Releasing my ankles, he reached up and grabbed my panties. With one quick move, he yanked them off and tossed them on the floor behind him. I scooted backwards on the mattress again while throwing him a look brimming with challenge.

His answering grin was pure villain.

The mattress dipped underneath me as Callan climbed up onto the bed. Taking a firm grip on my thighs, he held me in place and spread my legs while he moved up so that he straddled my right thigh.

I raised my eyebrows at him. "You know, I still have lots of thoughts inside my head. And none of them is your name."

"Impatient and arrogant." Leaning forward, he placed his hand against my chest and shoved me back down on the mattress. "You really never change, do you?"

"Would you want me to?"

"Never." A villainous smirk pulled at his lips. "It just makes it that much more satisfying when I finally draw those sweet pleas from your lips and make you beg me for mercy."

"You think I'm arrogant? If anyone's cocky it's—"

My words got cut off by a gasp as Callan suddenly pressed two vibrating fingers against my clit. Curling my fingers in the soft sheets, I stared up into the ceiling while I tried to suppress a moan of pleasure. It didn't work.

"You were saying?" Callan taunted while his fingers circled my clit, drawing another moan from me and making my body shiver.

I forced out a long shuddering breath.

Callan shifted his hand so that his thumb pressed against my clit instead, while his fingers slid down to tease my entrance. Desperate need washed over me, soaking my pussy, as he increased the strength of his vibrations.

My chest rose and fell rapidly.

A gasp tore from my throat as Callan pushed two fingers inside me. They were coated in his magic, and the vibrations pulsed against my inner walls as he slowly drew his fingers out and then pushed them in again.

I tightened my grip on the sheets.

The weight on my thigh shifted slightly, as if Callan had adjusted his position. His thumb continued circling my clit while his fingers lined up more properly with my pussy.

He drew them out once more and then pushed them back, and this time, the force magic extended from his fingers. I arched my back and groaned as the vibrating shaft penetrated me deeper.

It slowly retracted. Then shot back out again. I sucked in desperate breaths as pleasure pulsed through me in tune with the vibrations. Holding on to the sheets, I shifted my hips and ground my clit harder against Callan's thumb.

A low chuckle drifted through the air. "Want more, huh? Alright then."

Lights flickered in my brain as the force shaft inside me *expanded*.

"Oh, fuck," I breathed as it grew thicker, filling me completely.

Callan withdrew it to his fingertips and then shoved it back inside me again. I arched up from the bed. Using his other hand, he took my hip in a punishing grip, forcing my body back against the mattress as he pulled the vibrating shaft back and then pushed it out while expanding it a little bit more.

"Fuck," I gasped out again.

He increased the strength of the vibrations.

A violent lightning storm of tension crackled inside my body as pleasure thrummed through me, begging to be released.

The thick force shaft penetrated me mercilessly while intense vibrations pulsed against my clit. I squirmed against the mattress. Callan tightened his grip on my hip, trapping me in place while he pushed me farther and farther towards the edge without letting me fall off it.

I was clenching the sheets so hard that my fingers ached, and my whole body trembled with the desperate need for release. Callan shifted his thumb slightly. Blinding light flashed in my brain, and I sucked in a gasp.

"Oh, fuck..." I mumbled while writhing against the mattress. "Fuck. Please. Oh hell."

"No." Callan's commanding voice sliced through the fog in my brain. "My name. I want *my* name on your lips when you come. Understood?"

His thick force shaft expanded a little more as it pounded into me. "Oh, fuck. Callan. Please. Callan."

"Good girl."

My brain shattered. I moaned Callan's name up into the

ceiling as the orgasm shot through my body, making my limbs shake against the soft mattress. He kept sending pulsing magic against my clit until I thought the fractured remains of my mind were going to melt. Garbled pleas dripped from my mouth as the waves of pleasure rolled through me.

When the last of it left my body and he pulled his fingers out, I just lay there on the mattress and gulped down air for a while.

Once I had finished scraping together my shattered brain, I pushed myself up on my elbows and looked at my infuriating force mage.

He grinned back at me with the biggest fucking smirk on his face.

"As I said," he began in a smug voice. "When you play these games with me, *you* always lose."

"I'm not sure you can claim that as a win." I flashed him a smile full of wicked challenge. "When you weren't even the one fucking me."

He cocked his head. "Are you saying that you're unsatisfied with my performance?"

"I'm saying it wasn't *your* performance. Expanding the force shaft like that... Have you suddenly lost your edge and need to compensate for it?"

A lethal glint crept into his eyes. Moving forward, he shifted his position so that he was straddling me while he lined up his cock with my entrance.

I raised my eyebrows. "If you're going to prove me wrong, darling, you need to actually stick it in."

The words had barely left my mouth when he shoved his cock inside me. I groaned in pleasure.

Leaning forward, he braced one hand on the mattress next to me while he used the other to grip my chin. "I swear... That wicked mouth of yours..." He shook his head at me.

I smirked back at him. "Well, maybe you should do something else to shut me up then."

With his cock still buried deep inside me, he released my chin and drew his hand down my throat. His dark eyes glittered in the warm candlelight as he locked them on me. "Maybe I should."

Before I could reply, he wrapped his fingers around my throat and squeezed. My breath was cut off, his strong hand trapping the air in my lungs.

While holding my gaze, he slowly drew out and then pushed his cock inside me again. A strangled moan made it past my lips. I tried to suck in a deep breath, but his grip was like iron.

Pleasure crackled through me as Callan started up a rough pace. I reached up and wrapped my hands around his forearm, digging my fingers into his muscles while he shoved inside me again.

He eased the pressure on my throat.

Air flooded my lungs again as I sucked in desperate breaths.

Then he tightened his grip once more.

My body slid up and down the smooth sheets as Callan pounded into me with savage strength. Only his hand around my throat kept me in place on the mattress. I closed my eyes as a massive wave of pleasure rolled through me.

Callan gave my neck a firm squeeze. My eyes snapped open again.

"Eyes on me," he growled.

When I nodded, he relaxed his grip again, allowing me to draw in a few strained breaths. Then he tightened it once more.

Another crackling orgasm built inside me as Callan fucked me hard enough to make the bedframe thump against the wall. I dug my fingers into the corded muscles of his forearm. Pent-up tension pulsed inside me, and my lungs were begging for air.

"I promised you that the only thought left in your head was

going to be my name. So when I let you breathe again, you're going to say it," Callan commanded. "Only my name. Got it?"

While trying to blink my eyes back into focus, I nodded desperately.

He pounded into me another few times, pushing me farther and farther towards that sweet orgasm.

Then he released my throat.

"Callan."

I gasped his name out like a prayer while air rushed back into my lungs. His cock slammed inside me.

Release exploded through my soul.

My chest heaved and I gripped his forearm hard as lightning bolts of pleasure crackled through my every nerve.

Callan groaned as my tight pussy trembled around his thick cock.

Then pleasure flashed across his face as well.

Moaning each other's names, we came hard together in a moment that seemed to last a lifetime.

With my heart slamming against my ribs, I stared up into Callan's warm brown eyes. Eyes filled with pleasure and love and promises for the future.

I wanted this. I wanted this future. Us. Here in this house. Fucking and scheming and greedily wringing every imaginable pleasure and joy from life. Together.

But as a sudden fear crept into my chest, I couldn't help but wonder…

Did ruthless villains like us really get a happily ever after?

Chapter 31

Callan

Worry twisted inside my chest like strangling vines. Leaning forward, I glanced around the edge of the pale stone building and shot a quick look up and down the street. There was no sign of the others. I hadn't expected there to be, they were far too professional for that, but it would've calmed me a little to see their faces right now.

Pulling back, I pressed my body against the warm stone wall and blew out a long breath to steady myself. I tried to remind myself of what Audrey had told me back at Malcolm's mansion. She was worried too, but she handled it by remembering that I was lethal. So was she. And Henry. Both of them had survived this long because they were incredibly skilled, and they would survive this too.

I cast another glance around the corner.

The wide street just beyond the building was empty. After that flat stretch, the ground began sloping upwards, forming the massive hill in the middle of the city that housed the parliament building. White clouds drifted lazily over the sky, casting parts of the hill in shadow as they temporarily blocked out the sun. Only a few constables were moving about at the top of the hill, which meant that our ruse must have worked.

Chancellor Quill believed that we were still planning on attacking the academy in order to take the Blade of Equilibrium, and we had made sure to keep up that ruse. We had sent all of those disgruntled former mages that we recruited from the underworld to stage a fake attack on the academy. And to truly seal the deal, Paige had forged some official sightings of us so that the constables would have time to get into position on the other side of the city. That fake attack should have started half an hour ago, so the majority of Chancellor Quill's constables should be caught up in that fight by now. Leaving the parliament building practically unprotected.

I flicked yet another glance up towards the grand structure atop the hill. Flexing my fingers, I tried to dispel the impatience inside me. In order to increase our chances, all of us were going to charge up the hill from all sides at the exact same time. So now, we just had to wait for that damn clock tower to ring in the hour.

Forcing out another long breath, I tried to rip out the worry in my chest like the weed it was. But it stubbornly dug its thorns in.

Audrey and Henry would be fine. They *had to* be fine.

I'd spent so many years not caring about anyone. So many years convincing myself that having friends was beneath me. But then I met Henry. And then Audrey. I carefully edged that door open again. And they, like the merciless villains that they are, kicked the whole damn door in so that I wouldn't be able to deny that they had become my family. My people. So if I lost either of them now, I didn't think I would be able to survive it.

The ominous booming of giant bells split the air.

Alarm shot through me.

It was time.

After ripping out the last shreds of doubt by sheer force of will, I pushed off from the wall and sprinted across the street. All along the same road that circled the hill, dark mages darted out of the shadows and ran towards the grassy slopes. I knew that Audrey and Henry were somewhere on the other side. And so were Levi and his people, and Malcolm, and all the other dark mages of Eldar. Everyone except Sam and Paige, who remained at our rendezvous spot.

My heart pounded in my chest as I cleared the final bit of the street and leaped onto the grass. My boots sank into the soil, sending a spray of dirt shooting out behind me when I pushed off and hurtled up the slope.

Shouts rang out from atop the hill.

The constables had spotted us.

It didn't matter. Even though they had the high ground, they would never be able to fight off one hundred dark mages. Not when their own numbers were so few.

I slapped my palms together and called up a force wall while I continued sprinting towards them. Lightning crackled through the air.

The white bolts smacked into my force shield with a boom that echoed into the city. I immediately summoned another one when yellow flames roared down the hillside. They washed down the slope as I shoved them aside with my wall. Heat filled the air, making it vibrate from the power of the magic.

As soon as the flames had been pushed aside, I snapped my gaze back to the constables up on the hill, getting ready for their next futile attack.

Shock pulsed through my body like ice water.

Screeching to a halt halfway up the slope, I stared in utter disbelief at the scene playing out on the flat surface at the top of the hill.

Constables welled across the edge, sweeping down the sides

of the hill like a tidal wave. Row upon row poured over the ridge, and not just on my side. Around the whole hill, men and women charged down towards us while screaming battle cries into the warm summer air.

For a few insane moments, all I could do was stare at them.

They outnumbered us many times over, which meant that this had to be the bulk of Quill's army. But why the hell were they here? We had set up the perfect distraction at the academy, and the news of that attack had made it to Quill's ears from several different sources. Sources he should have trusted. So why hadn't he used his army to ambush us, or rather the people we sent to the academy instead of us, and take us all out once and for all? Why the hell had he hidden his army up here?

Based on how quickly all of the constables mobilized, they must have known that we were coming. But how? Not even those disgruntled people we recruited knew that we were coming here. They all thought that we would be joining them at the academy. The only people who had known that we were actually going to attack the hill were the dark mages of Eldar, along with Henry, Paige, and Levi and his people. And all of us were here, launching the attack. So how the hell had Quill known that we were coming?

Water and lightning magic shot towards me.

Snapping out of my stupidity, I yanked up a force shield to block the combined attack while I whipped my head from side to side. All around the hill, dark mages had come to abrupt halts as we all were forced to go on the defensive. I shoved aside another roaring wave of fire while trying to figure out my options.

Our plan had been to take the hill in a swift simultaneous attack and then work our way into the parliament building from there. That would never work now. Our momentum was halted. They had the high ground. And they outnumbered us.

Fuck.

A *crack* split the air as three lightning bolts slammed into my force shield. I summoned a massive spinning arc and hurled it at the sea of constables while I backed down the hill. Blood sprayed into the air as it cut the heads off the closest people, but the ones behind them just kept coming. I barely managed to throw up consecutive shields in order to block the mass of attacks they shot at me all at the same time.

Sweat ran down my spine.

Touching my hands together, I threw arc after arc and yanked up shield after shield to stem the tide of enemies while also trying to run backwards down the hill again. They knew that they would never be able to win against a dark mage in a ranged battle, so they did what they always did. They tried to rush us and force us into close combat instead.

Alarm blared inside my skull as I tried to buy myself enough time to launch a proper attack. But just blocking the shots coming from dozens of people at the same time was taking all of my concentration. Widening my force wall, I shoved it forward at the same time as they threw a combined attack of wind and fire.

Embers and yellow flames shot straight up into the air as the attacks hit my shield. It stopped the momentum of it on that side, but the other half of it went through. The constables let out a scream as my attack crashed into them, sending them flying backwards and slamming into their comrades behind.

But the ones who had thrown the torrent of fire escaped the hit.

I called up another wall to shove them back too, but it was already too late.

Air exploded from my lungs as three men launched themselves at me, tackling me to the ground. I landed on the thick grass with them on top of me.

Yanking up my elbow, I rammed it into the first guy's side while I drove my knee into someone else's stomach. Grunts tore from their throats, but it was almost drowned out by the pounding of boots coming down the hill.

I needed to get out before they could swarm me.

Hands wrapped around my forearm, trying to pin it to the ground. I shoved my other one upwards, slamming the heel of my hand into a chin. Blood burst from his mouth as he no doubt bit off part of his tongue.

He screamed and jerked back, removing some of the weight on my other arm. I immediately slammed my palms together, but before I could throw my magic, a knife glinted in the air right above me.

Jerking my head to the side at the last second, I barely managed to avoid the blade that would have taken my eye out. It sank into the grass a hair's breadth from my temple. I drew my palms apart and shoved a force scythe straight upwards.

Panicked screams were quickly silenced as it severed the two men's heads from their shoulders. I snapped my mouth shut as blood rained down on me.

Shoving the bodies aside, I struggled to my feet while the horde of constables welled down the hillside. While sucking in a desperate breath, I hurled a massive force wall towards them. Water and wind shot out to block it, but a few sections went flying backwards as it hit before they could shield.

I just needed to get—

A body slammed into me from the side.

Shock pulsed through me as I crashed down on the grass with a man on top of me. The hit sent the two of us rolling down the hill while both of us tried to gain the upper hand. Through the rapid rolling motion, I managed to catch sight of a man's pissed-off face where blood painted his chin.

Oh, of course. The guy who I'd gotten to bite off his own tongue. He was still alive.

Dirt and grass whirled around us as we tumbled towards the street below.

I tried to get him off me long enough to touch my hands together, but he was grappling me like a madman.

Dull pain pulsed through my shoulder as we at last hit the stone street at the bottom. I yanked my knee up and drove it into the man's side when he tried to climb up on top of me. It made him wince but didn't throw him off me. His hands scrabbled for purchase around my throat. I rammed my closed fists into his elbows, making his arms buckle. The move made him lose his balance slightly, and I slapped my palms together.

A force blade extended from my hand.

The man's brown eyes went wide as it punched straight through his chest.

More blood rained down on my already blood-splattered body.

Dragging the force blade downwards, I carved a hole straight through his chest and down his stomach for good measure before I released the blade. He slumped forward. I yanked up my hands and placed them against his shoulders before his whole weight could land on me. Gritting my teeth, I heaved his bleeding corpse off me.

Blood and dirt and grass covered my face. I dragged the back of my hand across my eyes to wipe off the worst while I climbed to my feet again. Snapping my gaze back towards the hill, I checked to make sure that the constables were still out of range. Luckily, they were.

But that was where our luck ended.

All along the hill, our forces were fighting the tide of constables while retreating down the slope. This was never going to work. We needed to regroup and figure out—

Fire and water and lightning shot up into the air from atop the hill in three separate torrents.

I stared up at them as they tore towards the sky.

Dread curled around my spine.

A signal. That was a signal.

Which meant that back-up was coming.

Chapter 32

Three columns of fire, water, and lightning shot into the air from atop the hill. I threw a massive cloud of poison towards the constables barreling down the slope while I flicked a quick look up at the magic tearing into the sky above.

That could only be a signal, which meant that reinforcements would soon be coming. A sudden flash of panic shot through me. Back-up was coming... from behind. They were going to trap us between the army on the hill and the reinforcements that were no doubt moving towards us this very second. *Shit*. We were supposed to be the ones launching the sneak attack. How the hell had we managed to fail this badly?

Men and women collapsed to the ground and tumbled down the hill as my poison magic slammed into their charging ranks. Lightning shot across the grass as the survivors aimed for me. I dove sideways, rolling out of the way. Before I had even gotten to my feet, I sent my fastest attack towards them.

I needed to get out of here. I needed to warn the others about the attack that would be coming from behind. We needed to figure out what the hell had gone wrong and how we were supposed to win this now.

Glittering green mist exploded across the grass, making the constables slam to a halt and throw up interlocking magic in order to avoid getting hit. I didn't hesitate a second. Whirling around, I sprinted the final bit down and leaped onto the street.

A jolt shot through my legs as I landed on the stones, but I just slapped my palms together and blindly threw another poison cloud behind me while darting towards the next street and the cover it would provide. Grabbing the edge of the building, I skidded around the corner while casting a glance over my shoulder.

The constables had trailed to a halt. Some of them were just standing there, staring after me, while others split off to attack some of Levi's dark mages who had been positioned to my left and right, and who were also trying to retreat now.

It made sense that they would want to remain on the hill. After all, they had the high ground and they knew that more of them would be coming to push us back towards the hill again.

But I still wasn't taking any chances, so I ran as fast as I could from them and towards our rendezvous spot.

The reinforcements would no doubt be the people that Quill had stationed at the academy, which meant that the former mages we had recruited no longer needed to keep up their ruse.

While darting around the next corner, I brushed my palms together and shot a glittering green column into the air. Since my magic was the easiest to both spot and distinguish from Quill's forces, we had told the people we had recruited that I would be the one sending up a flare if we needed them to come. Hopefully, they wouldn't chicken out on us now. We needed them to follow the constables and keep them distracted so that we could get up the hill before they could arrive and box us in.

My breath sawed through my chest as I took a left down the next street.

Right then, someone else ran around another corner up ahead and skidded to a halt just a few steps in front of me.

I called up a poison attack, but the mist dissipated when my eyes focused on the person's face. Slamming to a halt, I just stared at the dark-haired woman. Her chest was heaving, as if she had just sprinted here too.

"Audrey," she said.

Her voice snapped me out of my trance, and I lifted my chin slightly as I replied, "Jenny."

My sister watched me with sad gray eyes. Eyes full of pity. The sight of it made my blood boil, but I managed to restrain myself.

"Please stop this." She shook her head at me. "You can still come home with us, and things can go back to the way they were."

I could feel the steel creeping into my voice and the way my features hardened as I locked eyes with her. "And what makes you think that I would even want to?"

"Because we're your family."

"Really? Is that why you have pretended that I don't exist for the past six years?"

"You're a dark mage, Audrey!" She threw out her arms in an exasperated gesture. It made her long black hair ripple around her shoulders. "You betrayed the whole city. You betrayed *us*. What were we supposed to do?"

I didn't have an answer to that, and I was suddenly thoroughly done with this conversation, so I just shook my head at her and started forwards again. Clouds drifted over the sun, casting the pale stone street in temporary shadow. A few yellow flowers trembled on a windowsill as a gust swept between the stone buildings, making the colorful petals flutter.

"Look, I'm sorry that I didn't help you last time." Jenny took a couple of steps to the left until she was standing in front of me, blocking my way down the street. "But I'm here now."

"To do what?"

"To help you. It's like I always tell my students, it's never too late to start doing the right thing."

Anger rippled through me, and I bristled at the way she compared me to her students. As if I was some kind of troubled teen who didn't know what I was doing. I wasn't troubled. Or confused. I had chosen the dark mage path knowing full well the consequences it would have. That it would turn me into a person with dark morals and an even darker heart. That it would fill my life with threats and blood and violence. I knew all of that when I decided to escape Eldar. And now, six years later, I still wouldn't change a thing.

"Step aside, Jenny," I simply said in reply.

She threw her arms out wide, as if that would actually stop me. "No. I can't let you do this. I can't let you go back and hurt more people."

"*I* hurt people?" I stabbed a hand in the direction of the academy. "Quill sent students to attack us. Students! Maybe we're not the ones you need to worry about."

"Trust me, after you ran, Chancellor Quill got an earful from the rest of his parliament about that. Why do you think he had to move the—" Panic flashed across her features, and she abruptly snapped her mouth shut.

A smirk tugged at my lips as I raised an eyebrow and finished, "Why he had to move the Blade of Equilibrium to the parliament building instead of the academy?"

Embarrassment blew across her face, and she cleared her throat. "You knew about that?"

"Of course we do. Otherwise, why would we be here, attacking it?"

"Yes, well..." She trailed off. But she looked immensely relieved now that she knew that she hadn't just shared an important secret with us by accident. Pulling her usual confidence back around her, she raised her chin. "Chancellor Quill moved the blade to the parliament building to protect the students, who will remain at the academy until this is over. So he is not the one putting people in danger right now. You are."

Lifting an arm, I forcibly pushed her sideways and then took a step forward. Her hand shot up and grabbed my shoulder. I shrugged it off as I whirled around to face her again.

"Please, Audrey," she began before I could spit out the words on my tongue. "I can help you." Her gray eyes were pleading. "This is what I do all day. Helping troubled students find their path again."

Rage roared through me. "I am not your student. And I have already found my path." Brushing my hands together, I summoned a poison whip that snaked around my wrist while I locked hard eyes on my sister. "Now, get the hell out of my way."

"Please, you..." She trailed off as boots pounded against the ground. Relief flickered in her eyes.

I snapped my gaze towards the street that Jenny had come from. A moment later, four constables rounded the corner and poured out onto the street. I hurled my poison at them, making it expand into a cloud. Since my attack had already been ready and waiting while they were still rounding the corner, they didn't even have time to bring their hands together.

All four of them collapsed dead on the ground as my lethal magic forced its way down their throats.

A terrible coldness seeped into my chest as I dragged my gaze back to Jenny. "You knew they were coming." It was a statement, not a question. "You were just trying to keep me occupied until they got here."

Wind hit me in the chest. It was hard enough to make me stumble back several steps. I blinked at the scene before me while shock clanged through my head.

Jenny was standing on the pale cobblestones a short distance away. She had shifted into a battle position, and wind magic whooshed around her. I stared at her, dumbfounded.

Another blast of wind shot towards me.

I leaped aside, and it slammed into the stone wall on my left instead.

"You're going to fight me?" I asked, raising my eyebrows.

"You just killed four people!"

"All the more reason for you to back off."

"I am not afraid of you."

"You should be."

"Doing the right thing might be hard." She shot more wind at me. "But someone has to stand up against all the bad things. And good will always win against evil in the end."

I sidestepped the wind blasts and rolled my eyes while touching my hands together. "You sound like Lance Carmichael."

"Because he is right to—"

Green tendrils shot through the air. I slapped my hands together in rapid succession, shooting a hail of poison straight for her. Panic flashed in her eyes as she summoned wind to block it. But she had spent the past six years teaching people to do the right thing. I had spent them slaughtering anyone who got in my way. The difference in skill and power was ridiculous.

She sucked in a gasp as a poison tendril forced its way down her throat. I let the magic sweep through her body. Her arms dropped down by her sides and her knees buckled, sending her crashing down on the street.

Cocking my head, I watched her choke and dry heave there

on the ground for a few seconds. "I can't believe I wanted to be just like you."

Only strangled noises answered me.

"All that time, I tried so hard to live up to the insanely high bar you set. To be you. But here's the thing... I don't want to be *you*. Hell, why did—"

The back of my neck prickled, and I yanked my body sideways on pure instinct.

Pain burned through my side. I sucked in a gasp, losing the grip on my magic, as I whirled around. The clouds above blew clear, and sunlight glinted against a sharp sword.

Leaping backwards, I barely manage to avoid the second strike as the constable who had snuck up behind me swung his blade again. He pressed the advantage. My whole left side felt like it was on fire, and I couldn't stifle a cry of pain when I twisted sideways to avoid the next lunge.

Steel whooshed as the sword cleaved the air a mere inch from my chest.

Before he could get it back into position, I slammed a hard kick into the side of his knee. Pain flashed in his eyes as his leg buckled and he staggered a step to the side. I slapped my palms together and shot a poison cloud right into his face before he could recover.

Dark blue eyes widened in shock. Then he toppled backwards and hit the ground with a series of thuds.

I glanced down at my side. Blood welled out of a deep cut along the side of my ribs.

But before I could do anything about it, someone else moved at the corner of my eye. Jenny. Pushing to her feet, she moved her arms as if she was going to summon magic again.

Shit. I couldn't fight her while I was also bleeding out.

With great effort, I slammed my hands together and shot

another poison cloud before Jenny could even get fully on her feet.

"Audrey—" she gasped out.

Then she too crumpled to the ground.

My own legs hit the cobblestones a couple of seconds later. Gritting my teeth, I lifted a hand and pressed it against my side while pain burned through my body. Warm blood welled up over my fingers and ran down to form a small red pool on the stones.

Fuck.

After sucking in a bracing breath, I pushed to my feet again. I needed to get to Sam.

Pain ricocheted through my body, and I wobbled slightly. Throwing out an arm, I braced myself on the wall next to me. My hand left a red smear on the pale stones.

Then I looked back at Jenny.

She was only unconscious for now. A part of me wondered if I should just kill her too and be done with it. But in the end, I only turned my back on her and staggered towards the other side of the street.

Blood ran through my fingers, leaving the ground splattered in red behind me.

Chapter 33

Callan

"Take half of our people and form a barrier along these streets." Levi's commanding voice cut through the air like a blade. "We need to cut off their reinforcements before they can box us in."

Skidding to a halt, I whipped my head from side to side while the dark mage Levi had spoken to took off down the street. Sam and Paige had remained in this spot, just like we had instructed. And so far, Henry, Levi, Malcolm, and Grant had arrived as well. My heart constricted painfully when I couldn't find any trace of Audrey. But Sienna wasn't back yet either, so that didn't necessarily mean that something was wrong. I hoped.

"What the hell happened?" I snapped as I swept my gaze over them. "How did they know that we were coming?"

"That was my next question," Levi growled, his gray eyes flashing with anger and violence. "I have never seen a dark mage attack fail this badly. Are you people amateurs or what?"

Fury flickered in Malcolm's eyes. "Careful."

"Or what?"

"Enough," Grant interrupted. "What matters is what our

next move is. We all saw the signal. Reinforcements are coming from the academy. So how do we get up the hill before they arrive?"

"My people should be able to hold them off for a while," Levi said.

"And Audrey sent up that flare earlier too," Sam added. His worried gray eyes shifted from face to face. "Which means that all those angry people you recruited should be coming here to help too, right?"

Malcolm nodded. "Yes."

I just flicked another glance around the empty streets. Our rendezvous spot was tucked in between a small cluster of wooden buildings. It was far enough away from the hill to avoid attack, but because the ground that these streets were on rose up a bit, it still provided a partial view of what was going on.

"Where *is* Audrey?" I asked while terror carved its way through my ribcage.

"And Sienna?" Grant added.

"I spotted Sienna's dark red flames a short distance that way." Paige pointed towards the left side of the hill. "About three minutes ago." Worry swirled in her eyes as she slid her gaze to me. "No sight of Audrey's magic after that flare."

"We need to..." I trailed off as a figure staggered around the corner.

Ice spread through my veins.

Audrey was leaning heavily against the wall with her right hand, while her left was pressed against the side of her ribs. Her hand and the clothes on that side were covered in blood. Black strands had escaped her ponytail and they lay plastered to her face, which was sweaty and far too pale.

"Sam," I snapped while I took off in a sprint.

At the sound of my voice, Audrey lifted her head. Her normally so glittering green eyes were dull and glassy with pain, and for a moment, she just stared at me. Then her knees buckled.

I reached her right before she could hit the street. Scooping her up into my arms, I spun around and ran back towards Sam.

Audrey let out a pained groan and curled her fingers against my leather armor.

My heart almost shattered at the sound. This wasn't supposed to happen. She was supposed to be fine. I—

"Put her down on the ground," Sam's voice interrupted.

Yanked out of my despair, I realized that I had reached the others again. With careful movements, I crouched down and placed Audrey gently on the warm stones. She let out another small groan of pain between gritted teeth.

"You can fix this, right?" I asked, glancing up at Sam who knelt on her other side. "She'll be alright?"

"Yes. Now, stop distracting me and let me work."

Shimmering turquoise blue magic appeared between his hands before he shifted them so that they hovered over Audrey's side. He kept his eyes locked on the wound while a look of concentration descended on his features.

I just sat there, completely useless, and stared down at her pale face while I tried desperately to stop my heart from fracturing. Audrey. *My* Audrey. Reaching out, I placed my hand gently on hers. Her fingers curled around mine and gave it a small squeeze.

"You're not allowed to die, you know?" Paige said as she lowered herself to her knees next to Audrey's head. She lifted a hand and brushed the loose strands of hair from Audrey's face. "You left me for six years. You're not allowed to leave again."

Audrey laughed, which immediately made her wince in pain. After gasping in a breath, she managed to press out, "Guilt-tripping a dying girl, huh?"

"Oh you know me, nothing is beneath me."

Another strained laugh bubbled from her chest.

Sam shot her a sharp look. "Please stop moving so much."

She gave him a sheepish grin. "Sorry."

"What happened?" I asked.

Her eyes found mine again. "I got distracted."

Before she could elaborate further, another figure appeared from the opposite side of the street. Red hair whipped in the air as Sienna sprinted the final bit to us. Slamming to a halt, she whipped her head, flicking her long hair back behind her shoulder again.

Rage burned in her eyes. "This is why I hate people. I did them a favor, and this is how they repay me?"

A cold weight sank into my stomach.

But it was Malcolm who spoke up, his voice deceptively smooth. "What favor?"

"I told the people who live in the buildings closest to the hill to take their pets and leave before the fighting started."

She spoke the words as if it was the most natural thing in the world. Everyone else fell silent. Deadly silent. Ice sluiced through my veins. If I didn't do something to deescalate the situation, heads were going to roll within the next minute. As if she could sense it too, Audrey pushed against my hand in a silent command to get up and stop our allies from slaughtering each other.

After glancing down to make sure that Sam's magic was truly working, I gave her hand one more squeeze and then slowly pushed to my feet.

"Excuse me?" Malcolm said into the deafening silence. "I must have misheard you. Can you repeat that?"

Sienna frowned as if he was being an idiot. "I went to their houses earlier this morning and warned them to take their pets and leave."

Before the final word had even left her lips, Levi grabbed

her by the collar and slammed her up against the wall. Fear spiked up my spine when he growled, "You did what?"

I knew that voice. It meant that Sienna had exactly five seconds to explain herself before he cut her head off.

Dark red flames spread along Sienna's arms until it looked like she was wearing armor made of fire. Locking eyes with Levi, she said in a perfectly flat voice that was terrifyingly devoid of all emotion, "Take your hands off me, metal man. Or they will be washing what's left of your melted body from the streets tomorrow."

Alarm bells were blaring inside my skull. This was spinning out of control. If we didn't separate them now, they would kill each other. I took a step forward, but someone else beat me to it.

Henry placed one hand on Levi's shoulder and the other one on Sienna's. With calm movements, he used his massive frame to push the two of them apart. Both of them let out a low warning noise, but Henry only looked from face to face.

"We have more pressing problems right now," he said. "Remember?"

"There," Sam said from behind me. "All done."

I looked down to find him releasing his magic and rising to his feet. Audrey, who looked like herself again, drew in a deep breath and then let Paige help her to her feet.

"You have no idea what you've done," Malcolm said, his dark eyes still locked on Sienna. "This whole attack failed because of you. Because you warned people before our surprise attack!"

Levi had released her and taken a step back, but it looked like he was using all of his self-control to stop himself from murdering Sienna. Henry positioned himself slightly between the two of them, as if to prevent any lapses in judgement on their part.

"My fault?" Sienna snapped. "You think this is my fault?"

"Yes."

"This is not on me." Rage flared up in her eyes again, and she stabbed a hand towards me and Audrey. "You screwed up this mission long before I even got here."

I frowned at her while Audrey moved over to stand next to me. "What are you talking about?"

"The hostage exchange. You could've just killed those students when they ran out to attack you instead of sacrificing the whole bloody mission."

"So you would've killed thirteen-year-olds?"

"Yes!" She threw her arms out. "I don't care if the people who attack me are thirteen or eighty-three. If they willingly and knowingly attack me, they die. But hurting animals... *That's* where I draw the line." She flicked a hand towards the buildings around the hill. "I couldn't risk innocent animals getting burned alive in my flames during the fight. That's why I told the people who lived there to get their pets and go. We all draw the line somewhere, and that's where I draw mine."

"Fucking hell, Sienna." Tilting my head back, I forced out a long breath and raked my fingers through my hair.

Before she could say anything else, Grant spoke up. "We're getting off topic. Those reinforcements are coming, and we need a plan."

"How do we even know if the Blade of Equilibrium is still in the parliament building?" Paige looked from face to face. "Quill could've moved it the moment those people warned him about the coming attack."

Cold dread twisted in my stomach. She was right. There was no way to know whether the blade was still in there. Not now. And we were about to be trapped between two armies. If we charged up the hill only for the blade to not even be there...

Fuck.

"It's still in there."

We all turned towards Audrey and blinked in surprise.

"That distraction I mentioned?" She shrugged. "It was my sister. And she accidentally let slip that Quill moved the blade to the parliament building in order to keep the fighting away from the academy and protect the students."

Malcolm narrowed his eyes. "She could have been lying. It could be bait."

"It could have been. But she's a shitty liar, so I know it's not."

"Are you certain enough to stake all of our lives on it?"

"Yes," she replied without hesitation.

For a few seconds, no one said anything. Then we all nodded.

"Alright," I began. "Then we need—"

"Stop." Levi, who looked a bit less like he was going to slaughter us all, swept his gaze between all of us. "One thing at a time. Before we even begin planning how to get back up that hill, we need to handle the situation down here. My people will be able to hold those constables off for a bit, especially if those other people you recruited show up and help too. But we need something more. We can't fight our way up the hill if we have to worry about being shot in the back."

It was at times like these that I realized why I respected Levi as much as I did. He might be violent and arrogant and an utter bastard, but there was a reason why he had come to rule half of Malgrave. He was extremely good at what he did.

"I don't know this city like you do," Levi continued. "So if you have any suggestions, speak up now."

A light flared up behind Grant's blue eyes, and he turned to Sienna. "Do the constables who are coming in from the academy know that all of the houses around the hill are empty?"

We all shifted our attention to the fire mage.

She scrunched up her brows. "I don't think so."

"Good. Then we have an opportunity."

"What kind of opportunity?" Malcolm asked.

"Sienna," Grant began.

The fire mage frowned at him. "What?"

"Torch it."

"Torch what?"

A malicious smile spread across Grant's mouth. It was an expression I had rarely seen from the emotion mage. He usually kept his feelings well hidden, but now I could practically read the sneaky wickedness that hid behind his casual appearance.

"All of it."

Chapter 34

"They're coming!" Henry bellowed from up the street. Whipping around, he sprinted towards us. Callan and I were standing at the end of the street while the rest of our people were similarly placed in the mouths of the roads running parallel to ours. Only Paige and Sam remained a safe distance away.

When Henry was halfway down the street, the first constables rounded the corner.

My heart slammed against my ribs. This had better work. Otherwise, we'd be trapped in a battle we wouldn't be able to escape from.

Callan's half-translucent gray magic shot down the street when one of the constables hurled a fireball at Henry's back. Yellow flames exploded into the air as they slammed into the force wall.

A moment later, Henry skidded to a halt between me and Callan before whipping around to face our enemies again.

"Ready?" Callan asked without taking his eyes off the men and women marching towards us.

"Yeah," we answered in unison.

Thick white clouds currently blocked out the sun, which painted the whole street in gloomy gray light. No one spoke. The only sound was the thumping of boots that echoed between the wooden buildings, both from our road and the ones next to us.

I touched my hands together. Glittering green mist lit up the whole street as I threw the poison cloud towards the constables. Walls of water and wind rose up to shove it aside. But Callan shot a spinning force arc at them right after my attack.

Screams erupted as it slammed into a woman who didn't manage to block in time. Blood spurted from her severed arm. I shot a hail of poison tendrils towards them. Lightning and fire tore down the street as they began attacking in earnest.

Their attacks cracked into the wooden walls around us as Henry expertly used his wind magic to shove the blasts aside.

Callan and I increased the speed of our attacks. Green and gray magic shot through the air, twisting and spinning around to avoid each other before slamming into our enemies. It forced the soldiers to grind to a halt and focus on blocking our attacks.

Behind them, the rest of their company kept pouring into the street.

Since they couldn't very well shoot through their own comrades, only the first couple of rows were able to launch attacks at us.

Shouts and barked orders and whooshing magic came from the other streets as well, informing us that similar events were taking place there too.

Due to the sheer number of people facing us, very few of our attacks actually managed to slip through their mass of layered shields. But because of our fast and powerful attacks, they couldn't advance either. My pulse thrummed in my ears as the road in front of us grew more and more packed with people.

They would try to rush us soon. And we wouldn't survive that.

I shot poison cloud after poison cloud while anxiety tore at my chest. Where the hell was Sienna?

Three dark red fireballs shot into the air from our left and sailed across the partially blue sky above our heads.

Not hesitating a second, the three of us whipped around and ran like hell itself was chasing us.

Calls of pursuit echoed between the wooden buildings. They were followed by the pounding of boots and the whooshing of magic. Callan twisted around and threw a force wall behind us while he continued running. The move made him stumble slightly, and I had to throw out an arm to stop him from crashing into me.

Booms split the air and lightning flashed as their attacks slammed into his wall.

The end of the next street was so close now. We had to make it in time. I was falling behind Callan and Henry. Their legs were much longer than mine, so I couldn't run as fast. Fuck, I had to—

A yelp slipped from my lips as Callan grabbed my arm and practically threw me the final distance and onto the next street while he and Henry dove after me.

Pain shot through my shoulder as I landed hard on the cobblestones and rolled in behind the wide stone statue of a horse that we had picked out.

Merely a fraction of a second later, the world erupted in fire.

Dark red flames tore through the buildings on our left and crashed into the ones on the right. The massive wave of fire washed away the wooden walls as if they were thin sheets of paper.

Callan flung an arm over my back, keeping me down behind the base of the statue. But between the horse's white stone legs, I could see the incredible destruction that Sienna Hall was raining down on our enemies.

Screams were abruptly cut off as constables were burnt to ash in seconds. And the cries coming from the ones at the back, who had escaped the fiery wave, were drowned out by the roaring of the fire as it continued sweeping through the buildings.

Not for the first time, I thanked hell that I had never been stupid enough to go to war against Sienna. The sheer depth of her raw power was fucking terrifying.

When the dark red torrent at last faded out, the buildings closest to us were completely gone. As was the mass of constables who we had made sure were packed between them. The buildings farther back were still standing, but they were all on fire. It created a burning shield that kept the rest of the reinforcements from reaching us straight away.

"Let's go," Callan said as he jumped up from the ground.

Henry and I climbed to our feet as well.

After one last look at the smoking ruins, we turned around and jogged back to our rendezvous spot. Half of Levi's forces ran in the other direction. With a large section of the constables dead, and a flame barrier between them and us, those dark mages should be able to keep the rest at bay. Especially if the people we had recruited were also harassing them from behind. We had no way of knowing if they were, but this was as much protection as we would be able to create for ourselves, so we'd have to make do regardless.

Everyone except Sienna was already gathered in between the buildings. One shared look confirmed that we were all thinking the same thing. Thank hell that Sienna was on *our* side.

Sam was healing a cut on Grant's arm. I had no idea how he had gotten it, but it didn't look like he was in pain at all.

Though with Grant, it was hard to tell because of his mastery of emotion magic.

"Did it work?" Sienna called as she came running from the street from our left.

We all shared another long, knowing look.

"Yes," Malcolm replied, sliding his gaze to her. "Well done, Sienna."

She grinned at him.

"Alright, our backs are protected," Levi cut in. "Now, how do we get up the hill?"

Sienna flicked her hair behind her shoulder. "Why can't I just do the same thing I did now to those constables on the hill?"

"Because," Callan began, "as opposed to those idiots who were trapped between the buildings, the people on the hill can see an attack coming from miles away. Both because they have the high ground and also because it's a long way up from the street. I doubt even you could manage an attack from that range."

She pursed her lips, but then tipped her head to the side and nodded as if conceding the point.

"So how do we launch an attack that they don't see coming?" Sam asked.

"About that..." I began. "I think I have an idea."

Callan huffed out a short laugh. "Shocker."

I rammed my elbow into his ribs. "Shut up. Someone has to be the brains of the operation."

"The idea...?" Malcolm prompted, eyebrows raised in an exasperated expression, before Callan could retort.

"Since we don't have to fight fair, we might as well go all in with that. Listen up."

Most of them looked back at me with expressions that ranged from surprise to approval. From her place next to Henry,

Paige outright grinned at me. The King of Metal, on the other hand, scowled at me by the time I had finished.

"You want me to do *what*?" he demanded.

I raised my eyebrows at him. "Are you saying that you can't do it?"

"Of course I can do it." He shot me an affronted look before he went back to frowning. "But it's... ridiculous."

"I think you mean brilliant."

"If it works."

"It will work." I turned to Paige. "Can you get it done?"

She rolled her eyes at me. "Is that even a question? How many fake notes have I forged by now?"

A chuckle escaped my lips. "I'll take that as a yes." I slid my gaze to our healer, who had finished with Grant's arm. "Sam, stay close. This first wave is going to get messy."

He nodded.

"Alright, let's say it does work," Levi began, dragging the conversation back to his skepticism. "Then what? The whole corridor inside the doors is no doubt crawling with constables too. And once we're up there, we'll be vulnerable, so we can't stand around trying to come up with another plan. Once we get inside, we can bolt the door behind us if need be. But how do we make it into the first room inside the building?"

"Grant," Malcolm said. There was a smug smile playing at the corner of his lips as he turned towards the emotion mage. "You and I discovered a surprisingly effective attack out in the hills. What do you say we show them what we can do?"

Harvey Grant's mouth curled into a smile so cruel that the hairs on my arms rose. By all hell, I really hadn't known these people at all. Out in the hills, we had all been so busy fighting each other that we had never actually gotten to know one another. This war, for better or worse, had given me a glimpse into what the other dark mages were truly like. In some ways, it had made me even more wary of them. But it had also made me respect them more. Made me feel some kind of connection to them. And I was pretty sure that that wasn't a bad thing. After all, we villains of the world had to stick together if we wanted to survive the sweeping tide of heroism.

"Gladly," Grant replied, that terrifying smile still on his lips.

An idea flickered through my brain, and I turned towards Callan while an equally wicked grin slid home on my mouth.

He raised his eyebrows. "What?"

"Who said we need to use the front door?"

Chapter 35

Callan

The sun had climbed higher up in the sky and the thick white clouds were moving, which currently bathed the hill in sunlight that was only broken up by the occasional patches of shade. Behind us, buildings were on fire. Dark red flames licked the wooden structures greedily as the remnants of Sienna's attack kept spreading through the deserted houses. Sounds of battle rose behind the wall of flame where Levi's dark mages were fighting the surviving constables, who were also trying their best to put out the fires before they spread to the rest of the city.

I stood at the mouth of the final street separating the hill from the road that ran around its base. Tilting my head back, I stared up at the gleaming parliament building at the top. The constables up there were moving. It was difficult to tell from here, but it looked like they were shifting their forces so that they were clustered around the front of the building.

"Paige says it's done," Henry's voice suddenly rang out.

Turning around, I found him drawing in a deep breath and slowing to a walk as he closed the final distance to us. I swept my gaze over the others. A ripple of anticipation, and excitement, pulsed through the air.

"Alright then," Levi said, and gave him a nod before shifting his gaze to Audrey. "Let's see if this ridiculous plan of yours works then."

I could see her getting ready to say something snarky, so I spoke up before she could. "Henry, keep Sam safe."

"Yes, boss."

"The rest of you, you know what to do."

"And remember what I always say," Sam began, looking from face to face. "I can heal you..."

"But not if we're dead," we all finished with smiles that were half amusement, half exasperation.

"Exactly." His gray eyes locked on Audrey. "You especially were cutting it a bit too close earlier. Don't do that again."

Another stab of panic shot through my chest at the thought of Audrey almost bleeding to death on the street. All I had wanted to do after Sam had healed her was to wrap my arms around her and hold her until I could make sure that she was okay. But I didn't want her to feel as though she looked weak and frail in front of the other dark mages, so I had used every ounce of my willpower and simply squeezed her hand instead. The look of gratitude she had stealthily shot me afterwards informed me that I had made the right choice.

"I promise," Audrey said.

"Good."

"Do you people always stand around and talk this much?" Levi demanded, and shook his head at us. "Let's get this done already."

Before anyone could retort, he spun on his heel and took off towards the hill. I resisted the urge to hurl a force wall into his back, and instead turned to Audrey and raised my eyebrows in silent question. She nodded.

We started forwards as well. Behind us, Grant and Malcolm paired up to do the same. As did Sam and Henry. Sienna, to no one's surprise, sprinted towards the hill on her own. The rest of Levi's dark mages followed.

My heart thrummed in my chest as Audrey and I leaped onto the grass and ran up the slope. This time, I would make sure that she didn't get hurt.

Orders rang out from atop the hill.

And then the onslaught started.

Wind and water and lightning barreled down the hill. It crashed into Levi's metal wall with a deafening boom. I threw up a force shield in front of me and Audrey while Malcolm covered him and Grant with a mass of twisting shadows. Sienna just shot a torrent of flames up the hill to counter the attacks.

Magic whooshed and lights flashed across the grass as we tried to force our way up the main path in a combined assault. But the constables had been ready. They had shifted their troops from around the building so that the bulk of their force was located right in our path.

I yanked up force shield after force shield while Audrey shot her poison attacks between them. Screams rang out on our left as Sienna managed to burn a small section that wasn't able to shield in time. The rest of them threw up synchronized water walls.

White steam exploded across the grass as her flames met their mass of shields.

My heart pounded in my chest.

There was no way that we would ever make it through all these people. We were more powerful, and much more skilled, but there were simply too many of them. This had to work.

A scream split the air to my left. I snapped my gaze towards it to find Sienna clutching her arm. It hung limply by her side, probably due to a lightning strike. Sam and Henry rushed towards her, but I had to shift my gaze back to the path ahead. Fire roared through the air.

I yanked up a force wall right before it could wash over us. Yellow flames slammed into it before being redirected up into the sky. Next to me, Audrey didn't even flinch. As if she had never doubted that I would protect us in time.

It really was incredible how our relationship had changed these past few months. Before we went on that first mission to get Lance, she wouldn't have trusted me with a butter knife. Now, she placed her life in my hands without even batting an eye.

Battle cries echoed across the trampled grass.

I shoved the final waves of yellow flame aside to find the constables charging down the hill in force. Calling up another wall, I hurled it at them. But it was like trying to stop the tide. Boots pounded against the ground as row after row poured down the slope.

"Fall back!" Malcolm yelled across the deafening noise.

As one, we turned and ran down the hill again. To my left, Sam was dragging one of Levi's wounded dark mages with him while Henry covered their retreat. Sienna shot a massive torrent of fire towards our enemies, but they raised layered water walls to block it.

Steam hissed as the fire struck them.

I drew in a deep breath as I stopped by the stone wall outside the mouth of the street while Audrey and the others ran through the opening between the buildings.

The soldiers stopped their advance halfway down the hill, and cheers of victory rang out. Then they began retreating towards the parliament building again. From my position across the road, I simply watched them. They thought that they had won. But the fight was far from over.

Solid walls of metal shot up from the ground where Audrey

and Levi and the others had been standing. They formed a gigantic box that just barely fit between the buildings. I grinned at the constables up ahead as a ripple of confusion went through their ranks.

The massive metal box remained at the mouth of the street for another couple of minutes while the others got everything ready. Far behind us, red flames still consumed the buildings while Levi's dark mages fought the surviving reinforcements.

Then, the box moved forward.

With that grin still on my lips, I advanced as well, walking slightly to the side of the metal structure.

Let's see them try to counter this.

Metallic grinding filled the warm air as the box moved across the street and then started up the main stone path leading up the hill. I kept pace with it while staying on the grass to the right of it so that I would be able to shield it with my magic.

The confusion up ahead turned into alarm. Then shouted orders.

Touching my palms together, I called up a force wall.

Fire shot towards the metal box. I hurled my force wall in front of it, stopping the worst of the attacks. Embers sailed into the air as the flames licked the sky instead.

My pulse thrummed in my ears. *Fucking hell, Audrey. This had better work.*

The soldiers kept bombarding the box, and I tried my best to shield it and myself, while it continued moving up the hill. Sweat ran down my spine. It was taking every ounce of concentration I possessed to raise force walls in time to block both the attacks shot at the box, and the ones directed at me. My chest was heaving, and every nerve felt like it was crackling with pent-up tension.

Lightning zapped right past me.

I barely managed to yank my body out of the way in time.

Before I could call up another shield, the rows of soldiers broke. Screaming battle cries, they charged towards me. I cast a quick glance at the giant metal box next to me. Then I turned and sprinted down the hill.

Fire and wind slammed into the sides of the box as I left it unprotected while hurtling towards the safety of the street below. Ear-splitting booms echoed across the city as the constables swarmed the box and attacked it with everything they had. It ground to a halt halfway up the hill.

Leaping the final bit, I landed hard on the road below and then sprinted over to the mouth of the alley before swinging around to face the battle up on the slope. Except it wasn't exactly a battle since only one side was attacking.

My heart slammed against my ribs as I watched an entire horde of constables surround the metal box. Magic crashed into it from every direction, making it rock precariously.

I sucked in a deep breath to slow my heaving chest.

An unending hail of attacks bombarded the box.

From my position on the street, I watched as the four walls of the box suddenly snapped and toppled outwards. They landed on the stone path and the grass next to it with crashing booms that reverberated through the air.

Purple and orange light flashed.

And then the world exploded.

Throwing up an arm to shield my eyes, I twisted away as four massive explosions tore through the sea of soldiers.

Bloodcurdling screams ripped through the air, but most of them were abruptly silenced.

Once the flashing lights had faded, I lowered my arm and looked up at the carnage. The vast majority of the soldiers who had swarmed the metal box were gone. Blood painted the grass red, and torn limbs lay scattered up and down the hill. The surviving constables farther up had been blown backwards by the shock wave, and utter terror and dread pulsed on their faces as they staggered upright while staring down the hill.

A few steps behind me, someone threw up. Loudly.

I turned to find Paige bent over, hurling up the contents of her stomach while Sam gently patted her on the back.

"Told you it would work," Audrey said, and shot a smirk in Levi's direction as the two of them strode towards me.

Levi let out something between a scoff and a chuckle, but tilted his head in an acknowledging nod.

It really had been a brilliant plan. And an insane one.

First, we'd had Paige forge some messages that told the constables that we had been spotted organizing a combined attack up the main path. And to make sure that they bought it, we had to do just that. The first wave of attack was to make sure that they clustered in the way we wanted them to. Then, we retreated again.

While hidden from view by the buildings, Audrey and Levi and the others pretended to go inside that giant metal box. Then, all Levi had to do was to stand inside one of the buildings and move the metal up the hill while I protected it from the outside to make sure it got close enough to the constables. A couple of Levi's explosion mages had already rigged the inside with those massive explosions, so when Levi dropped the walls, all they had to do was to detonate them. With the constables all swarming it, thinking that dark mages were hiding inside, they didn't stand a chance when the explosions went off.

Indeed, a brilliant plan. And ruthless as fuck.

Another door creaked open, and Malcolm, Sienna, and Grant moved out of the building they had been hiding inside as well before approaching us. A couple of Levi's dark mages did the same, though they stopped and leaned against the wall behind us a respectful distance away.

"So, it's done?" Malcolm asked, turning to one of Levi's explosion mages.

The man, with dark hair and ice blue eyes, slid his gaze towards the hill.

I glanced up at the constables. Some of the ones farther up had run down the slope and were now trying to drag any survivors back up with them.

Another couple of seconds passed.

Then two more explosions tore through the air, killing the constables who had been trying to rescue the survivors as well.

Still leaning against the wall, the blue-eyed explosion mage slid his cool gaze back to us and lifted one shoulder in a shrug. "Now it's done."

Paige threw up again.

"How are you holding up?" Henry asked.

While bracing one hand on the wall, she waved the other in our general direction and croaked, "I'm fine."

"Great!" Sienna flashed us all a glittering smile that was tinged with a bit of madness. "Then let's go storm the parliament building."

Chapter 36

Paige, who couldn't stomach passing through the bloodbath on the grass, darted down the road on our left along with Levi and some of his people. To my relief, Henry joined them as well. I didn't exactly trust the King of Metal to keep my friend safe, but I knew that Henry would.

I glanced back at the small group that remained. Callan, Malcolm, Sienna, Grant, Sam, and me. The six dark mages of Eldar. We were the ones who had started all of this months ago when we sat down for a more or less unprecedented meeting in Essington's mansion. After that, we had schemed and plotted and traveled halfway across the world. We had fought and bled and killed together. And now, it was high time that we finished this.

After sharing a long look, we took off towards the parliament building above.

The walls from the metal box had disappeared into thin air now since Levi had released the grip on his magic. But blood smeared the pale path with streaks of red, and torn body parts littered the trampled grass. Running right through it, the six of us made our way towards the plateau at the top.

The constables who had survived the explosions were still waiting up there, and a nervous ripple went through their ranks when they saw us coming. They still outnumbered us by a lot, so we all called up magic, ready for another battle.

For a couple of seconds, the men and women on top of the hill only stared down at us as we plowed ahead with magic crackling around us.

Then they broke and ran.

Surprise flitted through me.

Whirling around, the whole mass of soldiers sprinted down the sides of the hill without looking back.

Though, after our little stunt with the box and the explosions, I supposed that I shouldn't have been surprised that morale was low and fear ran rampart.

We still kept our magic up, just in case it was a trap, while we ran towards the front doors. But the constables didn't turn back to ambush us. Instead, they fled down the hill and disappeared into the city.

I heaved a deep sigh. *Good.* I was getting a bit tired of fighting, and we still had to get through the actual building in order to reach Quill and the Blade of Equilibrium, so not having to engage in any more battles out here was a relief.

We slowed to a walk as we at last reached the top of the hill. Only some discarded swords lay scattered on the ground. Other than that, it was empty. I retied the string holding back my hair and then adjusted my metal corset.

After Sam had healed me, and before we set the trap where Sienna burned down those buildings, I had changed into the spare clothes I had kept stashed at our rendezvous spot. Previously, I had been wearing my tightfitting riding outfit. It had seemed the most practical choice since I knew that we would be running up a hill. But after that damn constable managed to stab me, I had come to my senses and gone back to my usual attire. They might be a bit less practical to run in, but at least my half armor dresses guarded against blades between my ribs.

"Well then, boys," Sienna said as she stopped in front of the doors and turned back to raise her eyebrows at Malcolm and Grant. "We're waiting with bated breath."

Grant gave her a sly smile as the two of them stepped up to the door. "Prepare to be dazzled, my dear."

The three of us took a step back to give them more space as they positioned themselves side by side in front of the closed door. As one, they touched their hands together.

Dark shadows twisted around Malcolm's wrists before dripping down from his hands like a stream of black water. Next to him, Grant held out his hands as well. The pale violet shimmer of his emotion magic tumbled down to join the shadows snaking across the ground.

My eyebrows shot up as the two powers mixed until they had formed a black mist with hints of violet glitter inside.

They shared a glance.

I blinked as the swirling magic shot in through the gap under the door.

"Hey!" someone yelled from inside. "What's that?"

"Watch out!"

"Wait!"

"I can't see."

"Fuck. Where is—"

"No. Stop. What are you—"

"Callan," Malcolm said while shadows continued pouring from his hands. "Would you hold the door shut, please?"

Lurching into motion, Callan threw his shoulder against the door and wrapped his arm around the handle. A second later, someone tried desperately to shove it open from inside.

"Open the doors!" someone screamed.

"I can't find them. I can't see anything!"

"Get them open! Now!"

Sam and I hurried over to the other door and threw our weight against it too. Sienna just remained standing on the stones, watching us with a curious expression on her face.

The shouting coming from inside was transforming from barked orders to cries of terror. People pounded against the doors. My feet slipped on the ground as I tried to keep them closed.

Steel clanked from somewhere inside. It was followed by more bloodcurdling screams and cries for help.

While struggling to keep the doors closed, I flicked a quick glance towards Grant and Malcolm. The two of them were just standing there side by side while the stream of their combined magic poured in under the door.

After a while, the pounding stopped. A few more screams rang out. Along with slashing sounds of blades meeting flesh. Then everything went silent. Eerily silent.

Malcolm and Grant turned and gave each other a nod before their magic dissipated.

"You can open the doors now," Grant said.

We exchanged a glance. After straightening again, I grabbed the left handle while Callan did the same with the right. Sam moved back to give us space to open them.

With a nod, we pulled at the same time.

My mouth dropped open at the sight we were met with.

Constables had been stationed down the length of the corridor, clearly waiting to ambush us the moment we stepped inside. Now, they were all dead. And by the looks of it, they had slaughtered *each other*.

The rest of us turned to stare at Malcolm and Grant. A slight smirk played over Grant's lips when he shrugged, as if it was no big deal. Malcolm just brushed some dirt off his black suit.

"You know..." Sam began. His wide gray eyes shifted from the mass slaughter in the corridor to the red flames still ravaging the city below and then back to us again. "This truce you all have with each other right now. Maybe you should keep it going afterwards too?"

The five of us exchanged a long look. Wicked smiles blew across all our faces.

"Yes," Malcolm said as he nodded. "Maybe we should."

"Then let's go finish this," Callan said.

We strode across the threshold and into the wide hallway. Blood splattered the walls and floor, ruining some of the paintings of previous Chancellors that hung on the marble walls. Stepping over the still bleeding corpses, we made our way deeper into the building.

"Remember, Quill should be keeping the blade in the Inner Chamber," Malcolm said. "It's the most protected place in the building since there is only one way in and out of it."

"And where do we find that again?" Sienna asked.

I arched an eyebrow. "Didn't you pay attention on the field trip that everyone at the academy has to go on?"

"I never went." Her eyes took on a dreamy look as she craned her neck to stare at everything we passed. "I burned down half of the greenhouse the week before, so I was suspended."

Callan chuckled under his breath.

"Focus," Malcolm cut in as we drew closer to a set of double doors. "There are bound to be more constables in here, but Grant and I can't use that same trick again in case the others have already arrived."

He was right. We were coming up on the Silver Hall. It wasn't nearly as grand as the Rose Hall where the ball had taken place all those months ago, but it was still large. The room was used as a kind of massive waiting room where officials who weren't part of the parliament could remain while those thirty-five members discussed and voted inside the Inner Chamber. If I knew anything about Godric Quill, he would have stationed soldiers inside the Silver Hall too.

My heart pattered against my ribs as we stopped in front of the silver-colored door. Callan and Malcolm called up magic to block any sudden attack. When they were ready, I sucked in a breath and shoved the door open.

Nothing happened.

I frowned as I glanced in through the door.

The Silver Hall was completely deserted. Only silver candelabras and glittering chandeliers stared back at me as I snuck across the threshold. I swept my gaze over the marble walls and floor.

Why wasn't it guarded? Dread crawled up my throat. Had we gotten it wrong? Had *I* gotten it wrong? Was it possible that Jenny had actually been lying and setting us up to come here even though Quill had already moved the blade again? The thought made me want to throw up.

This couldn't be it. We couldn't have gotten played this badly again. Not after everything we had just gone through to get here.

The others walked inside the room and stopped beside me as well. A few of them glanced my way, and even without looking at them, I could feel that they were thinking the same thing.

"I—"

Doors banged open.

All of us dropped into fight stances.

Magic swirled around our hands as we watched a horde of students pour out of the doors halfway down the hall.

Chapter 37

Callan

Shouts filled the Silver Hall as a mass of students thundered into the wide empty space from the adjacent rooms. I raised a force wall in front of all six of us, but none of the students attacked. They only raced out and organized themselves into what looked like a pre-rehearsed formation. A groan rolled from my throat when Lance, Jessica, Darren, and Leoni took up position at the front.

"I thought you said that all the students were still at the academy," Malcolm said without taking his eyes off the young men and women.

"They *were* supposed to be there," Audrey protested.

"They're here because I asked them to come," Leoni called from her place on Lance's left. Her brown eyes sparkled with satisfaction as she swept a hand to indicate the people behind them. "We were tipped off that you would be attacking the parliament building and not the academy."

We all flicked a quick glare at Sienna. She just shot us a sharp look as if saying, *what?*

"So I asked our whole class to come," Leoni continued. "And as you can see, most of them did."

I studied their faces again. Now that she mentioned it, these weren't just any random students. All of the young men and women across the floor looked to be around twenty years old. Sunlight shone in through the windows that covered the whole right wall, only to disappear again when another cloud drifted across the sun. It cast their faces in shifting shades and made them look even more resolute as they raised their chins and stared back at us.

"Congratulations," Audrey said in a voice dripping with sarcasm. "You've convinced them to follow you into an early grave." She turned towards Lance. "I can't believe that you, of all people, are on board with this. You've spent enough time with us to know how this ends. The vast majority of your classmates are going to die in the next ten minutes. Is that really what you want?"

A hint of uncertainty blew across his features, and he flicked his gaze up and down the row of people standing to his left and right. Then he squared his shoulders and raised his chin. "No one is going to die, because there won't be a fight."

"Oh? And why is that?"

"Look around you." He threw his arms out. "All of us are one month away from graduating, which means that we are at the height of our power. And there are fifty of us, and six of you." He nodded towards Sam. "Five, if you don't count your healer. Do you really think that you will win if you attack us now?"

Uneasiness slithered through my chest. He had a point. Fifty people with the power levels of dark mages, who were all at the height of their powers before graduation, and they outnumbered us ten to one. It wasn't going to be an easy win.

"Please." There was a pleading note to Lance's voice as he looked back at us with his big blue eyes. "Enough fighting. You can stop this right now."

Audrey gave him an almost sad look. "You know we can't do that."

Lightning zapped through the white marble room. My shield was already in place, hovering at waist level, so I just yanked it up to block the strike. White lights flashed through the room as Leoni's lightning bolt slammed into the force wall right in front of Audrey's face.

For a moment, no one moved. I wasn't even sure if the students were breathing. Lance and Jessica had whipped around to stare at their friend, but Leoni only glared at us as if we were demons who had crawled from the depths of hell itself. The problem was, of course, that in some ways she might actually be right about that.

"I told you that you can't reason with them," she said, her voice brimming with anger.

All hell broke loose.

I threw up another force wall as Darren hurled a massive wind blast towards us while a redhead to his left sent orange flames flying right on its tail.

Panic spiked through my chest as I realized that, out of the six of us, Malcolm, Sienna, and I were the only ones with magic capable of blocking attacks. Audrey, Grant, and Sam couldn't shield. And Sienna could disappear to crazy town at any point.

Shadows rose up to support my force wall as a host of attacks crashed into it.

"Sienna!" Sam called over the noise. "Remember that we're not fireproof."

Dark red flames burned along her arms and played in her hair. It looked like she had been one breath away from setting the whole room on fire, but at the sound of Sam's voice, she blinked. And then blinked again. As if she was coming back from the brink of insanity.

"Then stay out of my way," she snapped.

I barely had time to yank my force wall aside before her flames shot across the white stone floor. Malcolm didn't make it in time, and her fire burned off a section of his shadows. Angry cursing rolled off his tongue, but it was drowned out by battle cries from the other side of the room.

Raising another force wall, I shoved it towards the students that suddenly sprinted towards us. Wind and water magic slammed into it from the side, sending it crashing into the marble wall instead.

Audrey's poison magic shot through the air. As did Grant's emotion magic. Students fell as the attacks slipped through their defenses. But not enough. Not nearly enough. Once again, there were simply too many of them. And this time, they also had power levels that matched ours.

I yanked out my knife and threw it up in front of my face as Darren crashed into me with a sword. Metal clashed as the blades connected. Gritting my teeth, I shoved him backwards while shifting my grip on the knife so that I could touch my palms together.

A force blade appeared in my right hand.

Leaping sideways, I swung it towards Darren while the other students reached the rest of my companions. Sam edged farther back into the room while Audrey and Malcolm and Sienna and Grant all fought against the swarming students. Magic flashed through the air in a storm of light and darkness. Screams echoed between the walls as attacks hit home, but with the loss of range, we were at a disadvantage.

I landed on the floor again and rammed my force blade towards Darren's other side right as a blond man appeared beside him.

My heart leaped into my throat.

Aborting the attack, I threw myself backwards as Lance Carmichael lunged towards me with gold-glittering hands.

Terror seeped through my bones. One brush of his hands, and my magic would be sealed.

Wind slammed into my side as Darren hurled an attack. It sent me skidding across the floor towards the windows, and I had to throw my arms out to stay on my feet. With terrifying speed, Lance sprinted towards me with those damn gold-coated hands.

I dropped both my knife and my force blade and immediately smacked my palms together. A force wall barely managed to rise up in time for me to throw it into Lance's chest. His hand slashed through the air a mere inch from my arm when my attack hit him and shoved him backwards. But not far enough. Darren had thrown a wind blast that cancelled out part of my attack.

My heart pounded in my chest and alarm bells clanged inside my skull as Darren shot another blast at me that I barely dodged while Lance darted towards me again. Diving sideways, I rolled across the floor to escape his hands.

Fire roared somewhere behind me, and poison magic lit up the white walls in flashes of green.

Jumping to my feet, I hurled a spinning arc towards Lance. But Darren pushed it aside with a wind blast. It smacked into the marble wall with a *bang*, making cracks spider across the stone. I ducked while calling up another attack. Lance was getting closer. I barely managed to shove him aside with a force wall before his fingers could reach me.

Panic pulsed through my whole body like flaming waves. I couldn't fight back since one touch of his hands would doom me. But with Darren providing support, I also couldn't get Lance away from me. Blood rushed in my ears. It was only a matter of time before my luck ran out.

Glass exploded across the room.

Cries of pain and alarm ripped through the air as the

windows shattered, sending a storm of glass flying through the packed space. Shards slammed into my leather armor and clattered down on the floor, but I barely noticed it because intense relief washed over me.

Levi and Henry and Paige and at least twenty of Levi's dark mages leaped in through the broken windows. The King of Metal remained standing on the windowsill, no doubt holding up whatever construction he had raised in order for them to reach the windows from outside in the garden. But the others poured into the room and began hurling attacks at the shocked students.

"You're late," I called to Levi, but that relieved grin still tugged at my lips.

He snorted. "We had trouble finding the right windows." Flicking a glance behind me, he jerked his chin. "On your left."

I threw my body sideways right before another wind blast from Darren barreled through the space I had just been standing in. The students seemed to have recovered from the shock, and attacks shot through the room again. But they were losing ground now.

With the addition of twenty-odd dark mages, the tide had turned in our favor.

Lance seemed to be the first to realize that, because he gave up on trying to seal my magic and instead dragged Darren with him towards the door on the opposite side of the room. The door leading into the Inner Chamber.

"Fall back!" he bellowed across the noise of whooshing magic and pained screams and clashing steel. "Fall back to the chamber!"

Levi at last jumped down from the windowsill and began shooting sharp sheets of metal at them. Halfway down the room, Henry and Paige worked in tandem with him attacking with blasts of wind and her defending with water walls.

I whipped my head from side to side, looking for Audrey. There were slashes along her upper arm, but other than that she looked unharmed. Poison whips snapped through the room, aiming for our retreating enemies.

By the door, Lance shoved the panicked mass of students through.

"Darren," Leoni suddenly called when almost all of them had made it inside. "Dylan. Cassie. Sarah. Now!"

Alarm shot through me. I slapped my palms together at the same time as they did.

But they weren't aiming for us.

A massive blast of combined wind and lightning magic crashed into the ceiling with enough force to shatter the stone.

Panic crackled through my every nerve as I threw a wide force wall straight up as a shield. Levi's metal shot up a second later. But the ceiling was already collapsing.

White stones crashed down right on top of us.

The boom of the collision echoed through the whole building and made the shattered glass on the floor rattle. Gritting my teeth, I held the force wall up, hoping that I had everyone covered, while the cracked ceiling rained down.

Then, everything went silent.

A thick cloud of stone dust filled the whole room.

While coughing, I tilted my force wall to the right, sliding all of the broken stones towards the wall of windows. The grinding of stone against metal informed me that Levi was doing the same somewhere farther into the room.

"Audrey!" I called, blinking against the hazy air full of stone dust. "Henry!"

"I'm fine," Audrey's reply came from a short distance to my left.

A wind mage must have sent a gust whirling through the room, because all of the white dust that filled the air suddenly disappeared out the broken windows. I blinked at the scene before me.

By the wall on my right, a mass of broken stones lay piled on top of each other. But my and Levi's shields hadn't covered the whole room. Parts of the ceiling lay crumpled on the floor, along with what looked like broken metal pipes that must have run through it.

Bodies lay underneath the rubble. Some looked to be the students we had killed before Leoni dropped the ceiling on our heads, but a few of them I recognized as Levi's people.

My gaze darted around the room. Sam was crouching on the floor behind me. Grant and Sienna were standing close by. Between them were Audrey and Malcolm. And then Levi was positioned halfway down the room.

Cold fear crawled up my throat. Where was Henry? And Paige?

"NO!" A desperate voice sliced through the air. "No, no, no, no!"

I was already running by the time my eyes landed on the source of the voice.

The terror inside me was so intense that my whole soul was drowning in it.

Henry was on his hands and knees above Paige, who was lying on her back on the floor as if he had tackled her.

A metal pipe was speared through his chest.

The panic inside my head threatened to shut my entire brain off.

"SAM!" someone bellowed. I think it might have been me.

Throwing myself down on the floor, I grabbed Henry by the shoulders and gently moved his body up so that he sat on his knees instead. Paige, shock and fear flashing in her eyes, climbed up to her knees in front of him. I barely dared to turn and look at his face. If his eyes were already glassed over, I was going to die here with him.

A wet cough sounded.

I snapped my gaze to Henry's face.

Blood sprayed from his mouth and ran down his chin. But he had taken a breath, which meant that it wasn't too late. It couldn't be too late.

"Out of the way," Sam ordered as he dropped to his knees in front of Henry. His face betrayed nothing. All he said was, "Callan, pull the pipe out."

I scrambled around Henry's body and wrapped my hands around the cold metal. "Fast or slow?"

"Fast. One clean yank. Do it now."

The slight urgency in his voice at those last three words made another wave of fear crash over me. I tried my best to keep it at bay while I yanked the pipe from Henry's chest.

A cry of pain tore from his throat. It was immediately followed by wet coughing and strangled breaths.

Turquoise blue magic lit up the space between his chest and Sam.

I was vaguely aware of the others gathering around us, and I think Audrey squeezed my shoulder, but all I could see was the blood leaking out of the hole in Henry's back.

"What did you do?" Paige pressed out between sobs. "You shouldn't have protected me."

Her voice snapped me out of my trance enough that I managed to shift back into my previous position in front of Henry and slightly to the right. Paige was kneeling on Sam's other side, tears streaming down her face.

I reached out and placed a gentle hand on Henry's arm. He just sat there with blood dripping down his chin and his chest barely rising and falling. His normally so calm gray eyes slid in and out of focus.

"Hey," I said. "You're not allowed to die. Do you hear me?"

"Sor..." Henry gasped in a rattling breath and then coughed blood onto his shirt again, but his eyes slid to me. "...ry."

"No. You do not get to be sorry. You're going to live, and then I'm going to kick your fucking ass for this. Do you hear me? You're going to live." I flicked a glance towards Sam. "He's going to live, right?"

Sam said nothing. Concentration was etched into every line of his face as he stared at the wound in Henry's chest while his healing magic poured into it.

Dread spread through my body like acid.

"You're going to live," I repeated again with even more force.

Pain clouded his eyes, but I could see the doubt swirling in there too as he slid his gaze towards our silent healer.

"Hey." Reaching up, I grabbed his chin and turned his face back to me. "You do not give up. *We* do not give up. How many tight scrapes have we gotten through together already? This is just one in a long line of them. And then, once Sam has fixed you all up again, we're gonna go out and get into trouble again. And again. Together. Because that's what family does."

He smiled weakly and opened his mouth to respond, but another coughing fit racked his body. Blood sprayed into the air, splattering across Sam's face. Sam didn't so much as flinch. He just kept his hands hovering over the wound while his magic seeped into it.

My heart pounded in my chest. I didn't care that this made me look weak in front of the other dark mages. I couldn't lose Henry. I couldn't. He was family to me. He had to make it.

The minutes dragged on as if they were years.

My heart was fracturing more and more with every second that passed until I felt as though one small poke at it would make the whole thing shatter like brittle glass.

He had to make it. He had to make it. He had to make it.

Suddenly, the color began returning to Henry's face and the light to his eyes. I snapped my gaze to Sam. Our healer said nothing. Only continued working.

My pulse thrummed in my ears as I watched the wound at last begin to knit itself together. I tried to keep the hope at bay, but it fluttered in my chest like a flock of desperate birds.

After what felt like an eternity, Sam sucked in a deep breath. His turquoise blue magic faded out, and he dropped his hands in his lap.

I stared at Henry.

He only looked down at the round scar that was now all that remained of the wound. Looking up, he met Sam's gaze. "Thank you."

"What did I say about dying?" Sam snapped, a hint of annoyance in his voice.

Henry winced slightly. "How close was it?"

"Too close." Drawing a hand through his mop of blond hair, he heaved another deep sigh and shook his head. "Too bloody close."

"Thank you," Henry repeated.

I couldn't take my eyes off Henry even as I helped him to his feet. Disbelief still rang inside me. He was alive. This wasn't some illusion. Henry had actually made it through that.

As soon as we were on our feet, I yanked him towards me in a hard embrace. "Don't ever do that to me again."

His muscular arms wrapped around my back. "I won't. I'm sorry."

Relief washed over me like warm summer waves. I clapped Henry on the shoulder as we broke apart and then stepped back.

The moment I was gone, someone else took my spot.

My eyebrows shot up into my hairline as Paige raised her hand and slapped Henry across the face.

The slap was hard enough to snap his head to the side, and loud enough that it echoed between the white marble walls.

For a moment, we all just stared at her in shock.

Henry slowly turned his face back so that he met her gaze. The same stunned surprise shone in his eyes.

"Don't ever do something heroic like that again," she snapped, her voice full of steel.

Then she grabbed the front of his shirt and yanked him down in a desperate kiss.

Chapter 38

A wide grin spread across my mouth as I watched Paige kiss Henry like there was no tomorrow. After two seconds of stunned disbelief, he cupped her cheeks with both hands and answered the kiss with equal passion. Next to me, Sienna let out a short teasing whistle.

Pulling back, Paige flashed Henry a devilish smile and winked. "In case my subtle flirting wasn't clear enough."

Henry looked like he was still trying to piece his brain back together, so he just stood there staring down at her with his mouth slightly open.

On his other side, Callan snorted. "Subtle?"

She shot him a mock glare, but before she could retort, Malcolm spoke up.

"I hate to break up this touching display of emotions," he said in a voice that told us he wasn't sorry at all. "But we do have a war to win."

"I agree," Levi muttered.

After Sam had finished healing the other two dark mages who had survived being hit by some of the falling stones, we all moved over to the door at the far end of the room. I wasn't sure what metal it was made of, but it had a golden color and intricate designs were carved into it.

For a couple of seconds, we all just watched it.

"It will no doubt be locked," Grant said eventually.

Callan nodded. "Agreed."

"If we test the handle, we will as good as announce that we're attacking right now."

"I could melt it," Sienna offered.

"By all hell." Levi shot us a look of disbelief. "You people know that I'm a metal mage, correct?" Before we could retort, he jerked his chin. "Get ready. The moment I drop the door, they will attack."

"I say we let them tire themselves out a bit before we go inside," Malcolm said.

"I agree," I answered.

When the others also nodded, we split into two groups so that we were standing on either side of the door. Callan raised a force wall up to our chests while Malcolm did the same with his shadows on the other side. After checking to see that we were ready, Levi touched his hands together.

The door rippled as if it had turned liquid. In the span of a few seconds, the previously solid slab of metal turned into a puddle of gold on the floor.

Magic shot through the doorway.

Callan and Malcolm raised their shields to cover our whole bodies while lightning and fire and wind and water barreled out of the now open doorway. Inside, someone was yelling orders. I adjusted the bracers on my forearms and my metal corset while we waited for the idiots in the Inner Chamber to realize that they couldn't actually hit us with their attacks.

Thick clouds must have returned to fill the sky outside, because the light now falling in through the shattered windows had a pale gray hue to it. I swept a glance around the room, noting the mass of broken stone and shards of glass and dead bodies and nonexistent ceiling, and idly wondered which poor bastard would be charged with cleaning this mess up.

Eventually, the torrent of magic shooting through the doorway faded. Ringing silence took its place.

"Well then," I said. "Shall we?"

Levi snapped his fingers as he looked at some of his dark mages. "You. Keep us shielded. Anyone who lets an attack get through will answer to me when we're back in Malgrave."

Fear flickered in their eyes. Dipping their chins, they answered, "Yes, sir."

A layered shield of wind, water, shadows, and something I couldn't identify, rose up in front of the door. Immediately, the attacks began again. Lightning zapped against the other side, but nothing made it through so we all formed up in front of the door and started forwards.

The shield expanded to the sides as we all strode across the threshold and into the Inner Chamber.

Attacks pelted us while we walked through and positioned ourselves side by side with Levi's people behind us, and the barrage of magic continued for a solid minute after we were in place as well. The shield wobbled and rippled, but nothing made it through.

"Enough," a very familiar voice suddenly rang out.

The attacks stopped.

"Lower it," Levi ordered his people. "But be ready to raise it at a moment's notice. The consequence of failure still stands."

The layered wall before us slowly drew back down to the ground. I raised my eyebrows as the room came fully into view.

The Inner Chamber was shaped like a circle. Both the floor and the walls were made of pristine white marble with gold veins running through them. But there were no windows, so all illumination came from the massive gold chandelier that hung in the middle of the ceiling, as well as the gleaming candleholders mounted on the walls.

From my previous visit to this place when I was still a student at the academy, I knew that there were usually thirty-five tables and chairs arranged in a circle around the room. Now, all of that furniture had been placed like a barrier between the door we had come through and the rest of the space inside. Behind that frankly rather ridiculous barrier were the real threats.

Rolling my eyes, I muttered, "Seriously?"

All of the students we had fought in the Silver Hall stood positioned in two rows, with Leoni, Jessica, and Darren front and center. Behind them were five rows of constables. After that, the thirty-five members of Eldar's parliament flanked two men. Chancellor Godric Quill and Lance Carmichael. I glanced down at the Binder's hands to find him holding the Blade of Equilibrium.

Sweeping my gaze over the small army before us, I tried to calculate our odds. Even with the support of Levi and the sixteen dark mages who were currently with him, this was going to be an incredibly bloody battle. A little over forty students with dark mage level powers, one hundred constables trained for combat, thirty-five members of parliament who could use the Great Current as well, and one Binder. Forcing our way through was going to cost us dearly.

"You can't win this," Chancellor Quill called, as if he had read the calculations in my head. Lifting a hand, he motioned towards Lance. "And you will not be able to get the blade, because if you ever get close enough to take it from Lance's hands, he will be able to seal your magic."

Clever. Though I refused to tell him that.

"Have you forgotten that we don't need to get very close in order to kill people?" I replied instead.

"Yes, you do. Because there's no way your magic can reach us with all of these people in the way."

A vicious smile curled my lips. "Look at you. Hiding behind *students*."

Some of the other parliament members flicked quick glances at their Chancellor, as if this was something that they had argued about earlier.

"They're twenty years old," Quill said. His blue eyes were sharp as they locked on me from across the packed room. "They're one month away from graduation. They are not students anymore. They're full citizens of Eldar, and they're here of their own free will."

"When the fighting starts, they will be the first to die."

"They—"

"Are you truly willing to let them die for your stubbornness?"

Fury flashed across his face and candlelight shifted over his gray hair as he slashed a hand through the air. "They're willing to die for an *ideal*. For the belief that we are all equal. That we all deserve to have magic."

"And to achieve that you *steal it* from people against their will." I raised my eyebrows at him. "Yes, that sounds very fair and equal indeed."

"It's not stealing. It's distributing something fairly."

"Just like I'm sure you distribute all the money you make fairly too."

"That's not the same thing!" Leoni suddenly snapped from the front of their army. Her curly brown hair bounced around her face as she shook her head at us. "By the Current, are all of you dark mages really this dense? How can you not see that *you* are on the wrong side of history?"

Callan cocked his head while his gaze slid to her. "Careful with those insults."

"Of course." She shot us a vicious look. "We're back to threats again."

"Regardless of what you think about the redistribution of magic," Chancellor Quill cut in before any of us could reply. "It doesn't change the fact that this is a battle you cannot win. Even if you somehow managed to kill everyone in this room and take the blade for yourselves, you won't win. If you kill us, we will become martyrs, and the whole city will rise up against you. You will never know a moment of peace for the rest of your wicked lives."

"We know," I said.

Surprise rippled through the students and constables and parliament members as they all blinked at us in shock.

As much as Callan and I and the other dark mages of Eldar wanted to slaughter Quill's whole parliament, we still needed to be able to control the city even after Levi and his people had left. And six of us against a city in uproar would never work in our favor. The disgruntled former mages might be on our side, but it didn't change the fact that the majority of the city had been taught to fear and hate us selfish dark mages. So we needed the parliament... as a puppet, so that we could rule from the shadows.

I swept my gaze over the stunned faces staring back at me before I added the final sentence.

"Which is why we have come to once again offer you a deal."

Chapter 39

Callan

"We don't make deals with dark mages," Chancellor Quill snapped.

A sharp smile spread across Audrey's mouth. "No, you just send students, *children*, into a dark mage battle instead."

"You forced our hand. You had taken our loved ones hostage."

"What kind of deal?" another parliament member cut in. She had light brown hair, and pale green eyes that were currently brimming with both worry and hope.

"A deal that lets all of you walk out of this chamber alive." I locked eyes with her for a few seconds before sweeping my gaze over the rest of them too. "A deal that lets you all go home to your parents and your children."

Candlelight from the golden chandelier above their heads glittered in their eyes as many of the students and about half of the parliament members glanced around hesitantly.

"Don't listen to them!" Leoni's sharp voice echoed between the white marble walls. "I have seen firsthand how cruel they can be, so trust me when I tell you that these people cannot be trusted."

"Leoni," Lance said, speaking for the first time since we walked into the room. His voice was surprisingly gentle, and his blue eyes were soft as he looked towards her. "Hasn't there been enough killing? Enough death? If we can save our classmates from dying right here today, shouldn't we at least hear them out?"

"No!" She looked both furious and stunned as she twisted her head to stare at her friend. "What's gotten into you? You know that we can't trust anything these people say."

"I also think we should hear them out," another parliament member said.

A third one nodded. "I agree."

"We do not make deals with dark mages," Quill growled.

"Maybe we should."

"No, the Chancellor is right. We can't sell out our city's future just to save our lives."

"What city? Didn't you see outside the windows earlier? Everything is burning. There won't be a city left if we don't do something."

"You're just afraid."

"I'm not. I'm thinking of the future."

I scanned the students before us again while the parliament members kept arguing amongst themselves. Worry blew across a few sections, but they all remained standing resolutely on the gold-inlaid floor. Whatever decision Chancellor Quill and his parliament reached, they would abide by it.

"What are our odds for fighting our way through?" Grant murmured, softly enough so that only we would hear.

"Would we win in the end? Yes." I flicked a glance up and down our line. "Would all of us survive it? No."

"I figured as much."

"I will not die here," Sienna growled under her breath.

"Neither will I," Malcolm added.

"Then let's make sure to convince them," Audrey said.

The parliament members were still arguing, but it sounded like more and more of them were reaching the conclusion that a deal might be the best solution. Red splotches had appeared on Quill's cheeks as he angrily snapped back at them for even suggesting such a thing. Throughout it all, Lance Carmichael only stood there in the center, clutching the blade in his hands and staring at us with unreadable blue eyes.

"Last time we tried to make you a deal," Audrey called over the noise, "Quill sent children, your children, to attack us. We left, giving up our leverage, instead of killing them. So maybe we're not the ones you really need to worry about. If—"

"No!"

Everything happened so quickly that I had barely managed to touch my hands together before it was all over.

Leoni, her brown eyes flashing with rage, had whipped up a hand and shot a lightning bolt straight towards Audrey. But before our shields could even rise, someone else blocked it. The same person who had also screamed the word *no*.

I stared in utter disbelief as Jessica's body jerked back when the lightning bolt slammed into her left side instead after she had jumped out in front of it. Her blue eyes rolled back in her head and she crashed down on the ground while her slim body shook violently.

"*NO!*" Lance screamed from the other side of the room.

It tore out of him with such desperation that the hair on the back of my neck stood on end.

Chancellor Quill had hooked his arms around Lance's shoulders from behind, forcibly stopping him from running straight to her. Leoni was just staring at her friend with her mouth open and shock pulsing across her face.

"Bring her here," Audrey ordered in a voice that sliced through the stunned silence. "Sam."

"N-no," Leoni began, snapping out of her shock. "It's a trick."

"She will be dead in less than thirty seconds if you don't bring her here," Sam said in a calm voice.

Without hesitation, Darren dropped to his knees and scooped up Jessica's shaking body. He sprinted across the pale floor and immediately set her down in front of Sam's feet.

Brushing my palms together, I shifted my position and then placed a force blade to the side of Darren's neck. I didn't want any of them this close to our healer without some insurance. The wind mage, though, didn't even seem to notice. His brown eyes were locked on Sam's hands as the healer poured shimmering turquoise magic into Jessica's trembling body.

"See!" Leoni called from the other side. "It was a trap! A trick!"

But her voice sounded frayed and hollow. Behind the ranks of constables, Lance had stopped fighting against Quill's arms. Instead, he just hung there, staring at his girlfriend.

Jessica's body had stopped shaking, and her blue eyes shifted back so that they were staring up into the pale ceiling. For another minute, Sam kept pouring magic into her.

Then she sucked in a deep breath.

Letting his magic fade out, Sam rose to his feet again and took a step back.

No one said anything. In fact, I wasn't sure if their half of the room was even breathing anymore.

"Jessica," Lance called, shattering the silence like a broken mirror.

She drew in another deep breath and then sat up. Uncertainty washed over her features as she looked between all of us.

"Stand up," I said, both to her and to Darren. "Keep your arms spread."

Both of them rose slowly from the ground while holding their arms out at their sides.

Across the floor, Leoni stared at us and her friends with a mix of dread and panic and regret on her features.

No one moved.

I jerked my chin. "You can go back to your friends."

They blinked at us in disbelief. When we only looked back at them in silence, they exchanged a quick glance and then began slowly retreating towards their side of the room.

Keeping them as hostages would only have turned them all against us. At least now, we had a better chance of getting what we wanted without having to risk our own lives in the process.

"Why did you do that?" Leoni blurted out when Jessica and Darren reached her. "Why did you protect *her*? A dark mage? You could've died!"

"Because if that cheap shot you took at her had gone through," Jessica said, her voice surprisingly steady, "they would have slaughtered us all."

Quill at last released Lance and moved to stand next to him again. Drawing a hand through his gray hair, he smoothened it down. Lance only kept staring at Jessica as if making sure that she was truly still breathing.

"What's the deal?" a voice interrupted before Leoni could reply. It was that parliament member with light brown hair and green eyes from before. "What do you want?"

"The deal is the same one we gave you last time," I called back while letting my force blade fade out.

"We're giving you what you never gave us," Audrey filled in.

"A choice. If you had just let mages choose if they wanted to give up their magic or not, none of this would have happened. But your Chancellor refused to negotiate, and now your city is burning and your people are dying."

On my left, Malcolm raised his chin. "We want the Blade of Equilibrium and we want you to abolish the laws forcing mages to share their magic against their will. Do that, and we will stop the killing and the destruction."

"We do not negotiate with dark mages," Quill repeated.

But the green-eyed parliament member ignored him. "How do we know you won't just kill us all anyway once you have what you want?"

"Because you are the ones who started this war." Malcolm locked hard eyes on her. "*You* came into the hills and destroyed *our* homes and killed *our* people. All we have ever wanted was for you to leave us alone."

Well, to be fair, we were going to destroy the blade so that no one could use it even if they wanted to, we were going to kill Quill, and then we were going to use the parliament as a front while we ruled Eldar from the shadows. But they didn't need to know that.

"You love democracy, don't you?" Audrey called before she could reply. "So, put it to a vote. Anyone who votes to take our offer will be allowed to leave completely unharmed."

"This is not how we do things," Quill snapped, his furious eyes sweeping across his parliament.

But the woman only looked at the rest of her companions and said, "All in favor?"

For a few seconds, no one moved. Golden light from the multitude of candles flickered over their faces as they looked at one another. The rows of constables shifted uncomfortably on their feet, but none of them turned to look. The students, however, didn't have the same discipline. Several sections cast hesitant glances over their shoulders.

Then hands began rising.

A satisfied grin tugged at my lips as the vast majority of parliament members raised one hand in favor of the proposal.

"Would you look at that?" The smile on Audrey's lips was full of wicked smugness as she locked eyes with Quill and raised her eyebrows. "Democracy has spoken."

"It's not democracy when the decision is made under duress!" Quill spat back at her. His eyes burned like blue flames as he glared at his parliament. "I recognize that you acted in this way due to fear, but know that I will remember this when the war is over."

"The war *is* over," the green-eyed woman said. "We have already voted."

"I am the Chancellor, Marjorie. I can veto any decision. And I am vetoing this."

"You—"

"I know that you are afraid, but we will not bow to dark mages." Raising his voice, he called across the room. "Get ready for battle. We will fight to the last man."

The constables immediately straightened their spines and squared their shoulders while calling magic to their fingertips. It sent a ripple of certainty and purpose through the whole chamber. At the front, the students shifted into fight stances as well. The only one who looked uncertain was Jessica, who edged a step back while glancing over her shoulder at Lance. All the other students, Darren and Leoni included, were preparing themselves to go down swinging if need be.

Poison magic swirled in front of Audrey while black shadows flickered like snakes around Malcolm's wrists. Half of Sienna's body was already covered in dark red flames, and Grant's violet mist billowed around his shoulders. On my other side, Henry had summoned wind magic. Even Paige had water twisting in her hands. Levi hadn't summoned anything yet, but I was sure that was because his attack would be shooting up from underneath the floor.

My heart pounded in my chest.

We would most likely win this battle. But at what cost? I had almost lost Henry back there in the Silver Hall. I couldn't go through that again. If we started this battle now, some of us would die. There was no way around that.

Fuck! We had been so close. So close to convincing them to just give us what we wanted. And now some of us were going to die because Godric fucking Quill couldn't see past his own stupidity.

"We will not bow to dark mages!" Quill yelled again.

The constables let out a sound of agreement.

My pulse thrummed in my ears. I glanced up and down our row. Levi's people weren't used to fighting with us like this, so we wouldn't be able to rely on them to shield us in between our own attacks once the battle started. And due to the limited space, we would have to avoid hitting each other's attacks too. *Shit*. This was never going to work.

"We will fight for democracy!" Quill bellowed. "We will fight for equality! We will stand our ground and never let the forces of darkness win."

The constables, and some of the students this time too, let out an even stronger cry of agreement.

My body practically vibrated with pent-up tension. To my left, Levi dipped his chin in an almost imperceptible nod. Whatever sneak attack he had been preparing was finished now. The rest of us exchanged one last look. My heart pounded against my ribs. It was time.

Quill's eyes blazed with righteousness as he continued, "Someone has to stand up against evil! And today, that burden has fallen on you. Today, you—"

His words were abruptly cut off and his eyes went wide with shock as Lance Carmichael shoved the Blade of Equilibrium through the side of his neck.

Chapter 40

Deafening silence filled the Inner Chamber. For a few moments, it was as if time itself had stopped. Everyone just remained standing there like statues. Then, Lance yanked the Blade of Equilibrium out of Chancellor Quill's neck.

Blood spurted through the air from his severed artery.

With his mouth still hanging open, Quill managed to turn slightly to stare at his Binder. His hero. The young man who was supposed to save Eldar from dark mages. Utter disbelief shone on Quill's face.

Then his knees buckled and he collapsed to the floor with a thud that echoed between the gold-infused walls. Wet gurgling came from his mouth as he lay there on the ground while blood poured out and stained the white floor red.

That broke the spell.

Constables and students and parliament members whirled around to stare at the insane scene before them. Gasps rang out, and a few of them even jerked back in shock. Lance just stood there, looking down at his dying Chancellor. Blood ran down from the golden blade in his hand and dripped on the floor beside him.

When Godric Quill had stopped twitching on the floor, Lance dragged his eyes back up and locked them on us instead before speaking in a calm and confident voice.

"We accept the deal."

Wicked satisfaction pulsed through my body, and I couldn't stop the grin that spread across my lips.

It had been a long shot, and I hadn't known if it would actually work. We had all been fully ready to fight our way through this chamber, but I had always kept Lance as a sort of impossible back-up plan in my mind.

Ever since our journey to the dark mage mountain in Castlebourne, I had gotten the feeling that Lance wasn't as sure of his beliefs anymore. That he had begun to see the world a bit differently. So every time I had run into him since then, I had tried to fan that flame of doubt. To make it grow into a raging wildfire that would burn through his hero complex and all the grand destinies that had been forced upon his shoulders since he was a child. So that one day, when we needed it, he might be the final drop that tipped the scale in our favor.

"Lance," Leoni gasped as she stared at her friend while shaking her head. "What have you done?"

Lance held our gazes in silence for another few seconds before shifting his attention to her. "I've saved us. I have saved our city from the stubbornness of old men."

"You killed him!" Desperation flooded her voice, and she flung out an arm and stabbed a hand in our direction. "Why would you do that for *them*? Why?"

"Because I'm tired of fighting!" Something snapped in Lance's blue eyes. He threw his arms out, making blood fly from the tip of the blade and splatter the white stone farther away. "Going into battle isn't as glamorous and heroic as everyone makes it out to be. I don't want to fight anymore. I don't want to see any more people I care about die. I don't want to see any more one-handed dark mages who have been banished from their homes. I don't want to see any more children living in misery because they happened to be born to dark mages. I don't want to hear about another bright young man committing suicide because he was forced to give up his plant magic that could have brought the world so much joy if he would've been allowed to keep it."

On Callan's other side, Henry flinched slightly at the mention of his brother.

"I'm tired of killing people just because they refuse to let us steal from them." His eyes were wide as he swept them over the gathered crowd. "That's what we're doing, isn't it? We're taking something that's theirs against their will. Doesn't that make us just as bad as them?"

"It's not the same!" Leoni protested.

"Then where are we supposed to draw the line? Huh? Is taking other people's magic against their will the right thing to do? Or is letting parts of the population live without magic the right thing? I don't know! I don't know which side is good or bad anymore. But here is what I do know. Our city is on fire. Our people are dying. And every single person in this room is going to die too if we keep this up." His gaze slid back to me. "And I am not prepared to watch innocent strangers and people I care about die just to protect our right to steal someone else's magic."

Ringing silence descended on the room.

Our side exchanged a glance and a nod.

"Ben," Levi said, his voice booming into the tense silence. "Take the others and go tell our people to stand down."

The students on the front lines heaved a collective sigh of relief. Some of them even collapsed to the ground.

"Captain Olsen," Marjorie said. "Take your constables and do the same."

"Yes, Vice Chancellor." Captain Olsen cleared his throat. "I mean, Chancellor."

Boots pounded against the marble floor as all five rows of constables jogged out of the room. Once they were gone, Levi's dark mages disappeared too.

The students had all struggled back to their feet and were now clustered together on the left side of the room. Both they and the parliament members cast uncertain glances between us and each other.

Callan jerked his chin. "You're free to leave."

They hesitated for only a second. Then they hurried out of the Inner Chamber as well. We remained standing in front of the door, so that they had to walk around us to get out.

Once they were gone, the only people who remained in the room were the six dark mages of Eldar, Paige and Henry, Levi, and then Lance and his three friends.

Lance was still gripping the Blade of Equilibrium in his right hand as he walked up to stand between Jessica and Darren. Leoni stood a little to the side, casting wary glances between us and them.

I locked eyes with Lance. "The blade, please."

He said nothing. Only watched us with an unreadable expression on his face. Then he heaved a deep sigh and closed his eyes.

The golden blade began to glow.

We all tensed.

Opening his eyes again, Lance swept them from face to face, holding each of our gazes for a second. I frowned slightly at him.

With a tired smile on his lips, he raised the blade and drew it along his left palm.

Shock pulsed through me.

Blood welled up from the cut, but he only shifted the blade to his other hand and did the same thing to his right palm.

The moment that both cuts were in place, shimmering golden mist began to rise up from his palms. It was the exact same color as Lance's binding magic.

I watched as the golden mist rose up into the air above his head and twisted there while more kept pouring out of his hands.

Once the flow from his palms stopped, the glittering mist swirled for another few seconds. Then it dissipated into the air.

Lance Carmichael had just given up his powers as a Binder.

Without a word, he held out the blade to his friends. None of them took it.

Amusement flickered through me.

"Not so much for sharing anymore, huh?" I said.

Leoni shot me a withering glare, but said nothing. The other two just exchanged a guilty look.

Candlelight danced across Lance's features as he took a few steps forward. He still held the blade in his hand, and blood now smeared the gold and jewel-encrusted handle. Another ripple of tension coursed through our side. If he was going to change his mind and do something stupid right now, I might just kill them all.

But he didn't.

With one last sigh, Lance tossed the blade at our feet.

It clanked metallically as it bounced a couple of times before sliding to a halt in front of our boots.

"I can't bind magic anymore." Raising his hands, he looked back at us and swallowed. "So I'm no longer a threat to you."

There was a guarded sense of worry and uncertainty in his eyes as he watched us. As if he thought that we might still retaliate and decide to kill them all after all the trouble they had caused us. I had to admit, the thought had crossed my mind. But I wasn't going to. I might be a ruthless villain, but there were limits. And he had chosen the right side in the end.

When we didn't immediately reply, he pressed out, "Please. I don't want to fight. I just want to live in peace." He glanced back at his friends, and when he met our gazes again, there was a pleading look in his eyes. "Them too. Please."

I swept a glance up and down our line. When no one objected, I shifted my attention back to Lance.

"You and your friends are free to go. And as long as you stay out of our way, no one will touch you. Now or in the future."

He swallowed again and then nodded while relief blew across his features.

Twisting around, he held out a hand towards his friends. Jessica and Darren joined him immediately. After another few moments of glaring at us, Leoni grudgingly stalked after them as well.

Since we still blocked the door, they had to walk around us. Before they did, Jessica stopped in front of Sam. Her blue eyes locked on his gray ones with a sort of frank openness.

"Thank you," she said. "For healing me."

A small smile played over Sam's lips. "You're welcome."

And with that, the four of them walked around us and disappeared out the door once and for all.

I swore I could almost see the relief and smug satisfaction thrumming in the air as the nine of us turned to face each other.

Bending down, I picked up the Blade of Equilibrium.

It really was a remarkably beautiful blade. Both the hilt and the blade were made of gold, and gleaming gemstones in red, blue, and green were set into the twisting hilt. There were inscriptions on it too. Something about equality or some sort.

With a villainous grin on my lips, I held it out to Levi. "Would you do the honors?"

He took it while a sly smile pulled at his mouth. "A deal is a deal."

We all drew in a breath, and then apparently forgot to let it out again because we were all holding our breath as Levi touched his hands together and then shifted the blade so that it lay flat across his palms.

The blade began to glow with golden light, just like it had when Lance had activated it earlier. But this time, the color was a bit red-tinted, and the blade vibrated, as if it was angry. Or resisting.

Levi narrowed his eyes at it.

It shook even harder and the glow coming from within it turned an even angrier shade of red.

Then it stopped.

I finally let out that breath and sucked in a new one as the blade melted in Levi's hands. The golden metal turned liquid and ran through his fingers to drip down on the floor. Gemstones followed it.

When the last of it had left Levi's hands, all that remained was a now hardened pool of gold on the floor. Except now, it was dull and lifeless. All traces of magic were gone from it, leaving only ordinary metal.

"Well, I guess that concludes our business," Levi said. Brushing his hands off, he looked between me and Callan. "Callan. Audrey. If you ever show your faces in Malgrave again, I will kill you. Or buy you a drink. If you ever feel brave or stupid enough to risk finding out which one it is, you know where to find me."

Holding his gaze, Callan gave him a nod. "Thank you, Levi."

The King of Metal only looked back at him in silence for a few seconds. Then a slight smirk tugged at the corner of his lips.

"Traitor," he said. It wasn't a curse, or an accusation. More of a goodbye. He turned to me. "Poisonous snake."

I grinned. "Asshole."

Huffing out a short chuckle, he shook his head.

Without another word, the King of Metal turned around and strode out the door.

The rest of us stood there in silence for a while, looking from face to face.

"So, this... alliance we have," Malcolm began. "Should we perhaps extend it?"

Sienna flashed us a brilliant grin. "I had a lot of fun. So yeah, sure. I'm in."

"I can certainly see the benefits too," I said.

"Agreed," Callan added.

Grant shrugged. "I have never had any interest in war anyway."

A short silence fell as we looked from face to face.

"It's decided then?" Malcolm asked.

We all nodded. "Yes."

"Ha!" Sam elbowed Malcolm in the ribs before shooting us all a smile. "I knew it." A thoughtful look passed over his features. "Though, I'm not sure what that means for my future job prospects."

"We can live inside the walls of Eldar now," I pointed out. "So you now have an entire city full of potential clients."

"Oh. Ohh. You're right!"

I chuckled. As did some of the others too.

Without having to say anything, the eight of us turned towards the door and began walking back out of the parliament building. Gray light fell in through the broken windows and painted the mess of shattered stone in gloomy hues as we passed through the Silver Hall.

"The problem with immediate accommodations still

remains, though," Malcolm said to no one in particular as we made our way into the corridor. "Since they burned down my mansion."

"Shit," Sienna swore. "I didn't think about that."

"You're both welcome to stay with me for as long as you need," Grant offered. Amusement twinkled in his eyes as he looked over at Sienna. "Yes, even you, my dear pyromaniac."

"Are you sure you're okay?" Callan asked Henry while the three of them began discussing Grant's offer.

Henry nodded. "Yeah, I'm fine."

Keeping my voice low, I said to Paige, "So... nice move."

"What move?" she said, her face the epitome of innocence.

I rolled my eyes. "You know which move."

"Yes, well..." A hint of red crept into her cheeks as her gaze darted towards Henry. "He wasn't really noticing my subtle hints, so I figured I might as well spell it out for him."

A laugh rolled from my throat. "Oh you sure did."

"Shut up," she huffed, but happiness glittered in her eyes as she once again looked over at Henry.

Warm summer winds washed over us as we at last left the parliament building and stepped out onto the hill outside. Paige winked at me before sneaking over to Henry and sliding an arm through his. He blinked at her in surprise and then leaned down to kiss her on the forehead. My heart swelled in my chest.

The others began drifting off, walking back down the white steps and towards the city. But I lingered on the topmost step. Callan joined me.

For a while, we just stood there side by side, staring out at the city.

"So..." I began. "That went more or less according to plan."

Callan chuckled and glanced down at me. "Yeah, I suppose it did."

Another short silence fell.

"So this is it, huh?" I said. A flicker of both uncertainty and anticipation rippled through my chest. "This is the start of our new lives. In Eldar. Together."

"Yes, it is." He paused for a few seconds before adding, "Wife."

I snapped my gaze to him. He was standing there right next to me, watching me with hope and a slight hint of vulnerability in his eyes. Warmth spread through my chest.

With a smile on my lips, I replied, "What do you say we finally make that official, husband?"

Joy sparkled like glittering fireworks in his eyes. But then he flicked a glance around us. "Here?"

I swept my gaze over the area around us as well.

Abandoned swords from the constables who had fled littered the ground between us and the parliament building. Small streams of blood had run out from the mass slaughter in the corridor inside, trickling out from the front doors. Ahead, the city was still in chaos.

Red flames burned through the buildings farther down from the hill, making plumes of smoke rise up towards the gray sky above. The raging fires cast the city in a hellish glow, and people still yelled down there while trying to put out the flames. Between us and the end of the main steps below the hill was a sea of dead constables. Limbs and blood smeared the white stones and turned the green grass red.

A wicked grin curled my lips as I looked back at Callan. "What could be more romantic than conquering a city?"

He let out a dark laugh. Drawing a hand up my throat, he took my chin in a firm grip and then leaned down to steal a kiss from my lips. "My vicious little poisoner, I'm so glad I didn't kill you five years ago."

I smiled against his lips. "Likewise, pretty boy."

Another soft laugh escaped his throat before he released me and took a step back.

Steel sang into the air as he drew his knife from his thigh holster.

My heart began pounding in my chest as he held my gaze and then drew the blade across his palm.

"I, Callan Blackwell, swear by my blood and my power that I will love and protect you, Audrey Sable, for as long as I live. I will never betray you. I will share all of your joys and your sorrows, as I will share this life of mine with you."

My heart felt as though it was going to burst. Swallowing the wave of emotions that surged through my chest, I reached out and took the knife from his hand.

While holding his gaze, I drew the blade across my own palm.

"I, Audrey Sable, swear by my blood and my power that I will love and protect you, Callan Blackwell, for as long as I live. I will never betray you. I will share all of your joys and your sorrows, as I will share this life of mine with you."

This was it.

We had done it.

A blood oath.

He was mine. And I was his.

Love shone in his eyes as he looked back at me. "Wife."

I smiled. "Husband."

He wrapped his arms around me and kissed me deeply. The knife clattered to the stones beneath us as I released it and locked my hands around the back of his neck, answering the kiss and hoping that it could tell him all the things that I still didn't know how to put into words.

Based on the way he tightened his arms around me, he understood. And shared the feelings.

When we at last drew back, I was thoroughly out of breath.

My heart was slamming against my ribs and I felt as though I had just sprinted across the whole continent.

Drawing in a deep breath, I turned to face the city again.

Callan draped his arm around my shoulders.

For a while, we just stood there side by side, watching the burning city below.

We had done it. Chancellor Quill was dead. The parliament of Eldar belonged to us. And the Blade of Equilibrium was destroyed.

A villainous smile spread across my lips as I looked down at the city we had conquered.

The time for dark mages had come.

Acknowledgments

In real life, I think we all want good to triumph over evil in the end. We want everyone to be happy and live amazing fulfilled lives. But sometimes, it can be difficult to figure out how to make that happen. The world isn't as black and white as we are sometimes led to believe, so it can be difficult to decide which side is good and which is evil. In many cases, it depends on whose viewpoint the issue is seen from and what priorities that person has. And sometimes we just want the villains to win because it's fiction and the villains are hot and dark-haired with sharp cheekbones and a sad backstory that we can relate to, haha :)

I hope you enjoyed reading about my two unapologetic villains and all the wicked things they did during their mission to take over the city and secure the power they craved. I hope it made you scowl and laugh and blush and experience all kinds of emotions. And maybe question your own morals a bit too. Because in my books, ruthless villains really do get a happily ever after.

As always, I would like to start by saying a huge thank you to my family and loved ones. Mom, Dad, Mark, thank you for always being there for me. I truly don't know what I would do without you. Lasse, Ann, Karolina, Axel, Martina, I'm so glad I have all of you too. Spending time with you always makes me happy.

I would also like to thank my amazing best friend Oskar

Fransson for being such an incredible person. Thank you for always filling my life with light.

To my amazing copy editor and proofreader Julia Gibbs, thank you for all the hard work you always put into making my books shine. Your language expertise and attention to detail is fantastic and makes me feel confident that I'm publishing the very best version of my books.

A huge thank you to Claire Holt, the incredible designer from Luminescence Covers, who made this absolutely gorgeous cover. Your talent for creating beautiful covers is out of this world and I'm so lucky that I get to work with you.

To Jennifer Davis. Thank you for your unending support. You have no idea how much everything you do means to me. You really are an amazingly kind person and I'm so lucky that we have connected.

To Laura Bartlett, Faye Ostryzniuk, and Jayse Smith. Thank you for being the amazing people that you are. Thank you for your support and your kindness and for brightening my day.

To Catherine Bowser. Thank you for your continued support, both for this series and for Court of Elves, but most of all for The Oncoming Storm. Your support means the world, and it brings a smile to my face every time you recommend my books to others.

I am also very fortunate to have friends both close by and from all around the world. My friends, thank you for everything you've shared with me. Thank you for the laughs, the tears, the deep discussions, and the unforgettable memories. My life is a lot richer with you in it.

And lastly, thank you, all of you amazing readers who have followed me on this morally questionable journey. I hope that you had fun reading about my two stabby and violent, but also maybe a bit loveable, villains. And I hope that you will join me on many more adventures to come!

As always, if you have any questions or comments about the book, I would love to hear from you. You can find all the different ways of contacting me on my website, www.marionblackwood.com. There you can also sign up for my newsletter to receive updates about coming books. Lastly, if you liked this book and want to help me out so that I can continue writing, please consider leaving a review. It really does help tremendously. I hope you enjoyed the adventure!

Made in the USA
Las Vegas, NV
07 September 2023